HIS OTHER LOVER

By Lucy Dawson

His Other Lover

HIS OTHER LOVER

Lucy Dawson

AVON

An Imprint of HarperCollins*Publishers*

HIS OTHER LOVER. Copyright © 2009 by Lucy Dawson. All rights reserved. Printed in the United States of America. No part of this book may be used or reproduced in any manner whatsoever without written permission except in the case of brief quotations embodied in critical articles and reviews. For information address Harper-Collins Publishers, 10 East 53rd Street, New York, NY 10022.

HarperCollins books may be purchased for educational, business, or sales promotional use. For information please write: Special Markets Department, Harper-Collins Publishers, 10 East 53rd Street, New York, NY 10022.

FIRST AVON PAPERBACK EDITION PUBLISHED 2009.

Interior text designed by Rhea Braunstein

ISBN 978-0-06-170625-7

09 10 11 12 13 WBC/RRD 10 9 8 7 6 5 4 3 2 1

For Camilla

ACKNOWLEDGMENTS

*With thanks to Sarah Ballard, Joanne Dickinson,
Melissa Chinchillo, Lucia Macro,
and all at Avon Books/HarperCollins,
my family, friends and James for their support.*

HIS OTHER LOVER

ONE

I'm so tired by the time I get back into bed that I don't know where to put myself. I've reached a level of exhaustion where the room is swimming slightly and it feels a little like I'm walking on enormous lumps of cotton wool. Sliding noiselessly under the duvet next to Pete, I sink gratefully down into the warmth and, finally, close my eyes. I've been crying so much it's as if I've sandpapered them red raw. They ache on the inside.

I almost brained myself a second ago, creeping back into our bedroom and trying not to disturb Pete. Unfortunately I tripped over a picture frame that we haven't got round to hanging back up after the break-in and stubbed my toe on the edge of the bed. It really hurt and made me yelp, but he didn't wake up.

Earlier we were lying in bed talking before we went to sleep . . . well, before Pete went to sleep. He was remarking on how much damage the burglars had done in such a comparatively short space of time, probably mere minutes. I didn't say much to that and, misinterpreting my silence, he reached out and squeezed my hand in what I think was meant to be a reassuring "I'm here" sort of way. Then he started to snore.

I haven't found it so easy. Even now, when I'm desperately tired, I can't get comfy. I can't switch off.

Scrunching my eyes a little tighter I try to breathe deeply, focusing on emptying my head of horrible thoughts . . . but I can't. My brain is still blindly buzzing, like a bee trapped in a bottle.

Eventually I try to think about something happy and relaxing instead. A picture of my mum, my sister and me having a picnic on a beach pops into my head. God, life was simple as a child. I think about us just skipping around on the sand, laughing, and Mum watching us happily—but then thinking about Mum makes me want to cry again.

I want to get up now and ring her, confess everything, so someone knows what I've done. But I can imagine her pity and horror, her saying "Oh you poor, poor little thing . . . I'll be there just as soon as I can," but that would ruin her holiday and she so needs this break. I know that I won't tell her, not tonight, not tomorrow. Apart from anything else, it'd make it all real.

I still have a lot of tidying up to do tomorrow anyway. I found a small shard of glass embedded in the bottom of my shoe when I was walking through the hall earlier, even though I've hoovered thoroughly.

Pete was simply speechless when he got home from work and surveyed the damage. It's difficult to prepare someone for something like that over the phone, even though I tried. I'd explained how no room had been left untouched and how it had been a very thorough job, but he was still visibly shocked. He'd been especially gutted when he spied the elephant lying on the carpet in the sitting room, a snapped-off tusk lying miserably next to it.

"I can't believe it," he said incredulously. "They've even broken Bert. The bastards." He'd crunched over the cracked CD cases, mashing flowers from a broken vase into the rug en route.

"Who could do something like this? Don't they ever stop to think about the fact that all this stuff is someone else's memories, their lives?" He'd held Bert up to me sadly and said, "D'you remember that funny little guy who made him, the one with no teeth?"

I hadn't been able to say anything; I'd just nodded dumbly, trying not to let myself cry. I didn't trust myself to speak anyway.

He'd set Bert down carefully and shaken his head slowly. "How can someone be so evil? It's just mindless damage! I hope they get what they deserve—the fuckers."

We'd stood there and looked around our living room: smashed photo frames, ripped cushions, cupboard doors forlornly flapping open with the contents spewing out over the carpet. When we started to move from room to room, he gasped at each one. In the bathroom there were open bottles rolling on the tiles and dribbling puddles of shampoo on to the floor, squirts of sun cream up the walls and over the mirror, reams of loo roll festooning the shower. In our bedroom, clothes were strewn over the bed, the drawers upended, books and magazines flung wildly around, pictures at drunken angles.

"How could anyone just wreck everything with no thought for how much hurt it would cause?" Pete had said in disbelief.

And at that, I *had* cried. I hadn't been able to help it. I'd done a big gulping sob and tears had started to stream down my face. "Oh, don't!" Pete had begged as he rushed over and pulled me into his arms, hugging me fiercely. "It's just stuff. All that matters is that neither of us were hurt."

That had just made me cry even more. He had to hold me, make gentle shushing noises and rock me like a baby until I calmed down.

The memory of Pete holding me so sweetly makes my heart

thud painfully as I glance over at him lying right on the other side of the bed. There's a huge gap between us and he has taken practically all the duvet. I shiver slightly and wriggle over, reaching out for him. He flinches in his sleep as my cold feet touch his leg but doesn't protest as I wrap myself round him and huddle up for some warmth. We lie like that for a moment or two and then he shifts uncomfortably and turns over. I turn over too, facing away from him, but he reaches out for me as he always does and draws me toward him. We fit together and he sighs happily as he sinks back into deep sleep.

For as long as we've been together he has always liked to go to sleep with us hugging. It took a bit of getting used to, but now I don't drop off unless he *is* draped over me.

The first night we slept in the same bed together I instinctively rolled away when he switched the light off, as that was what I'd experienced with all other blokes. Pete had flicked the light back on and said in amazement, "What are you doing?"

I'd been a bit confused by that and said, "Er, going to sleep. Why, what are you doing?"

"Nothing. Just wondering why you've shot over to the furthest side of the mattress. Do I smell or something?"

I'd blushed and mumbled "No!," all embarrassed.

Pete had laughed good-naturedly and said, "Well, come here then!" So I'd snuggled into his open arms gratefully, my heart melting.

And that's how it's been ever since.

I tried to describe it recently to my younger sister, who was having bloke trouble. She'd spent about an hour snuffling into a tissue that she just wanted to meet the man who *was* right for her. Was that too much to ask?

"I just feel like it's never going to happen," she said desperately as I stroked her hair and she started to wail again. "I mean, I'm twenty-two! I can't keep getting it wrong, I'm running out of time! It won't be long before I start getting saggy and *no one* will want me." I'd ignored that and tried to think of something positive to say. After all, her boyfriends always seemed perfectly nice to me and I couldn't really see what the problem was.

"Well, you could just . . . ." I began gently.

"Don't tell me to put up with Jack! Just don't!" She'd sat up fiercely and looked warningly at me. "You don't understand. I just can't be with someone who doesn't get *why* I need to do this."

"But you're talking about a very big change here, Clare," I tried to reason, offering her a fresh tissue. "You've got to admit that not many people would want to give up studying law to be a . . . salsa instructor." I'd bitten the inside of my lip to try and stop myself smiling. It really wasn't funny; she already had enormous student loans.

She'd waved the tissue away and reached crossly for the Revels, shoving four in at once.

"I hate these," she said mutinously. "Don't buy them again."

"But it's fun . . . not knowing if you're going to get a coffee or a toffee or a . . ."

She rolled her eyes. "I'm so excited I'm going to wet myself. Anyway, we're talking about me and Jack. I just don't see what's wrong with me wanting to, to explore life more. To get out there . . . to—"

"But in fairness, Clare," I'd interrupted, "he didn't say you *couldn't* be a tango teacher . . ."

"*Salsa!*" she exploded through a mouthful. "It's sodding *salsa*! Not tango! They are two completely different things!"

"He didn't say you couldn't teach salsa," I continued sooth-ingly, "he said he didn't understand why you wanted to, but if it was important to you, it was important to him."

"Exactly!" Her eyes blazed. "Don't you see what is so wrong with that?"

I'd hesitated: the simple answer was no, I didn't.

"If the man I'm with can't understand *why* I need to do some-thing, if he doesn't *totally* get what makes me tick, if we're not *completely* on the same wavelength, then what's the point?"

I sighed inwardly and felt about a hundred. She had a lot to learn. Pete's and my puppy, Gloria, trotted in. I scooped her up and began to tickle her tummy.

"How did *you* know Pete was The One?" she demanded.

I shrugged. "I just knew. That's the thing, you just do. You'll know when it happens to you."

She shot me a cross look. "Don't be so patronizing." Then she was quiet for a moment and stared into space before adding in a smaller voice, "But *what* did you just know? I don't get it."

I sighed and tried to think. "We just get on."

"I get on with my boss at the restaurant, but I don't want to shag him. Any more."

I looked up in alarm and she rolled her eyes. "Joke. But seri-ously, what did attract you to Pete? I'm not saying he's not fit or anything, but what made him that little bit different?"

"His laugh and his smile," I said without hesitation.

She groaned. "God, you two are so sad. I want some more wine." With that, she'd got up and moodily stomped off to the kitchen.

But it's true: when we first met, one of the things I was im-mediately attracted to was this sort of glow around Pete. He had a spark in his eyes and looked lively, hungry for fun. The first time I saw him he was in a circle of people in a noisy, busy pub. He was telling a story and they were all listening to him eagerly, waiting for the punchline. When it came, the group erupted with laughter, him included, and he just grinned delightedly at all of them. He obviously liked making them laugh and that was, well, very sweet. Then he looked up and caught my eye and I blushed and dropped my gaze. I've always been hopeless at flirting like that. Anyway, after a bit he came up to the bar where I was sitting perched on a stool, trying to look alluring and not in fact like I was about to fall off, and asked me if I was someone who was likely to respond to crappy chat-up lines or not.

"Would you," he wondered as if it were a truly interesting question, "be the kind of girl who could appreciate a truly awful line and laugh, or would you be the kind of girl who would prefer just to politely be asked if I could buy her a drink?"

That would entirely depend on which awful line he chose, I said (I was a bit tipsy—there was a reason why I was staying seated). What lines had he got?

He understood the game immediately and pulled up a stool, asking if he could interest me in a cheeky little number that began with it being my lucky night. I pointed out that whenever a man says that to a girl it is rarely *her* lucky night, it is his, and he is unwittingly revealing that all he wants to do is shag you then leave—and that he is the kind of man who doesn't get to have sex often at all. (I would never had said that if I was sober. Never.)

He smiled and said he understood perfectly. What about a line that required props then? He could procure an ice cube and attempt to hit it, which would break the ice?

That, I said, would be lovely if he were George Clooney and we were in the Sky bar in LA, but a little ridiculous in the George and Dragon on what was, after all, quite a drizzly, cold night.

Hmm, he said. What about something a little more auda-
cious then? A "let's not waste time with small talk, let's just get
out of here and go someplace else *right now* . . ." Not bad, I re-
sponded thoughtfully, except he could be an ax murderer for
all I knew and, also, any man who doesn't bother with small talk
probably doesn't bother with foreplay—so no thanks. I remember him smiling and saying that he hadn't realized sex was in
the offing this early in the frame and had I considered playing
hard to get?

He almost lost me there. Had I been sober enough I would
have taken offense at that, or been unnerved talking about sex
with a perfect stranger, but I wasn't, I was enjoying myself. What
about something with humor? I suggested helpfully.

"Make my day, tell me you're Swedish, single and you've got a
twin sister?" he offered. I grimaced; absolutely not. If that was his
best shot at doing funny, he'd better try doing sweetly romantic.

He pondered this for a moment and said calmly, "You're the
kind of girl I'd like to come home to." I laughed at this and said
that I didn't mean to be rude but I'd kind of hoped for a little bit
more from life than sitting at home knitting and waiting for my
bloke to get in from t'mine to eat the rabbit pie I'd made him.

Heck, he said, biting his lip in mock fear, his repertoire was
running low. How about a plain and simple "I want to kiss you?,"
he went on, because it was true, he very much wanted to.

I stole a look at his gently smiling face, his kind, shiny brown
eyes with crinkly bits at the corners that showed he smiled a lot,
and felt myself melt a bit. Then I laughed again, a little nervously
this time because there was a moment where everything else
seemed to stop and go quiet, where we both realized something
was starting between us . . . and said firmly that would never
work. Did I look like the sort of girl who went around kissing

random men in pubs for goodness' sake? Of course not. Anyway it was a really cheesy line, it would never work. It would definitely never work.

It did work though. By the end of the night he'd given me his number and asked me please to call because he wanted to try his first-date lines on me. Purely in the spirit of research, I was to understand.

I left it all of three days before I got in touch and, two days after that, I was sitting in a restaurant opposite him peering at a menu and trying to think of something witty and amusing to say.

"I hate this bit," he said. "I should warn you that I'll probably blurt something out to try and start a conversation that will end up making me look a total idiot and you'll be sitting there wondering where the loos are and how big the windows might be."

That relaxed me a little. I assured him that he'd be okay. After all he had his first-date lines, didn't he? He looked a bit sheepish and said no, he didn't actually, they mostly consisted of "You look very nice" and "So tell me a bit more about yourself."

We both agreed that while these weren't wildly original, they were safe. Then we spent a fun twenty minutes composing a list of things that should *never* be said on a first date, which included "Well, I hope you like the food. My ex and I used to come here all the time," and "This is really embarrassing but I can't remember your name," as well as "You're a bit overdressed for the dogs."

We were getting on famously and then he said, just as the waiter arrived, "Or what about: 'I'm warning you now. It's not very big!'"

There was a silence that seemed to go on forever before the

waiter coughed in a crap attempt to cover a laugh, looked pity-ingly at me, took our order and then legged it back to the kitchen to tell everyone that the man at table ten had just told his date he had a small penis.

One of us had to speak and break the horribly uncomfortable social nightmare that had suddenly become our night out, so once I'd recovered myself I agreed that yes, he was right, that probably wouldn't be *such* a great thing to say. Not least because it assumed the evening was going to end a certain way. Which it wasn't.

He looked horrified. "Oh God, no," he flustered, utterly ap-palled at himself and flushing deep red. "I didn't mean I was expecting you to . . . although if you wanted to it would be . . . anyway. It's not true," he said quickly. "About me, I mean. It's okay . . . just in case you were wondering if it was . . . sufficient. Oh Jesus, I'm still talking . . . I can't believe I just said that." He stopped and exhaled deeply, and then tried to take a deep, calming breath. "I can't *believe* I just said that. You'd think that by now my brain would have stopped this, this verbal car crash happening, but no . . . words are still coming out . . ."

He took another deep breath. "Could we pretend I didn't just say all of that to you and could I ask you to tell me a little bit more about yourself instead?"

After I'd got over the initial shock and resisted the urge to do a mad sprint to the door (maybe it was just curiosity at how he was going to recover the evening after such a dreadful outburst of social Tourette's), we ended up having a surprisingly lovely time. He asked if he could see me again and I said yes without even hesitating.

Then it began. An evening here and there, a walk on a hot summer's afternoon in some quiet fields, just us, where we shyly began to talk about what we each wanted for the rest of our lives. When he said nervously that he had always imagined getting married and having children at a young age, I said *I'd* always wanted to have children too, with the right man . . . There was a silence where we both looked at each other, smiled gently and my heart felt so light and happy I just wanted to cry. It was as if we made an unspoken promise to each other there and then. I felt I was his from that moment onward and he hadn't even kissed me.

As time went on we became closer and closer . . . we talked several times a day and never ran out of things to say to each other. He made me laugh and laugh, and when he did first kiss me, it was the sweetest, gentlest kiss in the world. I wanted to be with him as much as I could. My heart would flip over when I heard his car pull up outside my flat . . . it was perfect and I fell very much in love with him.

We spent a first blissful summer together driving around country lanes and having pub lunches and after one, late in the afternoon as the sun was starting to sink, we stopped at the beach on the way back and he wrote "I love you" in the sand. Then he shouted it as loud as he could, to the alarm of the squawking seagulls circling overhead. I laughed like a loon and hugged him so hard we both fell over. I felt like I was in a film—cocooned in happiness.

That was what Clare just hadn't found yet—that being sure. That certain knowledge that it just didn't get any better. Knowing that the search could stop, you were a done deal.

Clare wandered back in carrying another bottle of wine and found me grinning to myself.

"God, you're thinking about him now, aren't you? Mr. Totally Wonderful."

I'd laughed. "He drives me totally nuts in lots of ways. You know he does."

"But you see, this is what I don't understand!" She'd started to wrestle with the cork. "If someone pisses me off, I'm out of there."

"Pete doesn't piss me off. Well, he does, but I don't spend all day wandering around thinking I've got to do something about it. If he does something twatty, sometimes I ignore it because it's not worth arguing about, sometimes I don't and we have words, then one of us says, 'Do you want a cup of tea?' and it's forgotten. That's what a real relationship is all about."

Clare wrinkled her nose. "Sounds really exciting. I'll have to check my diary and see if I can fit it in between rebellious university years and death . . . Oh, turns out I'm busy. What a shame."

That annoyed me a little and I started to get a bit more animated as I tipped Gloria off my lap and reached for the bottle myself. "Look, real love—*true* love—is about an awful lot more than roses, candlelight and remembering Valentine's Day."

Clare took a big gulp from her glass and put it unsteadily back down on the table. "What, it's about picking up his pants for the hundredth time and *still* loving him? Balls to that . . . I want passion, excitement, spontaneity. That can't be too much to expect." She'd started to look feisty and determined.

"It isn't." I'd gently leaned over to remove the bottle that she'd just picked up again from her hands, firmly putting the cork back in it. "It's just that all that stuff gives way to something much deeper, much more lasting. No one is perfect, every relationship takes a lot of work and once you meet the person that you really, truly love, it won't matter if he doesn't understand why you want to do something, it'll be enough that he's willing to support your choice *even though* he doesn't really understand why."

I listen to Pete breathing next to me, steady and untroubled, and I think about what I said to Clare and I know it to be true. I love him so much.

But I can't tell him what I did earlier.

Twelve hours ago, after he'd left for a meeting, I slammed from room to room in our house like a human sledgehammer, clutching one of his golf clubs with a grip so tight my fingers went white. It was hard to hear the shattering of glass and the crash of cascading CDs over my shrieking as photo frames, ornaments, Bert, all flew off shelves and tables, splintering into pieces. I threw things at walls, ripped apart anything I could get my hands on, pushed chairs over, kicked piles of DVDs. I was totally shattered when I finished and sank to the floor in a crumpled heap, breathing heavily.

Pete can't ever know that when I told him we'd been burgled I was lying. Tomorrow I will make everything okay. I know how to fix this mess. It *will* be all right. It has to be.

And with that thought I finally start to drift away, my body unable to fight sleep any longer.

TWO

A mere hour and a half later, I am wide awake again. I have literally jolted out of sleep back into my body, with an audible gasp. Pete doesn't stir next to me. My muscles are rigid as I breathe shallow, small breaths and then eventually they start to soften—my body has decided neither fight nor flight is required.

The only thing that can't ease is my mind. Despite it being 2:17 a.m., my mind is immediately alert and returning to the matter in question. Within seconds I am staring at the ceiling and sifting for clues through the sieve of my memory—I am trying to pinpoint the moment when it all began to go wrong, while I wait for the morning. Where was the bit when the winds started to pick up outside and swirl the leaves around lightly, those little troublesome gusts that lift skirts and whip hats off heads? The bit where, in a movie, wind chimes begin to ring eerily, shop signs creak and sway, dogs whine uneasily and the older, wiser townsfolk look suspiciously up at the sky? Because the immensely frustrating thing is, I can't remember anything out of the ordinary. There have been no giveaways, no warning signs. In fact

I specifically remember talking to Lottie at work about how comfortable Pete and I had become with each other. That was only three weeks ago! That's all!

It had been a very typical day in a very typical week. I was saying how annoyed I'd been at the weekend, as I'd had to go to a friend's wedding on my own because Pete had been working overtime.

"It was so crap," I'd said to Lottie. "Everyone had their boyfriends or husbands with them and I'm there playing with the stem of my champagne glass wishing Pete was too. I'd asked him specially to keep that weekend free as well. And as if that wasn't bad enough, it was a Celtic wedding with traditional dancing in a circle to a bloody fiddle and whistle."

Lottie made a face.

"Everyone got up with their other halves and my friend Amanda's bloke suddenly booms, 'Oh hang on, everyone! Look who isn't dancing!' and they all look over at me, minding my own business at a table trying to look inconspicuous, and he goes, 'Come on, Mia! Don't be a wallflower, come and dance!'"

Lottie groaned sympathetically, "Oh you're joking!"

"Nope," I retorted, "I'm not. So now everyone is looking at me, the whole band is waiting to start and I realize I'm going to have to go up there, I've got no choice. So I drag myself on to the dance floor feeling like a prat but thinking the sooner I get it over with etc., etc. . . . ."

Lottie nodded in agreement.

"But then, *then* he makes it worse by bellowing, 'Oh hang on, she hasn't got a partner! Come on, chaps! Step up!'"

Lottie gasped and put her hands over her mouth. "I can't bear it. I really can't. Why didn't Amanda shut him up?"

"I know! Wives are nudging their husbands and muttering

'Go on, poor girl . . . she's all on her own,' babies are being passed from boyfriends to girlfriends, much chair scraping ensues as the men start to reluctantly shuffle to their feet and then Tim, my mate Louise's husband, shoves the rest of his sausage roll in his mouth, wipes his hands down his waistcoat and cheerily shouts, 'Come on, old girl! I'll swing you round the floor!' to *cheers* from the rest of the wedding party, like he's a war hero or something. It was so embarrassing. I wanted to die."

Lottie held up a hand. "Stop, please. I can't listen to any more."

"I told Pete when I got home and he thought it was funny! Oh, hilarious. And not only that—he actually finished work earlier than he thought and had *time to go to the gym*."

Lottie looked gratifyingly horrified and whispered, "Then what happened?"

But at that point I had to stop because Spank Me, our boss, got back from his meeting and we needed to pretend we were working.

It was Lottie who came up with the nickname Spank Me after we discovered he'd been surfing some very unsavory Web sites after office hours. Why on earth he'd want to cruise gay porn at work and not do it in the privacy of his own home is beyond me, but to be honest we both try not to think about it too much. After all, as Lottie has pointed out, she has to sit in his chair sometimes and use that computer and it turns her stomach if she lets her mind dwell on what he might have been doing on it the evening before.

After what felt like forever, Spank Me announced he was going off to another meeting and would be back in an hour or two. Once his briefcase had whipped round the corner of the door, we waited for a moment to make sure he'd definitely gone and then turned back to each other.

"I can't believe Pete had been to the gym!" Lottie exclaimed.

"He's always at the gym at the moment. Apparently it helps him 'de-stress' while work is so full on." I shrugged. "I think what he actually means is he wants to up his beer consumption without getting fat, because he doesn't look any different to me, that's for sure."

Talking of drinking then made us decide we needed a cup of tea. Lottie and I spend quite a lot of time making tea. It's only the two of us in the office. Spank Me runs an operation that he calls a marketing consultancy, which means he does small-time promotional stuff for companies that they could do perfectly well themselves. I (in theory) follow up the meetings, book local advertising and update their databases and Lottie manages the Web sites. The only positive thing to be said for it is it just about pays the bills, while Lottie and I manage to keep each other sane. We get a lot of talking done.

"I can't even say I mind Jake's trainers being in the bedroom any more. I think I've acclimatized to the smell," Lottie mused later that afternoon. "But when I shook the sofa cushions the other day, a chopstick, a twenty-pence piece and a load of toe-nails fell out. He's so disgusting. Why can't he use a bin like anyone else?"

"I've seen Pete *eat* his toenails in front of the TV," I said idly.

"How charming." Lottie grimaced, standing up. "Do you want another?"

"Go on then. Can I have a bit more milk this time? It's weird, isn't it?"

"I suppose so. I mean, why cows? Were they just right place, right time?"

"No," I said contemplatively. "Weird how Pete can, on the one hand, do gross things like eat bits of himself in front of me and yet be the same bloke who used to whisper things that literally used to make me shiver they were so lovely."

Lottie snorted and adjusted her skirt, which had swiveled round. "That's not weird. The key word there is *used* to. They all do that at the beginning. Jake used to say things to me in bed like 'You're beyond beautiful.' Now it's 'What do you want me to do? Stick my arse out of the window? Well, don't lift the duvet up then.'" She groaned, gathered up our cups and walked to the kitchen.

That made me think about one night in Pete's room, in the flat that he lived in when I first met him. We hadn't been together very long. It was so close and muggy outside, even having the window fully open and the curtains pulled back made no difference, the air was utterly still. We'd had very quiet, slow sex, as I was paranoid about his flatmate and half the neighbors hearing us. Lit up by the moon and tangled in the sheets, with shallow moves that had increased the urgency and intensity, it was all barely audible gasps, tightly clasping hands, a shuddering groan that he couldn't help, lightly sweating skin . . . and I really did feel beautiful. Afterward he pulled me to him, wrapping his arms round my naked body and we just lay there in the silence.

"Did you know that heartbeats synchronize when they're this close?" he had said eventually and then kissed me lightly on the back of my neck.

I wanted to tell him I loved him right then and there, but I didn't—it still felt a little too soon—even though I knew, I just *knew* I did.

Lottie had carried our very full mugs back to the desk, swearing as she spilled a bit. She then sat herself down in her chair, but unfortunately slopped more tea down her front. "Bugger!" she muttered, reaching for a tissue. "What *is* the matter with me?" She rubbed at her top, but the tissue started to disintegrate and white bits began to shed all over her black jumper.

I got up, went to the kitchen, grabbed a damp cloth and threw it to her.

"Thanks. So what you up to tonight then?" she said. "Busy evening of dinner, TV and then bed?"

"Pretty much. Pete's going to the gym, I think, usual kind of crap."

"Familiarity holds hands with predictability . . ." Lottie said, absently sponging herself off.

I laughed. "Did you just make that up?"

Lottie looked up and grinned. "Probably. Maybe I meant better the devil you know . . . or a lazy-arse git at home is worth two in the bush? Can't live with 'em, so why won't they fuck off? I don't know."

I thought of Pete and smiled. "I'll settle for my devil. Anyway, I don't have the strength to break another one in. Pete'll do."

With a clarity that only comes in the dead of night when your brain is not cluttered with everyday work crap, bank statements and picking up something for tea, I am suddenly struck with the absolute knowledge that that was it. That was when I made my first huge mistake.

With all the complacency of familiarity, I had assumed that as a couple we had no surprises ahead. But as I have learned in the last twenty-seven hours, you *never* know all there is to know.

Equally, twenty-seven hours ago I would have said Pete and

I were invincible—utterly watertight—but now I can see that until you are actually tested, you have no idea what will happen when trouble approaches. Until then, you are in fact at your most vulnerable.

When your boat starts to rock slightly, you can either pull as a team and row away from the approaching huge black cloud together, or you can pretend it's not happening and it's your imagination—the wind isn't really getting up and there's nothing to worry about.

Or one of you can randomly decide to jump out of the boat. They think they've spied another, bigger ship that looks a better bet. And you're so busy sorting the sails, battening down the hatches and tightening the ropes, you don't hear the silent splash as they inexplicably throw themselves into the deep, dangerous, swirling sea.

THREE

As the clock on the chest of drawers next to my side of the bed hits 2:45, then eventually 3:15, I finally give in and get up again. There is not much point in going downstairs to watch TV, as I'm not going to be able to relax and switch off. I haven't got any control over my mind or body right now—my adrenaline levels are still high enough to keep thoughts madly leaping about my mind. I can, however, at least go and make a cup of hot milk and sit as quietly as possible, while I wait.

In four hours his alarm—on *his* side of the bed—is going to go off and he will get up. Then I will begin to sort everything out. He is not ever going to know I trashed the house. This has to pass, I tell myself as I pad barefoot downstairs, my heart as tight with worry as an overstretched drum—it has to. There is no other option, no other way forward. Any other outcome is just too scary to contemplate. I creep into the kitchen and switch the light on. Gloria wags her tail lightly but doesn't bother to get out of her basket. I'm the only restless one in this house tonight.

We will be happy again. I will not feel like this forever, life will return to normal. My birthday—when was that?—barely *two* weeks ago? We were happy then and we can be again! It was the happiest birthday I've had for years! I know it was real. I didn't imagine it and it was largely thanks to Pete.

Ironic, really. I spent an evening with Louise and Amanda the Wednesday before I turned twenty-nine, preparing my-self in advance for the crap present I felt sure he was going to get me.

"He might surprise you." Amanda shrugged. "Maybe this is the year he'll discover Tiffany & Co." She lit up a fag and her gentle big brown eyes—eyes that boys had frequently fallen helplessly into at uni—narrowed and hardened. More useful a look for the bank she works at, but it makes her look sharp around the edges sometimes, when actually she has one of the biggest hearts I know.

"I doubt it," I said. "I'll probably get the usual. A DVD of a film I've already seen, a CD he quite liked the look of and an item of clothing that doesn't fit and I don't really like . . . but hey, it could be worse. Remember the year he got his mum to buy my present?"

"Ah," said Louise, "the duvet set and the bowl of hyacinth bulbs."

"She totally did that on purpose," I said. "Old witch."

"What do you *hope* he'll get you this year then?" yawned Louise. "Sorry, I'm so bloody tired at the moment."

"Ben still not sleeping?" said Amanda.

"He is—just not at night when everyone else would like to. I think I've given birth to a hamster."

Amanda blinked uncomprehendingly.

"Hamsters are nocturnal," Louise explained patiently.

"Oh, I see. I was going to say . . . bit harsh to refer to your newborn as a rodent."

"Is that my phone?" Louise leaned over and peered anxiously into her bag. "No, it's not. Just thought it might have been my mum—she's babysitting—but it's not. We're fine. Oh, sorry—that *was* me."

Amanda's eyes widened. "Did you just fart?" she laughed.

"Yes," Louise said apologetically. "I'm like a small set of bagpipes at the moment and that's the least of my worries. Don't ever have children, either of you . . . Sorry, Mia—you were saying?"

"What I would *really* like for my birthday is a weekend away. A Cathy and Heathcliff-style cottage . . . wild, wintry walks on deserted sandy beaches, then just as your ears start to hurt and your noses are going red you go back to the cottage for hot chocolate by the roaring fire. Still—never mind."

"A dirty weekend," Amanda said wistfully. "God, I'd love Nick to take me away and give me a good seeing to. Although the chances of us both being in the same country at the same time and still knowing what bits go where are almost nonexistent."

"You can borrow Tim if you like." Louise took an enormous gulp of her wine. "He's desperate for a shag."

Amanda's jaw dropped. "God, Lou, it's been four months since you had Ben. You're not still *sore*, are you?"

"What?" Louise looked at her, confused, and then shook her head. "No, of course not! I'm just so knackered at the moment, most of the time I can see three of Tim and they *all* want to have sex with me . . . it's off-putting to say the least."

At that point an attractive, very young couple had walked into the bar, looking a little out of place, as if they were playing at being grown-ups. She was dressed up for dinner, holding her bag nervously. He had a protective palm in the small of her back and the other worriedly on his wallet. As they waited uncertainly by the bar he suddenly stole a look at her, as if he couldn't quite believe his luck, and with all of the uninhibited innocence of being about nineteen, just bent and kissed her in full view of everyone. Not a snog that meant sex, or a brief brush of lips, but an old-fashioned, romantic kiss.

"Ohhhhh!" we all went in unison, like sad old women let out of the care home for the evening. Louise—baby hormones running riot—practically misted over and even Amanda said, "How cute!" I had looked at the couple and thought back with a warm, rosy glow to when I first kissed Pete.

Oh God.

I halt in the dark kitchen, a mug in my hand and the saucepan already on the hob, the milk beginning to give off an unpleasantly sickly-sweet stench. Suppose we never kiss like that again? What if that's it? Suppose my plan doesn't work, suppose . . . Oh I do not want to stay stuck in this nightmare that feels like someone else's life and not mine! I want to go to sleep, wake up and find it was all a bad dream.

I set the mug down and lean both hands on the work surface to steady myself. I have to get a grip. I have very good reasons for not telling him that it was me who annihilated our house yesterday. And I certainly don't want to discuss *why* I did it.

Just breathe. Breathe. Think happy thoughts. I take myself back in my mind to the actual morning of my birthday. Pete has just told me he is taking me away for the weekend and I am delighted. I can see the smile on my face. It's a smile that suspects—

wrongly as it happens—that Amanda had something to do with him suggesting we have a much-needed night away together. I will focus just on the fact that I am smiling.

I exhale and feel calmer. This is better, this is definitely better. I force my eyes shut and picture myself tottering around our very sleek hotel suite with wet hair, looking for the dryer, getting ready to go out for dinner.

It was a room that I had felt slightly too fat for—all crisp lighting, clean lines and dark walnut furniture. I just didn't have the legs for such a swish boudoir. Happily, though, I had been feeling too blissfully relaxed to care that much. When we'd arrived at the hotel, Pete had confessed at reception to having booked me a massage.

That *had* been unexpected. I had been so flabbergasted that I wanted to call Clare then and there and tell her not to give up, the good guys were still out there and did really exist—and what was more her very own sister had bagged one!

"Just enjoy it," Pete had said sheepishly as I put my arms round his neck and pulled him toward me, planting an ecstatic kiss on his lips as the receptionists smiled indulgently.

"You are a very lovely man," I'd whispered. "I'll see if I can pick up any tips for later."

He'd decided to go for a workout in the hotel gym while I had my treatment, and finally arrived back, looking unattractively sweaty, just as I was switching the dryer off. I instinctively leaned away in case he tried to kiss me and ruined my makeup. He laughed, flicked me a V sign and said, "Wasn't going to anyway!" before walking purposefully into the bathroom. Seconds later the shower began.

I wandered in to look for my tweezers and glanced in the mirror to see him scrubbing himself vigorously. He looked up, smiled and then, pretending to be lofty, said, "Do you mind? I'd like to shower without being perved on." With that he stuck his nose in the air, winked at me and then pulled the curtain across.

I laughed and moved into the bedroom to get dressed, but standing in front of the mirror as I did up my bra, I'd felt the sudden but familiar twinge of stomach cramps.

I'd closed my eyes briefly and sent a curse to the god of crap timing. Why this weekend? Why couldn't I just be late for once? I decided not to tell Pete. It would only put the dampener on his evening, which no doubt he had planned would culminate in rampant hotel sex. Then I realized I had a bigger problem. I had nothing with me . . .

Which was how, two hours later, I was trotting downstairs with half a bog roll balanced in my g-string, praying it wouldn't fall out in the hotel lobby. Pete observed, quite correctly, that I was walking weirdly and asked if everything was okay. I assured him I was fine and concentrated on trying to move less like a geisha who had had her feet bound too tightly. Feeling very unglamorous I sat heavily down in the back of a taxi and we whizzed off into the evening London traffic.

The restaurant that he'd chosen was absolutely lovely: elegant and calming as we stepped into the warm interior from the chilly, busy street. Sadly, though, it was too upmarket for tampons in the loos. The only offering was—horror of horrors—a pantyliner delivered in a vile cardboard tray in exchange for a daylight robbery £4. I was convinced that everyone could hear me rustling back to the table, which probably accounted for my slightly distracted air over the starters.

However I started to relax and really enjoy myself during the main course. I was remembering just how much I loved chatting with Pete—he was such good fun when he was relaxed and not going on about work—when he looked at his watch, swore and said we had to get going or we'd miss the start of the show he'd booked.

I slowed us down—the pantyliner had readjusted during the meal and trapped a pube, making me walk like I had a hernia. Pete had rolled his eyes when I'd said I needed to pop to the loo and told me to hurry up, he'd wait outside. I had just enough time to sort it out and look in the mirror to discover the beginning of a big spot in the middle of my forehead. I artfully arranged a bit of hair over it (no time for cover-up) before dashing back and flinging myself into the back of our second cab of the night.

Having screeched up to the theater with none of our earlier sense of calm, we galloped to our seats, making it just as the house lights went down. It turned out to be a musical we were watching. The men all had curiously long hair (for reasons I didn't quite understand) and the girls, slinking around like predatory cats, were wearing barely anything. The girls all looked gorgeous, if unhealthily thin.

Pete seemed to enjoy the show immensely which slightly surprised, but delighted, me. I made a vow to do this sort of thing more often with him as I watched him poring over the program in the interval, and I felt a proud little glow when he got thrown a rose by a dancer at the end.

In the last cab of the evening, on the way back to the hotel, I snuggled up to him and rested my head on his shoulder. We stayed like that in comfortable silence until he asked if I'd had a nice time. I truthfully replied it had been a very nice night. "Good," he said. "I'm pleased. You deserve it."

Back in our room, I went to go and take my makeup off and heard his phone bleep. He was laughing as I came back into the room and said that he'd just had a puppy update from his mother—who was dog-sitting Gloria for the night—and that all was well. He switched it off and we fell into a hug. Everything was as it should be.

Almost. As we snuggled down into bed I apologetically explained the situation and said that we still could if he wanted to . . . while hoping that he would say he *didn't* want to as I had *really* bad tummy cramps. Luckily he was very sweet about it and said it didn't matter at all and he was just glad I'd enjoyed the evening so much. He looked at me, stroked a stray bit of hair from my face and said, "I'm very lucky to have you. You looked beautiful tonight."

I smiled, kissed him gratefully and murmured, "Love you." He said, "You too," and softly placed a gentle kiss on the end of my nose.

"Do you know heartbeats synchronize when they're this close . . ." I whispered.

He opened his eyes slightly and then frowned, a little puzzled. "What? I don't think they do actually. That wouldn't take into account people's fitness, sex, weight and height. It's just not physically possible. Where d'you read that?"

I'd laughed good-naturedly, said, "Never mind," and then we'd both happily gone to sleep.

I'd still been on a high the following Monday at work. "It was a perfect weekend," I'd boasted to Lottie, as we'd walked to get our lunch from the café round the corner. It had been so cold that we'd both squeaked into the biting wind as we turned on to the high street.

As we'd burst in through the café door and the heat from the kitchen hit us, our noses had started to run. The air was thick with the comforting smell of fry-ups and coffee, a blend of grease and steam clinging to the windows, forming little rivulets that coursed down the corners of the glass. The radio was blaring and a couple of blokes in paint-flicked jeans and Timberlands were idly thumbing through the newspapers while waiting for their orders.

Lottie had looked at the rows of sandwich fillings. "Yuck. I don't think salmon is *supposed* to be that color. So you really wouldn't have changed anything at all? Wow. Pete did well . . ."

Obviously she had meant would I have picked the same hotel as him, chosen a different place to have dinner?

In retrospect, I think now, as I pour the frothing hot milk into the cup—wondering how I am going to stomach it—I would change several things. We would have been able to make love, he would have remembered the significance of what I'd said about our heartbeats and we would have not gone to see that show. Not in a million fucking years.

FOUR

There are other things I would change, too. Mostly, I would also like to go back to Sunday. That was only thirty-three hours ago . . . and everything was normal then. In fact, Sunday had started *brilliantly*.

Over breakfast, Pete had said he wanted to see an exhibition up in town that he had read about. Did I want to go?

Of course I did! It certainly beat sitting around at home.

But it was while he was getting ready and I was messing around with Gloria in our bedroom that the day took a *really* unexpectedly lovely turn. Gloria had started yipping and growling under our bed. As I dragged her out, she brought the edge of a glossy bag with her. Reaching confusedly into it, a large, very beautiful, soft caramel Mulberry bag had slid out of its wrapping and into my hands. The rich smell of buttery leather had filled the room.

Gasping, as I knew how much it cost, my hand flew to my mouth in amazement. I saw the edge of a card poking out of the front pocket and snatched it out.

Because I know how much you'll love it. The best is yet to come, you'll see! P xxx

I was so excited that, clutching it, I had dashed to the bathroom door, knocked and squeaked, "Pete, I love it!"

He opened the door in a towel and a blast of blokey-smelling steam, all shower gel and deodorant. Even though he was wet, water droplets running down his chest, I threw my arms round him and covered his face in kisses.

"You are just the perfect boyfriend—it must have cost a fortune!"

"Eh?" he had laughed. "What's this in aid of?"

"I found the bag under the bed. Don't be cross! I know I've ruined your surprise, but I love it!" I slipped the bag over my shoulder and did a little twirl. "I'll take it to the gallery with me today! Oh God, I *love* it!" I stroked it incredulously and then grinned up at Pete, who was scratching his ear and frowning a little.

"Well, I'm just glad you like it," he said eventually. "It was supposed to be here in time for your birthday but it was late so . . ." he looked a little sheepish, "I was going to hang on to it for you until Christmas."

"Oh. Sorry!" I laughed, not sorry at all. "Well, you'll have to get me something else for Christmas because I can't possibly put this back under the bed and pretend it's not there until then. I'm going to put all my stuff in it now," I finished quickly, and then legged it downstairs in case he insisted I hand it back.

A few hours later I was delightedly parading my new bag around the exhibition with a false nonchalance, as if I spent every Sunday being terribly cultured and sophisticated.

Of the pieces on show, I especially liked a cushion covered in glass that had been artfully shattered to coincide with the paisley print of the material. Pete admired a big pink blob that managed to look like a giant squid and a human bottom at the same time. It came as no surprise to me that he liked it: it looked like his mother.

Halfway round the exhibition we wandered into a small room that appeared to hold only a blank screen. We sat down and tinny music started, softly at first, a sort of slow, grinding gramophone winding up eerily before gathering pace and morphing into a jolly 1920s number. A picture of a woman dancing flickered on to the screen. She was dressed in a flapper dress and the style of film was a silent-movie pastiche. She looked pretty, but sad, like a small, breakable doll who would rather not be played with.

Her skin was very pale with huge, luminous, almost dead eyes and a big ink blob of full pouty lips. The crystals on her dress caught the light as she twisted mournfully, horribly out of place with the merry tune. It was a little creepy at first, but then I just became rather bored. Nothing much seemed to happen apart from her dancing and just as I was getting really impatient and wasn't sure I understood the point of it all, she suddenly jerked to a stop, pulled down the front of her demure sparkly dress and just stood there half naked. Traced over her tiny breasts was a copy of the very recognizable David Beckham "Brooklyn" tattoo. Her mouth curled into an unpleasant leer and she started to laugh—only I couldn't hear her, just the music bashing away. She was definitely supposed to be laughing at me though.

Then the picture flickered off and the music stopped. Everyone else started to file out but Pete stayed.

"I'm just going to watch it again," he whispered, trying to look earnest and arty.

I rolled my eyes and giggled—what, just to see them again? Why bother? But the music had already started. I'd wandered slowly outside and read the gumph about the artist. The piece was apparently intended to highlight the "banality of the fascination with celebrity, who lack substance and real beauty and who are themselves being manipulated . . . Just who is being exploited?"

Hmm. Not just an excuse to get a young girl to take her top off then? The model was an E. Andersen. Were Mr. and Mrs. Andersen proud, I wondered? Then I got fed up of being pious and thought whoever she was, she was more than capable of looking after herself, and if she was stupid enough to get her kit off to further her career that was her problem.

Once Pete re-emerged, he quickly developed gallery fatigue and it wasn't long before we were back out on the street. I switched my phone on again and it immediately buzzed with a new voicemail.

It was Clare. Her breathless voice tumbled through the message; she was obviously hurrying somewhere when she left it.

"Hi! I *forgot* to tell you that Mum's gone on a two-week cruise to Miami. I was supposed to let you know. She's gone bunty hunting with Auntie Joan. I tried to get her to take me but she wasn't having a bar of it. I could do with a bit of fun at sea at the moment too, she's such a selfish old cow. Except it would be all old men in banana hammocks. How sick is that? Anyway, sorry I forgot to tell you about Mum and that she forgot to tell you herself in the first place. She thought she had if that makes you feel any better. See you, chick."

I hung up. "My mum's gone to Miami," I said to Pete. "Bit random."

"Your mother *is* a bit random," Pete said, glancing at his watch. "Shall we head home?"

My phone buzzed again. Text message. It was from Patrick. "Today is International Good-Looking Day," it read. "Send this text to someone you think is gorgeous. Don't send it back to me, I've had hundreds." I laughed.

"Who's that this time?" Pete nodded at the phone.

"Patrick," I said simply and Pete rolled his eyes, muttering, "Say hi from me."

I'd ignored that. Pete doesn't like Patrick. He's deeply skeptical that we can have been mates since school and not once has anything happened between us. I did toy with the idea briefly, but Patrick was always with someone else, or I was. The moment didn't so much pass as never really arrived and we happily settled into being friends, which is where we've been ever since.

"So what do you want to do now?" I asked cheerily, putting my phone back in my lovely designer bag.

"We need to get back for the dog, really," Pete said. It had started to rain lightly, getting steadily heavier. People around us were starting to look for shelter. There was a cozy little café to our right and I suddenly fancied diving in there to drink a hot chocolate, watch the windows steam up and listen to the hiss of the cappuccino makers until the rain passed. "Quick hot choc?" I suggested hopefully.

He looked at the coffee shop and wrinkled his nose. "Nah. It's really busy. Anyway, it's a rip-off. I can make you a hot chocolate at home. Come on."

On the train home I was happily flicking through the Sunday papers, as Pete gazed out of the wetly streaked window.

"Do you remember that day we went to the beach with the dog?" he said suddenly. "We were trying to hit that big rock with the pebbles and you nearly took out that old couple's corgi? The one with the really saggy tummy?"

I looked up at him in surprise. "What made you think of that?"

"No particular reason. It was just a nice day. That's all."

I smiled and reached for his hand. I gave it a quick squeeze then returned back to the papers.

"Actually we were trying to get the stones in the sea." He looked thoughtful. "I remember now. You were rubbish."

I let the paper drop in my lap and shot him a deadpan look. "I think you'll find I was *not* rubbish. My throw had velocity—it just lacked distance. I could have had a very promising cricket career, thank you very much."

He snorted and shifted uncomfortably in his seat, trying to reposition his long legs under the table. "And you threw it right up in the air," he laughed. "Typical girl, throwing it underarm so hard your feet left the ground." He shook his head lightly at the memory and smiled. "It was a fun day . . ." He trailed off, and then gave himself a little shake. "Right," he said determinedly, crossing his arms. "I'm going to have a nap. Wake me up when we get home." With that, he closed his eyes and was silent for the rest of the journey.

Later that evening, having enjoyed a long soak in the bath, I walked into the sitting room to find him on the phone. He looked up and saw me and said immediately, "Well, Mia's here now so I better go. Bye now."

"Who was that?" I asked, rubbing my wet hair with a towel as I sank on to the sofa.

"My mum, they're going to Kenya tomorrow, on safari."

"God, my mum's in Miami, yours is off to Kenya. There's something wrong with this picture." I smiled. "Why did you say you had to go because I'd come back in? She's going to think I have a problem with you talking to her. She already doesn't like me."

He frowned. "She loves you, don't be stupid. I said I had to go because . . . well, I've messed up, Mi."

I stopped drying my hair. "What have you done? I *knew* you were looking shady when I came back in just then!"

"Yeah well." He shifted awkwardly in his seat. "I forgot to tell you we're supposed to go to my cousin's wedding in my mum and dad's place. Family representatives and all that. I said yes ages ago—sorry."

"Oh, Pete," I sighed. "When is it?"

"Next week I think, maybe the week after."

"Is there a present list?"

"No idea."

"Well, we need to know, Pete, we can't just turn up without—"

"Okay, okay," he cut across me tiredly. "I'll sort it."

I nodded and picked the phone up to put it back in its holder. Then it occurred to me that of course he wouldn't sort it and I might as well do it now before his mum went on holiday. Standing up to go and put the kettle on, I dialed 1471 and hit three. As I walked toward the kitchen it began to ring.

"Hello?" said a voice.

"Shirley?" I was a bit confused, it didn't sound like her at all. "It's me."

"Er, this isn't Shirley. I think you might have the wrong number."

"Oh, I'm so sorry!" I said immediately. "Sorry to disturb." I hung up. How the hell had I managed that?

I decided to just dial instead and was tapping the number in as I wandered back into the sitting room. Pete sighed as he saw me. "Who are you ringing now?"

"Your mum," I said. Bugger, he'd made me tap the last number in wrong. I started again.

"Don't bother now," Pete said irritably. "She'll keep you on there for ages."

Seeing as Shirley had barely said more than a paragraph to me in three years, I somehow doubted that. I gave him a funny look and frowned. "I'll just be five—" I started, but quick as a flash he was off the sofa and wrestling the phone away from me.

He flung it behind him, grabbed me passionately and for some reason best known to himself growled in a mock-Russian accent, "You vill do as I say, voman! I vant you to myself!"

I'd squealed in delighted shock and we fell to the floor in a tangle of arms and legs. Then he kissed me again. A deep, urgent kiss. I felt my hands curl up around the back of his neck. He began to lightly suck my bottom lip, then pulled away and slipped my dressing gown off. His hands were touching my skin, still damp from the bath.

I got carpet burns, but not once did I take my eyes off him. It was sexy as hell to watch him and know it was me making him feel that good. I delightedly watched the man I loved, eyes closed, hoarsely breathing, "Oh God, oh God, what are you doing to me?" as he began to lose control.

Later in bed, sleepy and peaceful, I watched him dozing. I looked at his eyelashes, the slope of his nose, his lips. How many times had those lips kissed me? Hundreds, maybe thousands?

"Do you love me?" I whispered.

He reached out for my hand and murmured, "Do you even have to ask?" Then he rolled over. Thrilling head to toe, I snuggled into his back. He fell asleep quickly. I, however, didn't. I'd left the heating on too long and my mouth was dry. I needed a drink of water.

Getting up quietly, I tiptoed into the hall to go down to the kitchen. I didn't want to wake Pete, but that object was defeated as I noisily tripped over something lying on the floor by the stairs. It lit up and I realized it was his mobile, charging. Panicking that I'd broken it, I picked it up and peered anxiously at the screen. Thankfully it wasn't cracked. It was, however, very clearly displaying:

New Message: Liz

FIVE

I carry my steaming mug of milk into the cold, still sitting room and perch on the edge of the sofa in the dark. It's burning my hands slightly and as I raise it to my mouth, trying not to breathe in the smell of the liquid, the first touch of it scalds my dry lips. I have to pull away sharply, setting the cup quickly down on the carpet to cool. I put my head in my hands and massage my temples tiredly. I can feel the heat of my fingers and the sharp edge of one slightly too long nail as it digs into my skin. Was it really only last night that I was down here, having tripped over his phone? It feels like that happened an age ago. I can see myself now, confusedly picking up the phone and staring at the screen reading "New Message: Liz," and the information just not computing.

My first thought had innocently been, Why on earth was a client texting him so late at night? It must be an emergency.

But Pete is an architect, not a banker brokering a deal or a doctor on call. There was, of course, absolutely no reason why a client should be contacting him that late on a Sunday night.

All the same, I had stood there for a moment in the dark and wondered, Should I go and tell him so he could take a look?

But he was tired, I didn't want to have to disturb him. I decided I'd open it and if it was that important I'd wake him up.

I clicked open and read:

Don't worry! U can get me another one can't U?! Same brown?! was v v v sweet of you tho. Night night xx

And in that split second, it was as if the room flipped upside down and shrunk all at the same time. An instinctive chill crept across my shoulders like someone had draped a cold, damp towel round me. My heart did an extra thump thump.

Get her what in the same brown? Night night? And kisses?

My brain couldn't seem to catch up and work fast enough, I just stared at the type dully. Finally my fingers got fed up with waiting and darted to his inbox. I stood there, wearing just knickers and one of his old T-shirts, with the neon screen lighting up my face as I started to scrawl through names that I mostly didn't recognize, apart from my own.

An icy, bony hand clutched around my heart and squeezed tightly as I saw "Liz" roll into view.

With shallow breath, I opened it. It simply read:

Can't now xx

I scrolled through some more names and there was Liz again:

On way, running late, will be there xx

Hurriedly I rolled through the rest of the list, my eyes darting to her name again:

I do too xx

And with that, my legs suddenly turned into hollow bendy tubes under me that wouldn't support my weight. I wobbled over to the stairs, not taking my eyes off the small screen, and sat down heavily. My throat had started to constrict. I could hear my own heart pounding like waves in my chest and blood crashing in my ears.

I desperately clicked on some other names. In contrast, they seemed incredibly businesslike.

Paula:

By lunchtime tomorrow hopefully. Deadline Friday max.

Seb:

Not a chance, don't think it's viable at all. Suggest a rethink.

Then there were ones from me that read things like:

What time are you back for tea?

and

Get milk on way home pls?

The lack of kisses jumped out at me straight away.

I scrolled back to the list again and then I noticed what times Liz had texted him: 1:20 in the morning and 11:45 at night.

Hardly the time to be talking shop.

I took a couple of deep breaths and tried to calm myself down. There would be a logical explanation, a good reason for some woman to be texting my boyfriend late at night.

But at the same time, as I stood there holding Pete's phone, I got a rush of pictures of him in my head. All the times I'd seen him with his mobile lately—just finishing a call, snapping it shut, throwing it casually on the bed as I came into the bedroom, checking it as I came out of the bathroom in the hotel . . .

A small ripple of fear coursed through me and I started to feel dizzy and sick, the same nausea as when you realize you've got way too drunk and you don't want to be any more; the room is spinning and you'd give anything not to be feeling so foul and out of control.

Acid started to gurgle in my gut. I took some deep breaths and tried to think rationally and calmly. Don't jump to stupid conclusions, I told myself.

I looked again at the texts. After all, that one could just be her running late for a meeting with Pete to talk business, couldn't it? And she was probably one of those addicted-to-her job types who worked into the night, hence why they were sent so late.

But that didn't explain *what* had been very sweet of him, and "night night?" It was so familiar, relaxed and suggested such intimacy. Something was very wrong.

I went back into his outbox, his sent texts. There were a lot, but I soon saw what I was looking for: To Liz, sent at two in the afternoon:

What u up to? can talk now if you like.

I felt a wash of relief when I realized he hadn't put any kisses. I scanned furiously up and down the rest of the list, but there was nothing else. That was the only text to her.

I went to his call list. Nothing at all. No incoming or outgoing. The relief started to ebb away . . . for a man who spent so much time on the phone, why was it all clear? What did he have to hide?

I stared so hard at the screen that her name started to swim in front of my eyes. I needed more information.

Phone bills. That was what I needed. His phone bills. I grabbed a pen and scribbled her number down on the inside of my hand. Then I had to decide what to do with the new message . . . I couldn't leave it, he'd know I'd seen it. I clicked delete and it silently vanished without trace.

I plugged the phone back in and quietly began to creep upstairs. Having tiptoed past our bedroom, I listened carefully for any letup in his snoring and then opened the door to his office. Slowly, I pushed it shut until it clicked gently behind me. Then I switched the light on, took a deep breath and began to look around.

SIX

The small room was an absolute tip. His drawing board was covered in sheets, the bin overflowing with balled-up bits of paper. Books were spilling out of shelves, half-full cups of coffee were glued with sticky bottoms to piles of files and as for the desk, it was a total mess. The curtains were half open so the darkness could nose in. I made myself jump when I looked up to see my reflection staring guiltily back at me in the glass.

Pulling the curtains shut I looked around disbelievingly. It was far from the room of someone with an uncluttered mind, that was certain. More like walking into a teenage boy's pit of a bedroom, or the lab of a mad professor. How the hell, I thought as I stepped over a pile of magazines on the floor, was I going to find *anything*?

I sat down gingerly at the desk and started to leaf through a pile of loose papers, but they slid through my fingers and cascaded on to the floor in a slippery mess, making what sounded to me like a *huge* noise. I froze and held my breath . . . but there were no resulting footsteps across the landing, no opening door and no accusative Pete standing there saying, "What the hell are you doing?"

And what *was* I doing? I knew I shouldn't be snooping in his stuff, but I'd gone past the having morals stage: it was proof I wanted. Proof that I was wrong, that I'd made a stupid mistake and could go back to bed feeling a little bit silly and bloody glad I hadn't woken him up.

But there was nothing to reassure me. Just a list of quotes and notes for a job, tile quantities and wiring requirements.

I opened a filing box: nothing much in there either. Accountants' letters, tax receipts. I turned back to his desk and another stack of papers.

I came across the receipt for our weekend away and on careful inspection realized we'd been billed wrongly—there was a room service order on there we didn't have. I tucked it in my dressing-gown pocket and made a mental note to ring the hotel in the morning and get it refunded.

I still couldn't find the phone bills, though, and that worried me even more than the prospect of finding them. He *had* got something to hide. Otherwise why weren't they on view with everything else? I sat at his desk wondering what to do next, when I noticed out of the corner of my eye that the light of his laptop was still on. I lifted the lid up and it whirred loudly as it restarted. My heart stopped again and I froze but, after a second of sitting there holding my breath and waiting, he didn't appear at the door. Cautiously I looked at the screen.

There were a number of files on his desktop, but it was all work stuff. There was one called personal, but it was just his CV.

I clicked on his e-mail icon and scanned through hundreds of mails, but there was nothing from or to Liz.

So if she was a client, I thought to myself quickly—*if* she was a client—where was the correspondence from her? There were no quotes, no nothing. Doesn't everyone use e-mail for work these days?

I looked in some box files round his desk; none of them had anything that made reference to Liz. Who *was* this woman?

I stood up and accidentally stood on a slippery magazine that resulted in my nearly doing the splits on the carpet. When I glanced down to see what I'd trodden on, I saw the program for the show he took me to on our weekend away.

My heart softened. We *had* had a really good time . . . I picked it up and ran my fingers down the spine of the glossy cover. It was such a great weekend. I started to absently flick through the pages, glancing at the pictures. Perhaps I could just talk to him about the text? Surely it could be explained . . .

But just as I was on the brink of dismissing it all, resolving just to ask him who she was in the morning and going back to bed, something caught my eye.

A photo was smiling out of the page. It was a girl with long, blonde hair and a familiar face. I knew I'd seen her before. I was frowning and puzzling when it dawned on me. It was the gallery girl, the one with the tattoo from the film about exploitation that I'd seen that very afternoon.

I studied the picture. She looked different, as she would in a contemporary outfit—in an outfit full stop—but it was definitely her. Same full lips, almost feline features and arched eyebrows. My eyes dropped down to the bio under the picture. It read: *Teasel—Elizabeth Andersen.*

It took a moment. I stared at the picture and the words for what felt like a full five minutes before my brain ground into action: Hang on a minute . . . *that's* a coincidence . . . A girl you recognize from a gallery exhibit that *Pete* took you to is in a program in *Pete's* office and it just turns out that her name is *Elizabeth*, just as you happen to be searching for *Pete's* phone bills to find out who a mystery *Liz* is . . . whaddya know? Whadda the chances, eh? Pete and Liz, Pete and Liz, Liz and Pete . . .

I looked at the photo again and she stared back at me, a knowing, seductive smile. I slowly started to realize that this was the woman I was looking for. *This* was Liz. Scanning disbelievingly through her bio notes, my eyes flickered and skimmed over the words:

Teasel—Elizabeth Andersen

Lizzie trained at the Doreen Lightfoot Academy in Woking, having grown up around song and dance from a young age. On graduation, Lizzie took on her first role in *Annie Get Your Gun* at the Left Way Theatre in Rhyl, then the title role of *Aladdin* in Croydon. Lizzie has toured extensively with Princely Cruises and has appeared in the tour of *Night of a Thousand Voices* for Tin Pot Productions. Lizzie has performed at numerous trade fairs and appeared in pop videos for A1 and Sam and Mark from *Pop Idol*. The role of Teasel is Lizzie's first West End appearance and she is thrilled to be part of such a demanding and respected show. She would like to thank God for giving her the gift of song and dance, her parents for their support and endless love and her special boy for just being him, love ya always! xxxx

It was then I remembered a dancer throwing a rose at Pete at the end of the show. It was her.

Pulling at the pages of the program frantically, I flipped through them, but there was nothing else, just her smug, diamond-hard little face staring back at me.

I sat down and tried to think. Someone called Liz was texting Pete at odd times of the day. Inexplicably I had found a program in his office with the picture in it of a girl I know threw a rose at him—a girl we happened to have seen in a gallery installation. It was just too much of a coincidence.

I needed his fucking phone bills.

After an hour of searching I finally found one. It was shoved inside a book called *Truss Construction*, deliberately hidden. It had been opened.

My hands trembled as I slid it out of the envelope and unfolded it. The date revealed it was his bill for the month just passed. The list of numbers ran over several pages, but it didn't take long to spot what I was looking for.

Like clusters of little poisonous berries, I could see bundles of one number. I checked the number on my hand—it was hers. In one afternoon alone he had texted her ten times.

I let out a gasp and my mouth began to go dry. I could feel a sticky coating on my lips.

Flicking quickly to the week before, again, I could see over and over:

Text Message
Text Message
Text Message
Text Message

And all of the numbers my boyfriend had texted were hers. My eyes scanned the page; it was full of her.

Then I noticed the calls. An hour here, half an hour there and on one afternoon a call lasting two hours. *Two hours?*

It suddenly occurred to me that the night before, when I had done 1471 thinking I was going to get his mum, I'd got someone else. A girl. Was that her? It must have been.

I realized that he hadn't been on the phone to Shirley at all, he'd been talking to *her* while I was in the bath. That was why he didn't want me to call Shirley back, because I'd have caught him out. He was never on the phone to his mum in the first place.

He had lied to me, and Liz was very obviously much, much more than just a client.

Standing frozen in the small room, at last my mind began to gather speed like a runaway train; wheels started to steam, metal ground on metal, whistles shrieked warnings as it started to hurtle out of control downhill . . . I stared wildly at her picture in the program . . . What about the trips to the gym and him not getting much slimmer . . . him getting me nice but unusually thoughtful treats, suggesting days out . . . but things had been good lately . . . we'd hardly been going through a rough patch . . . had we? *Wooooo! Woooooo! Get out of the way! Train with no brakes!* I tried to stand up but the room had started swirling and spinning in the opposite direction . . . we'd had sex only hours earlier . . . I felt like I was being whirled down a plughole. Things hadn't been perfect, but what is? *She could still be a client, she could still be a client . . . Couldn't she?* Even when I knew, I knew that I had nothing left to cling on to, I still wanted to believe that I was wrong. Not Pete, not my Pete.

The train crashed through rickety wooden barriers daubed with red paint and a sign that said, "Warning, do not enter! Danger!" like a bad Wild West movie. It plunged over the cliff and sailed through the air, pistons pumping pointlessly, bell clanging and smoke rushing out of its chimney up to the sky. It arched silently then plummeted to the dustbowl below. Everything went quiet for a moment, the moment of sterile calm before impact . . . then there was an almighty crash, a ball of fire as it exploded and then a billowing mushroom smoke cloud. No survivors. Couldn't be. Just a lump of twisted, mangled metal and an eerie silence.

I looked at the evidence of the secret little conversations they'd had, conversations I had known nothing about, and felt like I was staring over the edge of that cliff into the wreckage of my life.

The man I'd lain next to each night, undressed in front of, cleaned my teeth with in the bathroom, had this secret little world that I had no part of and didn't even know existed. How could this be? *How?*

Through a chink in the curtain, I could see a sliver of my reflection. Hot, shocked, scared tears started to slip down my cheeks and her number on the bill swam in front of my eyes. I had a sudden image of her sitting in her flapper dress, swinging her legs, phone to her ear, waiting, phoning my boyfriend. I pictured him answering, them both smiling and laughing happily.

I looked again at the times of the messages and the calls he had made to her. They were all when I would have been at work during the day or very late at night when I would have probably gone to bed. I could see him in my mind, creeping into the bathroom, sitting down on the edge of the bath with the door locked, texting away while I lay sleeping in the room next door.

I had stepped into a parallel room, a reflected, twisted one full of the objects of my life, but all in the wrong places. In under a minute Pete, the man who I have spent not an inconsiderable part of my life with—the man I've danced in crappy discos with, who sang *My Girl* to me at a friend's karaoke party, the man with whom I have had both my best and worst holiday ever, the man who can recite most of the lines from *Dumb and Dumber*, the man who I chose sofas with, the man who can't eat eggs because they make him hurl, the one who I never dreamed in a million years would do this to me—had become someone I didn't know at all.

I forced my eyes shut and they burned on the inside with the tears that I'd trapped . . . all I could see was her fucking face, her smiling, laughing face. Looking at the bill again, I noticed there were even texts on the night of my birthday. *My birthday!*

I tasted blood in my mouth. Reaching my fingers up, I touched my lip and realized that I had bitten it so hard I had noticed the skin.

I don't really remember how long I sat there with tears escaping down my face, staring dumbly into space, wracked with a physical pain that I could barely breathe through, but it felt like forever. Finally, when I couldn't cry any more and I had given up hope that he was going to hear me, come and tell me it was all a bad dream and take me back to bed, I tried to stand up.

My legs were stiff and my toes so cold they felt like stubs of ice.

I tucked away the bill just as I had found it and arranged the room so that he had no idea I'd been in there. Then I walked noiselessly to the bathroom. The small strip light above the mirror flickered on and my blotchy red face stared back at me, puffy and swollen. I could see her perfect face in my mind—lips that had almost certainly kissed him.

The thought of him touching this other woman made me literally sick. I retched silently, the half-digested chicken and red wine that we had for supper splashed quietly into the loo. I hung there for a moment gasping, my eyes streaming. Then I stood up, glanced in the mirror again, brushed my teeth, blew my nose, wiped my face. There was nothing to do but go back to our bedroom.

I opened the door and stood in the doorway. From there I could see the outline of his body in the bed, hear his breathing, smell the fuggyness and sleep in the room.

"I'd boot him out."

I could hear my own voice, laced with the conviction of a couple of glasses of wine, back in the bar with Amanda and Louise. We had tutted disapprovingly over a colleague of Amanda's who was conducting an affair behind his very nice wife's back, to the full knowledge of everyone in his office. "I'd absolutely get rid of him if I were her," I'd said firmly as I passed my verdict—no room for error, no choice to be made.

But when it was suddenly real, not just a stupid idle conversation I hadn't given any real thought to, I didn't shake him awake, shout and cry and ask him how he could do it to me. I felt desolate. He hadn't just drunkenly shagged someone else. This was obviously an emotional involvement, someone he had *feelings* for . . . someone he might have fallen in love with.

The free-falling hurt and confusion was almost unbearable and it froze all of my anger. I just stared at him lying there and, despite knowing for how long and how much I had loved him and how he had broken it all, how he had ruined everything that was so precious and real to me, had taken it all away without giving me any say in the matter—despite that, and knowing he had been so careless with us and our lives—when I should have been outraged and angry, all I saw was him simply lying there, breathing softly. All I wanted—all I *needed*—was to be in bed with him. To hold him and have him hold me.

I wanted to blot her out, have it not be real.

So I went and got into our bed and felt the warmth begin to spread through me as I pressed silently up against him. In his sleep, the chill of my skin made him shift gently, but he eased his back into the crook of my body. We fitted together and as he slid back into deep and restful sleep, I tried not to get tears on his back.

I attempted to force away the image of him lying in bed with her. There was someone out there so powerful, with such a pull on his heart that he had forgotten about me and risked it all for something with her.

My hands reached out and I clung helplessly to him.

SEVEN

B y 4:07 I've given in and have quietly put the TV on, but I'm so paranoid about waking Pete that I've got the sound down so low I can barely hear it. Despite a relentless search, there is nothing worth watching on over thirty channels. Finally I settle for a repeat of a property show and lean back into the sofa, pulling my dressing gown tightly around me as the pictures flicker and light up my tired face. I must look appalling. Oddly, though, I can't say I feel very much worse for two nights of no sleep, just more numb, perhaps.

Yesterday morning, however, I had felt raw when my eyes opened to the sound of heavy rain. There was a deep, taut knot in my tummy that somehow seemed to have been there since before I woke up, and a pulsing ache raged behind my dry eyes.

I had lain completely immobile in our bed, my mind already running blindly down corridors. I stared through the chink in the curtains at the chimney pots and roofs and wondered what I was going to do about what I had found on his phone and in his study, and how it was going to be all right. The alarm clicked on and I automatically reached out and slapped my hand down on it. Pete stirred, but we stayed in silence; me afraid to say any of the hundred things I wanted to, him barely awake. Finally he heaved himself out of the bed and, seeing him leave the imprint of his body behind on the sheet, it was all I could do not to shout hoarsely after him, beg him to come back and hold me while I cried and cried.

So I just lay there, very still, listening to my boyfriend move around our house as if nothing was wrong. After the shower stopped there was the hiss of the iron steaming over his fresh shirt, a clatter of a cereal bowl, breakfast TV, the gush of the tap and whir of his electric toothbrush. All I could do was stare at the ceiling and wonder how this could be happening. Finally he appeared next to me.

"Are you okay? How come you're not getting up?" He looked at me in concern.

I rolled my head listlessly toward him. "I feel sick," I muttered, which wasn't a lie.

"Poor baby." He sat down on the edge of the mattress. "Would you like some water or anything?" He reached out and stroked my face.

I wanted to grab his hand, to hold it to me fiercely and smack it away both at the same time. I shook my head. "No, thank you."

"Are you going to work today?"

I shook my head again. "Will you phone them for me and tell them I won't be in?"

His face clouded over slightly before he smiled sympathetically and said, "Yeah, sure." I suddenly realized my being ill was inconveniencing him in some way. Had he been planning to see her? Just as the horrific thought occurred to me that she might have already been in my house, in our *bed*, he said that he was sorry but he had a meeting that he couldn't move so he wouldn't be at home all day.

I shrugged wordlessly and turned my head away from him because I could feel tears flooding my eyes and I didn't want him to see me cry. He leaned over and kissed me lightly on the forehead.

"I'll be back this evening. Try to get some sleep and call me if you want me."

I didn't look at him, I just heard the bedroom door close quietly.

He bounded downstairs and then the front door slammed. As I heard the window frames rattle, a flood of panic set in. I hadn't asked where he was going, or who the meeting was with! I leaped out of bed, grabbed my dressing gown, rushed to the spare-room window and watched him drive down the road. I wanted to ring him straight away, tell him to stop the car, turn around and come back. Stay with me, comfort me, tell me I was wrong.

I craned my neck for the last sight of him as the car turned right and then slipped out of view. He was gone. Where was he going? *Where was he going?*

I started to weep and leaned my forehead against the cool glass of the window, forcing my eyes fiercely shut. But as I did, Liz seeped unwanted into my mind, smiling smugly. I gasped out loud with the pain. My eyes flew open; anything, anything to get her out.

It was pouring outside; straight, determined rods that battered off the leaves. There were no signs of life in the street apart from one small bird miserably hunched on a branch, trying to keep dry.

I could still see her, laughing, sparkling in her dress. I

couldn't believe I'd actually spoken to her last night. I dashed to the phone and dialed with shaking fingers. I had to know that it had definitely been her. I had to.

It rang and I waited with a thumping heart, willing her to pick up.

"Hello?" said a female voice.

"Hello," I said, forcing the tremor out of my voice. "Sorry to disturb you, I know you're probably a bit rushed, but I wanted to catch you before you left."

"Well, you've got me, Mia," said Pete's mother. "How can I help?" she asked in the tone of voice that starchily meant, "I've got a hundred and one things to do, so hurry up."

"It's just this wedding," I said carefully. "When Pete spoke to you last night I wanted him to ask you if there's a gift list, but I don't think he did, did he? I was going to ring you back, but it was a bit late, so I just wanted to check this morning before you went."

There was a bit of noise in the background and she said bossily, "Not that one, Eric, that's the hand luggage bag. Oh just leave it! I'll do it in a minute!" Then she snapped back to me. "I didn't speak to Peter last night," she said irritably.

"Last night?!" I forced a merry laugh. "Listen to me! I meant morning. When you *last* spoke to him . . ."

It was painful, it really was. I can't believe that someone as sharp as her didn't realize that something was wrong. She probably would have done if she hadn't been so distracted, but she had other things on her mind than her son's girlfriend wittering on about wedding presents.

"I told him to tell you not to worry about a gift. I bought one from the list several weeks ago and put our names on it. Didn't he say anything?"

"No, he didn't." I tried to sound bright. "He is dreadful! Well, thank you for that."

"Not at all," she said with a slight snort, to indicate my mistake at thinking she made the effort for me.

"Well, thank you anyway. Have fun on safari," I said as sincerely as I could manage.

"Thank you," she said stiffly, and hung up.

I sat there in the silence of our room. Funnily enough I felt no better at all for having the irrefutable truth that he lied to me last night. He had called her from *our* phone. On *our* bill.

I didn't know what to do next. I just sat there thinking this must be what being in shock felt like: a numb, empty, frozen space.

Sinking back on to the bed, I heard the crinkle of paper. Reaching into my dressing-gown pocket, I pulled the receipt for the hotel out and stared at it. Room service that I never had. I wasn't paying for that too. I suddenly felt irrationally angry. I wasn't having it! How did people think they could get away with things like this?

I dialed furiously and a very well-spoken man answered. I told him in no uncertain terms that an error had been made on our bill and I wanted him to sort it out immediately. He apologized smoothly and asked me to hold while he checked his records. Then he came back and said kindly, no, madam, there was no error, a bottle of champagne had been correctly charged to room 105. Angrily I told him that was ridiculous. When had it been signed for and by whom? It certainly hadn't been me! He asked me, in a slightly less kindly tone, if I could hold the line again.

I clutched the receiver tightly to my ear as thoughts jostled for room in my head. An affair, Pete was having an affair. What had I done wrong? How long had it been going on? I stared at the rain and waited.

"Hello, madam. I'm sorry to have kept you." The clipped voice sliced into my thoughts and dragged me back to the room.

The champagne had been signed for at 4:30 in the afternoon by Pete, apparently. I explained hotly I knew that was not possible, because I was definitely having a massage at that time and I think I might have noticed if my boyfriend had drunk an entire bottle of champagne. But then, just as I was about to ask to speak to the manager, a horrible, dreadful thought slammed into my head. With a sickening sense of foreboding I asked slowly where he was when he signed for it.

The man sighed and said he couldn't possibly say, all he knew was that they had a signature and it was charged to our room.

Hating myself for asking, and with my eyes squeezed shut, I asked him tremulously if I could give him a name, and could he tell me if that person was staying in the hotel at the same time as us? There was a pause while he digested the implications of my suggestion. Softening, he gently said no, madam, he could not divulge that information. There was an uncomfortable silence and then I said, "Please . . . I need to know."

"I'm so sorry, madam. I wish I could help you. Is there perhaps anything else I can do for you?"

I thanked him flatly, but said no, no there wasn't. With palpable relief he wished me a good day and then he was gone, out of my life forever.

But I couldn't leave it there. With my heart starting to hammer and a leaping, visible pulse fluttering at my wrist, I took a few deep breaths and called back. This time a woman answered. I said as calmly as I could that my name was Liz Andersen, I had stayed in the hotel the weekend of the 7th and 8th and I thought I had left a necklace behind—I just couldn't remember what room I had stayed in. The lie came remarkably easily to me. Not at all, madam, she assured me, she would just be one moment. She disappeared off the line and I held my breath for what felt like eternity, willing and silently pleading with God that I was wrong. The phone clattered as she picked it up again and cheerily informed me I had been in room 315. What was the necklace like?

I didn't say anything, I just clicked the phone off and it slipped from my hands.

I shut my eyes and tried to breathe. She had been there on our weekend away. She had been at the hotel.

My head started to spin and everything became light and nauseous at the same time. *She'd been there.*

Had he slipped out of the room that night when I was asleep to go and find her? Was she waiting with their bottle of champagne in room 315, or did they drink that while I was packed off for my massage? No wonder he didn't mind about not having sex with me . . . he was upstairs fucking someone else.

It made me retch. I didn't want to get it on my pillow, so I leaned over the edge of the bed and tried to aim on some magazines . . . but nothing came out, just bile. I hadn't eaten anything so there was nothing to come up.

I hung there and gasped, eyes running, a string of spit dangling from my lip.

Then I remembered him sitting in the dark room at the gallery, staring up at the screen, transfixed, gazing at her as the music played. Her eyes boring into him, her smile not faltering. I thought that day out was for us . . . had it been just so he could see her on screen? Even though he was getting her in the flesh?

I retched again, my body still confused and going through the motions. Again there was nothing there.

Spitting on to the magazines, I wiped my nose with the back of my hand, pushed my hair out of my face and waited, wanting to make sure I was all done. The airbrushed face of a cover model pouted back up at me. Perfect skin, eyes all false, just like Liz.

I could see her again, all makeup and costume, waving down at him from the stage, throwing him a rose. Had she known I was at the hotel too? She must have. Had she pitied me? Had she even thought of me at all? The fucking bitch. The fucking *whore*.

The intense anger and jealousy seemed to rise from the pit of my gut, right from the core of me. I jumped up violently and crashed off down the hall to his office. Flinging open the door, it bashed back off the wall, chipping the plaster. I wanted to know more about this woman who I now suddenly hated more than anyone on the face of the earth. I paused on the threshold of the room. I had no idea of what it was I was looking for but whatever it was, I was going to find it.

Descending on his desk, I started to rifle through the piles of papers, sending them crashing to the floor. I crunched over files, not caring as they sprung open, spewing out pages. I heard discs snap under my determined feet, kicked his DVDs out of the way. I pulled books off the desk; papers were fluttering in the air like confetti—I didn't care about the mess, I just wanted to know *everything*.

My search didn't take long. For a man who was careful enough to delete his call lists and make sure he had no explicit texts on his phone that would prove anything, he was heartbreakingly bad at hiding other huge giveaways. All I had needed to know was that I had to look for them.

First of all there was the program. I stared so long and hard at her face that the page went blurry and I had to restrain myself from ripping it out. After another exhaustive and reckless search I found bills for two credit cards I didn't even know he had (the disadvantage of leaving before the post arrives and him always being at home to intercept it). And then I found a card. It had a small puppy on the front. Inside, in big, floral show-off writing it said:

Thank you SO much! I LOVE her AND you! We can go for walks now with you and Gloria! Liz xxxx

I sat down heavily. What had he done? Bought her a puppy? Moaning slightly, I rocked back and forth on the spot, hugging my knees into my chest trying to force the pain out. Had he taken my dog out with his bitch? It was sick!

I lost the plot completely then and wrecked his office. Jumping to my feet, enraged, I grabbed his Stanley knife and punctured his desk with pock holes and mad slashes. I swept everything off the desk, I ripped up the card into tiny shreds. I violently tore up some of his papers, the sound of it ripping through me. I stuck the knife through a picture of him and me on his desk. I sliced the blade through the program, screaming and screaming, flinging books around and kicking his chair over.

Then I heard Gloria barking downstairs and I stopped, breathing heavily, a light sweat on my brow. I could tell she was frightened; I could hear her scratching and whining, she knew something was wrong.

I went downstairs and discovered she'd weed everywhere, so I cleaned her up before shutting her out in the garden. Once everything was tidy downstairs, I went back upstairs and looked at the mess there.

His office was devastated. Not merely trashed—totally flattened.

That's when it occurred to me that when Pete got home and saw the mess, he would know that I'd found out. I'd forced his hand, backed him into a corner. We were going to have to talk about it. It was all going to come out.

And the thought of that was suddenly terrifying.

I realized with a jolt that I had never properly imagined being without Pete, not having him as part of my everyday life. Not having the right to go up and fling my arms round him and kiss him when he walked into a room. Not being able to pick up the phone and call him when something happened. Pete is the first person I call when something good or bad happens to me. Who would that person be if it wasn't him?

And what if this was just the excuse he'd been waiting for? Suppose he'd been trying to decide what to do—if he should stay, or leave me and go to her? The night before, I'd chosen not to wake him up and yell at him to get out. For all I knew, the choice about what would happen next might not actually be mine at all.

If he got home, saw the mess and then I had to tell him that I knew, would he deny it? Would he *want* to stay with me, or would he say, "Actually, you're right, there *is* something I want to talk to you about. I'm so sorry, I never wanted this to happen but it has, and I just want to be with her?"

I tried to imagine life without Pete as I stood there in the mess of his office, but since I met him he has been pretty much the first thing I think of when I wake up, the last thing I think of at night and, quite often, the thing I think about in between, too. He's the structure that my family and friends—my life—is woven into. He's the someone I come home to who has somehow always been there and I don't really remember what it was like before him. He is my best friend, the person who knows me better than I know myself.

He just *can't* be that with someone else. It doesn't make any sense. Where would I live? What would I do? I don't think I could even afford the house on my own. I'd have to start again. *Really* on my own.

The steadily rising alarm in my chest started to pound on the inside of my ribs. I looked wildly round the room and decided then and there that he simply couldn't see what I had done. I felt like Alice falling down the rabbit hole: weddings, children, couples, houses, all whisking past my outstretched fingers. I knew I had to do something to cover up what I had done or I'd be trapped by my own hands in a future that I didn't want, one that wouldn't include him.

And that's when the idea leaped into my head. A burglary . . . that would cover it up. All I had to do was total the rest of the house too, so it looked convincing.

My first deception.

EIGHT

A t least you weren't at home when he came calling," said the younger of the two policemen, trying to be helpful. "You should see what can happen if people disturb raids in action . . ."

His thickset, older colleague gave him a tired look. "But there'll be no need to worry about that now. He'll be long gone. I think he was an opportunist, madam. He didn't take anything other than the two items of jewelry?"

I curled my fingers tightly around the brooches in my pocket. "That's right," I said a little jerkily. "Two brooches that were my grandmother's."

"You see, if he'd have really known what he was doing, he'd have taken a lot more than that. I know it feels horrible to think of a stranger going through your things, but I really think this was a one-off, probably a kid." The policeman smiled at me kindly but obviously wanted to finish things up so he could go and have some lunch. "We'll do all the paperwork and here's your crime reference number, but other than that . . ." He tailed off.

"Thank you for your help," Pete held open our front door, "and we'll certainly look into getting that alarm fitted."

I watched the policemen walk down the drive and get into their car, my hands still in my pockets—jewelry in one, the ripped-up pieces of her card to Pete in the other. I'd have to remember to get rid of those.

Pete closed the door as they drove off, turned to me and said, "Come here, you!" as he pulled me to him. He said lovely things like, "You poor baby, you must have been so scared" and, "Thank God you'd taken Gloria out for a walk. You're so brave finding that on your own, and being ill as well . . ."

I stand up and move quietly to the window, picking up the edge of the curtain and looking out on to the quiet street and the same drive that the policemen sauntered down yesterday lunchtime. It is starting to get light. I don't have much longer to wait. Pete will be getting up soon. I let the curtain drop and move back to the sofa, being careful not to kick over the full, now cold, mug of milk that is still sitting on the floor at my feet. Even if I *had* drunk it, I'm sure it wouldn't have helped me sleep. I pick it up and inspect it. There is a disgusting skin over the surface that bulges slightly as I tip the contents gently to one side, not quite enough to let the milk underneath burst through.

I think about my saying to Pete yesterday in a strangulated voice, "I *was* scared Pete, I was more scared than I've ever been in my life," and I set the cup down unsteadily. Thankfully it doesn't fall over.

Pete had had to hold me tightly for at least a full five minutes after the police left, soothing me worriedly. He started by whispering things like, "It's okay, sweetheart, I'm here, I'm here—I'm not going to let anyone hurt you," but that made me cry harder, and I sobbed into the lapel of his jacket with his arms round me as if my heart would break.

Eventually he pulled away and led me into the sitting room. Shoving a pile of crap off the sofa, he gently sat me down and bustled off into the kitchen to make me a hot, sweet tea.

It was an overwhelming relief to have him next to me, gently rubbing my back as I sipped the tea in silence. I didn't want to say anything in case I gave myself away, so it was left to him to suppose out loud that we ought to start clearing everything up.

He stood up, took off his jacket, pulled his tie loose and hung them both over the banisters. Looking around him he whistled and shrugged rather helplessly. "God, I don't know where to start!"

How about with where you met her? Or what she's got that I haven't? How long has it been going on? Do you love her? Has she been here, in our house?

"We could use some help really, couldn't we? I'd ring Mum and Dad but they'll be in Africa by now." He glanced at his watch, as if that was going to tell him exactly what time Shirley had touched down on another continent. "What about your mum, shall I call her?"

I shook my head dumbly. "She's in Miami, isn't she?"

"Shit! I'd forgotten about that. What stunning timing on both their parts."

"Just one of those things," I said, totally exhausted. I wondered dully if he was thinking about her right now . . . it felt so odd. Sitting silently with my hands wrapped round a scalding cup of tea, thinking that I could be throwing it at his head. I could be opening my mouth, having it all out, screaming and shouting . . .

By the time he started going on about how much mess the burglars had made and not understanding how someone could be so heartless, I wasn't really listening. All I was thinking about was how if it wasn't for her everything would be okay. She danced through my mind in her little flapper slapper dress, smiling nastily at me and I loathed her for it.

Shaking slightly, I tried to calm down, making myself grip the burning hot cup, trying to drag my thoughts away from her and on to the heat of my hands instead. Something to focus on would stop me going to pieces.

As we got dustbin bags and began to clean up, Pete chattered away to me to fill the silence, shooting me worried glances every now and then. I just listened to him, not really hearing the words. The easiest thing to do was to play along and act like I was very shaken up—which wasn't much of a stretch.

When I tripped over the edge of a chair that I'd flung across the room only hours earlier, he shot out a hand to steady me. I grabbed back at his arm and he smiled and said, "It's okay, you've got me!"

I just managed not to laugh hysterically, but against my will tears started to slip out of my eyes again. He pulled me to his chest. "Oh, baby! You've got to stop it. Come on! Otherwise they've won." A sharp little stab dug into me when he said that, and I saw her face grinning back out from the pages of the program, laughing at me. I could smell his tangy lemon aftershave mixed with the washing powder we always use as he held me to him. "Hey!" he went on. "It'll be okay, we'll sort this!"

I clung to him for ages because I didn't know what else to do and he waited patiently until eventually he had to prise himself away from me. "Come on, soldier!" he smiled. "I'm here, the perimeter is secure!"

The rest of the day passed slowly and painfully. We carried

on clearing up and he made us sandwiches that we had on our laps in front of the TV. An item came on the local news about an old couple celebrating their golden wedding anniversary. Looking at them so happy, so contented, I felt jealous—of an *old* couple. That was all I wanted: togetherness, trust, honesty, not both of us sitting here with dirty secrets.

Then I heard the bleep of his phone from the dining room.

A text message.

My heart thudded. *Was that her?*

He'd heard it too because he subtly removed his arms from around my shoulders. But he didn't get up, he just carried on watching TV. Then after a little stretch and a yawn, he reached for his glass and pretended to be surprised to find it empty. "I need another drink," he announced, getting up. "Want one?"

I shook my head silently. *Liar!* He didn't need one at all, he was off to the dining room to check his phone!

Pete walked casually out of the room and I sat stiffly on the sofa, trying to look as if I was focusing on the TV. All I could think was, "it's her, it's her." He came back in with a full glass of water and I forced a bright smile. "Who was that?" I asked. "I heard your phone go."

He didn't look me in the eye but sat down on the sofa. "No one important," he said. "Just a message that someone had called for me at the office." He yawned tiredly. "We should make a start on upstairs. Are you sure you feel well enough to help?"

"Absolutely. Why don't we tackle your study next?" I said quietly.

"Oh I can do that later," he replied calmly. "More important to get the bedroom sorted so you can have a nap later if you need one."

"Well, you go and get started then and I'll be right up, just need a wee." I managed to smile at him and he squeezed my hand, hauled himself up and trawled upstairs.

Sitting frozen on the sofa listening intently, I heard the floorboards squeak. He wasn't in our bedroom, he'd gone straight to the office to make sure nothing was lying around that shouldn't have been, just as I knew he would. I walked quickly into the dining room, grabbed his phone from the table and slammed into the downstairs loo, locking the door sharply behind me. Moving fast, I located the inbox, clicked on it and there it was. Top of the list—*Liz*. The office my fucking arse. It read:

Is all ok? Nothing too wrecked? Gloria all right? U ok? Xx

I wanted to scream, punch the wall, kick the door and flush the phone down the loo all at the same time. What the *fuck* had it got to do with her? It was *my* house and *my* dog and *MY* boyfriend! How *dare* she? "U ok?" *Fuck off!* It's not *her* that makes sure he's okay, it's *me*, *ME*! I hurled the phone on to a towel on the floor in disgust.

My blood pumped madly, making my scalp prickle. I was wired with hatred for her, a balled-up energy that had nowhere to go. In the tiny downstairs loo, still half tiled, I couldn't even pace. I was boxed in totally. Looking at the phone screen, staring furiously at the words, I could have killed her, I swear to God. Instead I just thumped the wall with the flat of my fists and leaned my head against the spiky peaks of the chipped grout.

I heard Pete shout, "You okay?"

He must have heard the thump. I jerked my head up and listened carefully. Was he coming downstairs? He *couldn't* catch me with his phone. I flushed the loo, picked up the mobile and cautiously opened the door. I heard the creak of the boards again as he moved from the office to our room. He must have heard the loo and was making *his* way back. It was like being stuck in a bad spy movie, only not funny at all, just utterly horrible.

"Be right up!" I shouted and adjusted the phone so it was back to the screensaver. I put it back on the table and ran upstairs. Then I slowed down again as I remembered I was supposed to be ill.

He was making the bed as I went into our room. I walked round to the other side and grabbed the opposite corners. In a practiced routine we smoothed the duvet together, then he plumped the pillows and I got the cushions from the floor. We moved in silence until I broke it.

"Hadn't you better call work?"

He frowned and looked puzzled. "Why?"

"You said you had a message that someone had called for you?"

"And?"

"Don't you want to find out who?"

He started to gather up underwear from the drawers that I had pulled it out of earlier. "No, the message told me who it was that called."

"Oh, I see—who was it then?"

He straightened up and looked at me. "A bloke about his conversion. Why the questions?"

Bloke about a conversion . . . bitch called Liz, more like. How dare she ask him if he was all right?

"Just interested . . . making conversation." As I spoke, I realized that in order for her to have been asking if he was all right, he must have already told her about the break-in. That's how close they were . . . she was looking out for him . . . she knew what was going on in his life. It was definitely not just some one-off shag.

"Hey! Sweetheart!" Pete snapped my attention back. "I said we've just got time to go and buy some new frames for the pic-tures, and I think all they really broke in the kitchen was some cups and plates. Thank God they didn't do the TV, eh? You well enough to come into town or shall I go on my own?"

What, and have you call Liz the second you leave? I thought quickly. No chance.

"I'll come. Maybe we could go to the cinema afterward, watch something fun. I'd like to get out of the house. I just don't want to think about anything for a couple of hours." There was no way he'd be able to get messages or anything in the cinema.

He looked a little surprised but said okay, if that was what I wanted. I sorted Gloria out with water and some food and watched her leap about excitedly, thinking she was getting a walk. I didn't want to be near her—she just made me think of Liz.

Pete wandered back in and patted his pockets like he'd for-gotten something. "Oh! Wallet and phone," he said absently, making for the door again.

"Leave them!" I interjected quickly. "My treat for the cinema and I'll get the other stuff too. Anyway, you don't need the mo-bile, you'll have to have it switched off anyway at the cinema."

He couldn't argue with that, it would have looked obvious. So he just smiled a slightly tight smile and said, "Come on then! Let's get you medicinal ice cream and popcorn."

And off we went, just like any other normal, happy couple.

The trip was sadly not a success. I tried to hold his hand in the cinema and he pulled it away to rummage for some pick-and-mix and didn't put it back in mine afterward. I tried to lean my head on his shoulder but the armrest got in the way and it felt awkward. I knew I was reading into everything with far more significance than it probably held for him, but I couldn't help it. I wanted a sign—any sign—that he still loved me and not her.

In the car on the way back, he was very quiet and withdrawn. Totally different to how he had been earlier, as if he was deep in thought. He was barely monosyllabic and the harder I seemed to try, the more absent he became.

I kept looking at him, wondering what he was thinking, if she'd called him while we'd been out. I was silently devastated when he didn't automatically curl his fingers around mine and hold my hand when I rested it on his lap as he drove. He just left it sitting forlornly on his knee and I felt pathetically needy, hating myself for willing him to pick up my hand. I had to tell myself he needed two hands to change gear and hold the wheel, that it didn't mean anything. Forty-eight hours earlier, I probably wouldn't have noticed if he'd put *his* hand on *my* knee.

Then I tried to ignore the fact that he didn't seem to notice I was only just managing to hold it together next to him, and focused on looking out of the windscreen instead, like I used to when I was much younger and car sick. "Just stare straight ahead," my mum would say. "Don't look left or right, just straight in front of you, and keep breathing. No, darling, we can't stop just yet. Let's get home before it gets dark. Just keep breathing, in and out. Good girl."

When we got home I was tired and wanted to go straight to bed, but I knew that was probably what he wanted me to do so he could text or call her. It had seemed a good idea, getting him to myself for a few hours, but it had achieved nothing, merely delayed everything.

I couldn't leave him alone downstairs. We sat silently

watching TV. There was still a lot of cleaning up to do, but neither of us felt like doing it. When I started to fall asleep on the
sofa, he woke me up with a little nudge and gently told me to go
to bed.

"Will you come too?" I rubbed my eyes sleepily.

In a bit, he said firmly, he just wasn't quite tired enough and
Gloria needed a wee.

I had no choice. I trailed upstairs and got into our cold, big
bed. I sat hunched up, clutching my knees to my chest, craning
to see if I could hear talking or not. I barely noticed when my
own mobile rumbled on the bedside table next to me. It was a
text from Clare:

Whatcha doin? R U watchin Ghost? Is on TV now. P Swayze
with no top on. Woof. Call me—haven't spoken to you forever.

Then I noticed I had another text, this one from Lottie:

Hi hon. Soz you feel rough. Must be bad to have to get Pete
to call, unless you're pulling a fast one? Bitch if you are.
Spanky in well bad mood. See you tom. Xxx

I barely registered them as I put the phone back on the table.
I managed another five minutes before I crept noiselessly downstairs again and waited for a second behind the closed sitting-
room door, listening. I couldn't hear anything, so I opened the
door.

Pete jumped and looked up, startled. I wasn't looking at him
though—his phone was beside him on the sofa. It hadn't been
there when I'd left.

"You all right?" he said.

I couldn't help myself. I shook my head and, to my disgust, up came the tears *again*. I opened my mouth to say, "I can't do this. I can't act like I don't know." I wanted to say it, but I couldn't get it out.

He jumped up and said, "Hey! Hey! It's not that bad!"

"Not that bad! *Not that bad?!*" I exploded at him. "My whole fucking life has been ripped apart. I don't know what to do, I don't feel safe . . . I don't know where to put myself . . ." My voice was heaving with jumbled words and hiccups.

He clutched me to him and said, "Shh! I'm here. You *are* safe. I'm such a dickhead! Of course you don't want to be upstairs on your own! And you're ill, too. I'm so sorry. I'll come to bed now."

He reached for his phone and switched it off. Then he flung it on to the sofa.

I watched it sitting there dead and still as he rocked me again for what felt like the hundredth time—and a tiny flicker of spirit sparked somewhere in me.

Fuck you, Liz, he's coming to bed with me, I thought savagely as I looked at the lifeless mobile, no merrily twinkling lights or buzzing exciting messages. That thought made me feel a little calmer as I allowed him to lead me upstairs like an invalid.

We talked for a bit about the mess everywhere and he stroked my hair softly, which, oddly, made me feel not soothed at all, although I did a happy little sigh anyway.

"Is that nice?" he asked, smiling at me. I nodded gratefully and then felt disgusted with myself for being so limp and useless, so I lay there, tried not to think at all and just closed my eyes. I tried just to enjoy him stroking me. It didn't last long though, he drifted off pretty quickly.

Not that it really mattered anyway. All I could think about was his phone lying downstairs on the sofa and what he'd sent her and what she'd sent him. I waited until I was sure he was asleep and then I quietly slipped out of bed.

NINE

Silently picking up his mobile, I took it into the downstairs loo, locking the door behind me and switching it on. I started to scroll through his messages, but before I had the chance to look for her, she came to me. The phone rumbled in my hand as three new texts delivered. *Three!* The first one said:

Where r u? all ok? Xx

Fine thanks, you whore.
The next one was:

Please text me bk—crap show—could do with chat.

The bitch. What a stupid, selfish, self-obsessed little bitch. As far as she knew his house had been wrecked. Bit more important than her shit show.
Then the last one said:

Know it doesn't help, but am thinking about you right now.
Xxx

Oh, she had *no right* to be thinking about him, texting him,
doing *anything*! I felt insane with anger.

But then, to my horror, the phone buzzed in my hand again.
New message:

Hey! You're still up! Left phone on, it woke me up as mssge
delivered! Bn worried. Know you had to be at home but don't
forget me! U know I need u too! x

That had almost made me roar out loud with rage. The
sheer force of the anger the words unleashed in me was fright-
ening. I'd started to fumble with the keypad, trying to call her
back to tell her to get out of my life and to leave my boyfriend
alone, but I was so angry my fingers couldn't hit the right but-
tons. She had no right to need him—he wasn't hers to need.

The phone rumbled again.

OK, guess you're asleep. Call me in morning when you are
free. xx

I'd stared furiously at the phone. Five messages in the inbox.
Five! Fucking obsessive.

Then it had occurred to me that they were five messages he
was going to know I'd seen. I couldn't just switch it off and go
back to bed . . . but I couldn't just delete them either, she'd have
a delivery report to show him. It would be impossible to explain
away five texts. One was coverable, but five . . .

I took a deep breath and tried to calm down. I had no choice but to break the phone.

I deleted his inbox—all of it. I checked his sent mail, nothing there at all. Switching it off, I crept into the kitchen and turned on the light. Gloria had sat up and eyed me with interest, pleased to see that I'd come to play. I got her half-opened tin of food out of the fridge and dipped Pete's phone in it. Then I held it out to Gloria.

She looked at it, sniffed it and then curiously touched the tip of her tongue to it.

"Don't lick it, you prat, *chew* it," I hissed at her.

I had to wiggle it around a bit before she got the idea, but finally there were some evident tooth marks and a cracked screen. Before she cut herself I took it away, rinsed the food off and dried it carefully. I removed the back and dropped the SIM card in Gloria's water bowl. Then I pulled it out again because I wasn't really sure if it could still work having been dipped in water, so to be on the safe side I pocketed the card, put the battery under the blanket in Gloria's basket and the actual phone by it. She sniffed it once or twice and then ignored it. Which was good because I didn't want her to chew it once I was back in bed and die or anything.

After I washed my hands, I eased exhaustedly back into bed beside Pete. My head ached dully with tiredness and my eyes hurt from my earlier crying but the satisfaction of knowing he wouldn't be calling her in the morning was immense. I imagined her pouting sulkily by the phone, kicking her chair and twisting her hair . . . *five fucking texts* . . . and "crap show could do with a chat," as if her bloody play was important—who gave a shit? I shivered with anger. I'd outwitted her. I didn't have to just roll over, I wasn't just helplessly stuck. I could fight.

But then I saw myself in my mind's eye, pathetically crouched next to Gloria's basket in the dead of night in my dark kitchen, desperately trying to make her leave teeth marks on the phone screen. How was that fighting? That was just mad. What had this person done to my life? She had me creeping round my own house . . . I was a grown woman! I had a good job, nice friends, a family whom I loved. Was I really going to be forced into behaving like a lunatic who was losing control? I had to have faced—and beaten—worse in my life than this girl, surely?

It was then, with a sickening thud, that I suddenly thought of Katie.

And, for the first time ever, I wondered if all those years ago she had been telling me the truth.

TEN

The first time I met Katie properly was at a First Holy Communion class when we were five years old. She was perched on the edge of Sister Ann's stiff sofa cushions in a sitting room that smelled faintly of boiled cabbage. She was wearing a deep-blue pinafore dress with a red roll neck under it, and her feet couldn't quite touch the ground. She had her Silver Book clutched tightly to her chest and a small, furry, neon-pink pencil case next to her. Just by looking at her I knew that in that pencil case there was going to be a full selection of neat, non-chewed felt-tip pens with the right lids on them. And none of them would be dried up.

I also noticed, with admiration and envy, her earrings glinting. I wasn't allowed my ears pierced as my mum said it was common on little girls and that I had to wait until I was twelve.

I must have been staring, because finally Katie said to me, "You're at my school, aren't you, in Mrs. Piper's class? I'm in Mrs. Tundal's. I read up to page seventeen of the Silver Book already, the bit on loving your neighbor. How far did *you* get?"

I teased her about that for years later. So typically Katie; competitive from the word go.

Despite that first meeting, we didn't really spend much time together at primary school. Different classes back then were different worlds, we just occasionally went round to each other's houses for tea.

It all changed when we went to secondary school. We stuck together nervously on our first day because we sort of knew each other, her in her pristine long white socks and slip-on shoes, me in the brown T-bar monstrosities from Jones the Bootmaker that my mother had insisted on making me wear because my feet rolled in. I looked like I was wearing a giant shit on each foot. But Katie stuck by me and even stood up for me when I got teased about the shoes *and* my A-line skirt and tight cardigan.

"She can't help it," Katie would say, her pencil skirt pulled tight as she stuck one hip out defiantly, baggy cardigan slipping off her shoulder, "her mum makes her. It's not *her* fault."

I got teased mercilessly about those bloody shoes. I was sent to deliver a message to a teacher who was teaching a sixth-form class and the whole room fell silent when I walked shyly in.

"Oh my God!" cried a girl with spiky hair and electric-blue eyeshadow. "What *has* that first year got on her feet?" Twenty pairs of eyes swiveled to look at me and then the whole room fell about laughing. I felt my face flush bright red and I tripped slightly in my haste as I stumbled out of the room. "She can't even stand up in them!" someone else shouted as I desperately tried to close the door behind me. I cried for hours in the loos afterward with Katie patiently holding out tissues. "They're all stupid," she said helpfully. "Ignore them. I could help you look better . . . if you like."

"You know, you could be pretty," she said in her bedroom several days later. We were sitting on her bed, ready to commence my makeover. "You look a bit like her," she went on, pointing to a girl dressed in a tartan puffball skirt in the latest *Jackie* we were flicking through. It had been a satisfying day of messing around with Katie's mum's hundred bottles of different-colored nail varnishes and going through her jewelry box, followed by us recording ourselves doing a pretend radio show on Katie's cassette player, before Katie had decided it was time to get down to business. "You've got nice hair, but it's too long," she said knowledgeably. "You should get it cut, and maybe perm it." She looked at my dead-straight, thick brown hair thoughtfully. "That would be cool."

"My mum wouldn't let me," I protested.

"How comes your mum is so strict?" Katie said, reaching for her makeup bag and pulling me to the edge of the bed. "I'm going to do your eyes first. Browns or blues?"

"Blues, please. She's not strict really. Although I wish she'd let me go to the cinema with you and watch *Ghost*!"

"Yeah, it was good. Keep still."

"Mum said it wasn't suitable. *Oww!*"

"Hmm. I think these eyelash curlers need a new rubber bit—did I pinch the skin?"

"A little bit." I winced, my eyes watering. "Okay—I'm all right now."

"So do you think it's cos you don't have a dad?"

I kept very still. "I don't think so," I said slowly.

"Mum says your dad lives in another country now with new children."

I didn't say anything, I just sat there silently hating Katie's mum more than I thought possible.

"I wish my dad would go and live in another country," Katie sighed. "He's grumpy, fat and we never get to watch what we want on TV. I think you're lucky." She smiled at me. I smiled back and suddenly it was all okay again. "So," she said, reaching for the frosted-pink lipstick, "if you had to choose between New Kids on the Block Joey or Jordan Knight, which would it be?"

In the second year, Katie continued my conversion from geek to Little Miss Popular by taking me to Freeman Hardy Willis and helping me choose a pair of white plastic slip-on shoes which I proudly changed into at the end of my road every day. My poor mum never was any the wiser and remained utterly confused as to why my feet continued to roll in.

It was Katie who showed me how to roll my skirt up. It was Katie who eventually persuaded my mum to let me have my waist-long hair cut to shoulder length and Katie who held my hand when I finally got my ears pierced. Katie who I made up a dance routine to Madonna's "Vogue" with—that I can probably still do. Katie who used to wait outside McDonald's for me so we could hang around town aimlessly every Saturday. Katie who I went to my first disco with. Katie who told me about her first kiss in lurid detail, Katie who I made laugh so much once she was actually sick. Katie who held my hand when I puked everywhere after first getting drunk on Taboo. Katie who I went on holiday to Ibiza with after our A-levels. Katie who helped me choose my uni course and Katie who broke my heart twice over by purposefully going to bed with my then boyfriend Dan.

I can remember it like it was yesterday, running breathlessly and excitedly up the stairs in Dan's halls of residence, the straps of my overnight bag digging into my shoulder. Ringing the doorbell, one of his friends opening the front door and going, "Mia? Er . . ." his eyes darting nervously toward Dan's closed door, "he's not in right now." Me saying confusedly, "But I can hear his stereo." Him looking embarrassed and me suddenly realizing there was something in that room I wasn't meant to see. Pushing past him, calling, "Dan? Hello? It's me!" and shoving the door open. Dan's horrified face as he reached for his T-shirt, shouting "Mia! Don't! It's not what it looks like! We just got drunk and fell asleep!" Me realizing someone was in bed with him and somehow getting across his room while Jay-Z blared out "Hard Knock Life," my bag slipping off my shoulders and my train ticket falling from my fingers as he scrabbled out of bed, knocking over a can of lager and an ashtray, still in his jeans, the stale smell of cigarettes and musty boys' clothes in the air. Me shouting, "What's going on?," hot tears springing to my eyes as I tried to pull back the duvet cover while this girl clasped it tightly around her. Dan's arms around me, attempting to hold me back, me wriggling free, him going "Shit! Oh shit!" as I tore desperately at the duvet and ripped it back . . . to reveal Katie's frightened face.

The funny thing is I can't remember how on earth I got back to university after that. I just remember walking back into the student kitchen in our halls and Louise looking up from the magazine she was reading and exclaiming, "You're back? Wasn't he there?" as I promptly burst into tears.

I cried solidly for about twenty-four hours with Louise and Amanda sitting beside me, fending off nosy parkers on our corridor and random people knocking on my door shouting, "phone call." Louise finally went down when Katie rang for the hundredth time and told her I never wanted to speak to her again and that she was a fucking bitch. Amanda shouted, "You're a two-timing lying shit!" out of the window when Dan imploringly shouted up, begging to be let in, saying that he'd traveled all the way from Newcastle to see me—that he had to see me, had to explain, needed me to take him back. Amanda chucked some cold noodles down at him and he gave up in the end and went home.

I never saw Dan again after that, apart from once in Birmingham New Street Station, of all places, about four years later. I glanced up and there he was in a suit, clutching a newspaper, a couple of platforms away, just staring at me. It was one of those weird moments that feel like everything and nothing all in one go. I looked at the first boy I ever had sex with and who had passionately kissed me for a whole afternoon once, only pausing to tell me he loved me and that we'd be together forever—and he smiled politely. He half waved and I half waved back. Then my train pulled in and that was it.

As for Katie, I didn't see her at all for five years after that afternoon. It was quite easy to avoid her. I stayed in when I went home for the holidays and got used to hearing my mum say, "She won't come to the phone, Katherine, I'm afraid." I took a year out after university that I spent traveling and when I finally moved back to England, penniless and desperate for a bed that was clean and in one place, I built my social life in London with my old uni friends. Our paths simply never crossed.

Until one day I walked into a café to get a coffee and, bizarrely, there was Katie, sitting on her own, reading a magazine. She looked up as I walked in and saw her and we both froze.

Neither of us spoke for what felt like forever, until she finally said, "Well, what a small world. Or fate. One of the two. Why don't you join me?"

I think I was so stunned to see her after all this time that I did as I was told. We talked about where she was living, how her mum and dad were, where I worked, what I was up to. Everything but what had happened all those years ago.

We carried on for about half an hour like that, politely trading stories and inconsequential details when she suddenly blurted, "I never properly slept with him, you know."

The air sucked out of the space around us and I looked at her directly. "I saw you in his bed. I was there, remember?"

She looked at me pleadingly. "I really didn't set out to do anything. I just went up to see him, he was my friend first if you remember. We all went out and got trashed, came back blind pissed and I slept in his bed. I woke up to find him kissing me."

"So it was his fault?"

She sighed. "No, it was my fault too. I should have told you I was going up there. Neither of us should have got pissed. I should have told him to get off . . ."

"But you didn't," I said quietly.

There was silence.

She looked at the table. "I should have done. I'm sorry." Reaching for a sugar wrapper she began to play with it. "It's not like you would have stayed with him anyway," she said eventually.

"How do you know?" I said quickly. "I might have."

We fell silent again.

I picked up a ketchup sachet and fiddled with the corners of it as I stared at the table and thought about Dan. "Suppose it had all happened differently." I looked up at her challengingly. "If I hadn't come up for that weekend to surprise him, would I ever have known? Would you ever have told me?"

She looked back at me unflinchingly. "Probably not. Because it meant nothing."

"It didn't mean nothing—it meant everything! I lost my boyfriend . . . and my best mate."

She went quiet for a moment. "I lost you, too." She ripped fiercely at the sugar wrapper and stared at the table. "And I really missed you."

Then she looked up. "I'm sorry," she said simply. "Can you forgive me?"

ELEVEN

I make my way back into the kitchen to pour the milk down the sink and wash up the saucepan. This time Gloria positively ignores me. She's also ignored the phone on the floor next to her though, which is good. I ease the kitchen door gently shut behind me and slowly let the sink fill. Amanda and Louise always said I made a mistake in letting Katie back in after the first time she betrayed me. I wonder what they would say now?

At the time, they accepted my decision to forgive her with good grace, even though they both made it clear they thought I was mad. Slowly but surely Katie came back into my life—and became an important part of it. Ironically it was because of her that I met Pete. It was Katie I had been waiting for at the bar that night when Pete came over to me. Had she not stood me up, I may never have met him.

"Do you like him?" I asked her shyly, after I'd introduced them for the first time.

"He seems very nice," she said.

"It's just—I think he could be The One." I'd blushed and my face split into a broad grin.

Her eyes widened. "Bloody hell! Really?"

"Oh God—I don't know! I hope so . . . it's really early still but . . . I think so . . . yeah."

"Wow! Well, if you're happy, then I'm happy." She smiled at me and I reached out and gave her hand a quick, grateful squeeze.

"You deserve it," she said.

Pete had seemed to like Katie, too. "She's very funny," he said when I quizzed him.

"Do you think she's pretty?" I asked.

He shrugged. "She's all right . . . very girly. She dresses a bit—weird."

I couldn't help but feel a little secretly pleased. "She likes to stand out from the crowd."

He looked at me and grinned. "Well, I didn't notice if anyone was looking at her, I was too busy looking at you."

When Katie's relationship with her boyfriend fizzled out, I was actually pleased. He was an idiot and anyway I wanted Katie to hook up with Pete's flatmate, who I was convinced was perfect for her. I had happy thoughts about the four of us going on double dates, then eventually holidays . . . it was all mapped out. I invited Katie round for dinner with Pete to lay the foundations. I wanted to suss out her feelings and get Pete's input.

I'd known I was going to be a little later back than planned, but that hadn't mattered to me. Pete had a key to my flat and I knew he would let Katie in.

And that's exactly what happened. Holding a bottle of wine I pushed the front door open to hear Pete talking and Katie laughing. The sound of them getting on together was nice. I kicked my shoes off and padded into the sitting room.

I don't know what suddenly made me feel so uneasy. The

room looked just as I had left it that morning. They were sitting at opposite ends of the sofa and Pete jumped up immediately and said, "Hi, babe! You're back! Wine? We've got a bottle on the go," before kissing me and going to get an extra glass. I looked at Katie. Her cheeks were flushed and her eyes had gone glittery—always a sign with her that she was a couple of drinks up.

"Hello, you!" She stood up to hug me. I thought I saw something hidden behind her smile, but I said nothing. Just watched her quietly as she flicked her hair over her shoulder and sat back down on the sofa, not quite meeting my eyes as she began to tell me about her day.

After supper Pete and I snuggled up on the sofa, him affectionately stroking my hair. Katie was being witty about a guy who wanted to date her at work, but I was quieter than usual. We got on to Pete's flatmate and she said she'd love to meet him. When her cab finally arrived she started to gather her things, asking me if I was around the following day and promising she'd call me in the morning. She hugged me tightly on the doorstep and looked at me just long enough to make my heart lurch, before turning and clattering off up the steps.

Closing the door I walked back into the sitting room, where Pete had flicked the TV on. I hesitated for a moment but then I heard my voice say, surprisingly calmly, "Is there something going on with you and Katie?"

An hour later we were still arguing.

"You're not listening to me! I'm not trying to say that what she did was okay, but I think she was a little bit lonely, a bit drunk." Pete looked at me earnestly. "She very badly misread the situation. That's all."

"*That's all?*" I looked at him incredulously. "So let me get this straight. One minute she's telling you about how sad she is that her bloke has dumped her and the next she's trying to kiss you? I'm sorry, but I'm really, deeply confused as to what fucking part of that is all right!"

"Okay, okay," Pete soothed. "I can totally see why you're angry."

A strangulated laugh escaped from me. "Oh you can? That's big of you—thanks!"

"Hey!" He looked surprised. "It's not my fault this happened."

There was an ugly silence.

"Oh hang on," Pete stood up and looked directly at me. "You can't actually think what I *think* you're thinking?"

"I don't know *what* to think!" I shouted. "One minute everything is fine, the next you're telling me this. I can't take it in . . . I . . ."

I couldn't look at him. I just had a picture in my head of Katie on my sofa, fingers curled round the bowl of a wineglass, red liquid swirling gently as she moved forward to kiss him. It made me feel sick. Sick to the core of my being.

"I *told* you!" Pete said, starting to get annoyed again. "We were sitting on the sofa, she was rabbiting on about this bloke who's dumped her and how she couldn't even get a total twat to stay with her. I said that she'd meet someone nice if she just hung on in there and that, honestly, there are good blokes out there. Then I patted her leg. It was just a friendly gesture!" He threw his arms up in exasperation. "I'd do that to anyone—your mum, Clare, *my* mum for God's sake! Then she gave me this weird look, I felt uncomfy and I asked if she'd like another drink. Just as I went to stand up, she leaned over and kissed me."

"On the mouth?"

"Yes, Mia, on the mouth."

"And you're sure it wasn't just a friendly 'thanks for being nice' kiss?"

"Er no, I think I'm long enough in the tooth to tell the difference between that sort of kiss and the kind she tried to give me."

I flushed hot with anger and said nothing. He stayed quiet too and just looked at me.

"You're absolutely sure that's what happened?" I said rigidly.

"Yes. I'm sure."

"Because you did say she was pretty."

"Oh my God!" He threw his arms heavenward again. "I said I thought she was all right! What did you want me to say? Actually as it happens, I don't especially think she's pretty—I don't think about her full stop. She's your mate, who I was trying to be nice to because of you. Jesus!" He dropped down on to the sofa and threw a cushion to one side. "Cut me some slack!"

"How would you feel if one of your mates tried to kiss me?" I exclaimed.

"I'd fucking kill them," he said instantly, "but I wouldn't be angry with you."

I said nothing, just looked at him.

He looked really pissed off. "Funnily enough, Mia, I trust you. I trust you 150 percent and that's everything to me. Have I ever, *ever* given you any reason to doubt me?"

"No," I said truthfully.

"Well then." He glowered. "I can't believe you'd even think I'd do something like that to you. And with your best friend of all people! Thanks very much."

"Just calm down," I said, suddenly tired. "Don't get angry with me."

"I'm not! I'm just . . . I try to be nice to her . . . I listen to her, even though she's seriously boring. She tries it on, I tell you and in return I get this! You know what I honestly think about her? I think anyone who treats you with that little respect doesn't deserve to be your friend. I certainly wouldn't want someone like that in my life and, yes, I have a problem with her now, because she's done something that's made trouble between you and me. I'm not having that. You're too important to me." With that, he got up and strode out of the room.

I just sat still for a moment, trying to stop the out-of-control roundabout of thoughts in my head. Finally I got up and went to find him.

He was standing in the dark kitchen, leaning his hands on the work surface and looking out of the window. I went up behind him and gently put my hand on his arm, slowly turning him to face me.

"You promise me that's what happened?" I said.

He sighed again and made a helpless gesture. "How many times? Yes! That's what happened! I'm really sorry that your friend tried it on with me, but I'm not going to take the blame for something that wasn't my fault. I could have lied and I could have pretended nothing happened and in some ways that would have been easier because it would have saved you being hurt by Katie, and I never want to see you hurt. But it still wouldn't have been the right thing to do." With that, he padded sadly off to bed.

Half an hour later I was outside Katie's front door hammering like mad and ringing the bell repeatedly. Nothing.

I thumped my fist on the door again and finally a light came on. A shadowy figure moved down the hall to the door. "Who is it?" she called.

"It's me."

"Mia?" I heard locks unbolt and she threw open the door, rubbing her eyes sleepily and pulling her dressing gown tighter round her. "Are you okay?"

I pushed past her into the hall. She closed the door behind me and turned to face me, looking confused. "Is something wrong?"

"Yes, something's wrong!" I burst. "How *could* you?"

Her hair was slightly disheveled and she hadn't bothered to take her makeup off before getting into bed; she had a black smear of mascara down one cheek like war paint.

"Look, I've just woken up, come in and sit down." She moved toward the living room but I blocked her.

"I don't want to come in! I want you to tell me just what you thought you were doing?"

"About what?"

"Don't 'about what' me! You *know* what! About Pete and you, tonight!"

She sighed. "I thought this was going to happen." She shook her head slightly, almost as if she was somehow disappointed at the predictability of it all.

"You thought this was going to happen . . . What's *that* supposed to mean?"

"I saw it in your eyes the second you got home tonight that you knew something was wrong. You forget how well I know you, Mia—how long we've been friends."

"*Friends?* Don't you *dare* talk to me about friendship!" I was incredulous. "No friend would do what you did to me tonight."

She didn't flinch. "And what did I do?" she asked.

"Don't play games with me." I raised my voice. "You kissed Pete."

"Just calm down. You're very angry and you're not thinking straight."

"Don't patronize me!" I shouted. "You kissed my boyfriend."

"Keep your voice down!" she instructed bossily. "It's 11:30 at night and I don't want the neighbors hearing you wailing like a teenager. Jesus, Mia, we're not at school any more. Listen to yourself! And for your information I didn't kiss Pete—*he* kissed *me*."

"You liar! You bloody liar!"

"Fine, have it your way." She tiredly walked past me into the living room.

"Don't walk away when I'm talking to you!" I followed her in and grabbed her arm, spinning her round to face me.

"Please let go of my arm, Mia. I know you're angry but it's not okay to pull me about like that."

"Oh shut up!" I yelled. "Just for once, stop being Katie-fucking-knows-it-all-and-knows-best. Just admit it! At least do me the courtesy of admitting it."

"Admit what?" She started raising her voice, needled by my comments. "That I kissed him and he didn't in fact try to kiss me?"

"Yes! That you've done it again! Not content with one of my boyfriends, you had to make it an even two? Why Pete? You could have any bloke you wanted. Why does it have to be him?"

She rolled her eyes at me. "It doesn't have to be him! I don't want him! And you shouldn't want him either. I wouldn't want to be with anyone who would cheat on me."

"Shut up!" I hissed.

"No, *you* shut up!" she said, rattled now. "It's the truth, your precious boyfriend tried it on with me tonight and if I'd have let him, I don't think he would have wanted to stop at a kiss either."

My hand shot up, she saw it and her eyes widened slightly.

"Go on then," she said softly. "Do it if it'll make you feel better." She twisted her face toward me and tapped her cheek lightly with her finger. "Go on, hit me."

My hand trembled. "Do it!" she cried. "What the fuck are you waiting for? If I'm such a cow, just do it!"

Against my will I felt tears start to rush to my eyes. "I wouldn't give you the satisfaction!" I said desperately.

We just stood there looking at each other. Then I did start to cry.

"Oh, Mia!" she said, her voice breaking. "Come here!" and she reached out her arms and pulled me toward her. Just for a brief second I let her hug me, but then I pushed her off and stumbled away from her. "Don't touch me!" I said brokenly. "I just want to know what happened. Tell me the truth."

"I don't want to! I don't want to hurt you."

"What? More than I am already?" I said hoarsely. "Just tell me."

"I got to yours, Pete let me in and we had a drink. He asked me how I was feeling after the breakup, was I okay? I said I was, but that I just felt I was in danger of never getting it right with anyone. I said I hoped I would have a relationship one day like you two and he said to hang on in there, that good blokes did exist, I just had to believe it. Then I said thanks to him for being nice to me and he said it was very easy to be nice to me. Then he leaned forward and kissed me."

I said nothing, just looked at her.

"I pushed him off," she continued, "and said how could he? He said sorry over and over again, and was I going to tell you?"

"And what did you say?"

"I said I didn't know," she admitted. "He begged me not to—said that he'd just felt so bad for me, sitting there looking so sad, he didn't know what had come over him and that he'd never do it again. I said we'd just forget about it and pretend it never happened. Then I had a glass of wine very quickly as I felt so shocked and soon after that you got back."

"You'd pretend it never happened," I repeated slowly. "Why do I somehow feel like I've been here before?"

"This isn't the same as Dan! I *was* going to tell you. I said to you I'd call you."

"Why didn't you just tell me then and there?"

"I didn't want a scene."

"How thoughtful of you."

"Look," she said quickly, moving toward me, reaching out her hands and clasping mine, "I know how much you love him. I can see it written all over your face, but how can he be right for you if he does this? If he does this now, he'll do it again, Mia—it doesn't matter that it was me."

"Oh you're wrong there. It matters very much. Because you've done this to me before, haven't you? *Haven't you?*" I shouted in her face, pulling my hands away.

"And how many times can I say I'm sorry for that?" she said, getting louder and slower with each word, like I was an exceptionally stupid child. "Are you going to make me feel shit about it for the rest of my life?"

"I'm not making you do anything!" I cried. "You keep doing it all on your own!"

"Do you know how bad I still feel about Dan? Even though— even though I was *only twenty*? For the last fucking time *I'm sorry!*"

"You don't need to say sorry, you just need to stop doing it!" I laughed hysterically. "It's not hard. I get a boyfriend, you don't kiss him! How easy is that?"

"I'm not saying sorry for Pete, because I didn't do anything. It wasn't me," she said bluntly. "It was him."

"But it's your word against his and I know he wants to be with me and I know you lie to me!"

"Look," she said urgently. "*He's not telling you the truth.* I know it'll hurt like hell—but just walk away while you still can, it's still early days, you're young. You'll meet someone else who really will love you, who can stay faithful. It'll be fun! You and me, single girls living it up. Come on! What do you say?" She looked at me eagerly.

I stared back in astonishment. "Is that what this is about? You're newly single and you want someone to hang out with?"

"Oh grow up!" Katie said in disgust. "What do you think I am?"

"I don't know any more," I said truthfully. "But I do know that I don't trust you."

I made toward the door. She followed me and as I marched down the hall she called out after me.

"I didn't want to hurt you, Mia—that's why I didn't say anything."

I opened the front door.

"If you go back to him, I'll . . ."

I turned back to her. "You'll what?"

"I won't be able to be in your life any more. I'm not going to sit around and watch you get hurt."

"So it's you or him? Now who's sounding immature?" I laughed in disbelief. "Stay away from me and stay away from

Pete. You're trouble and I don't want you near us ever again. You get that? *Ever again!*"

I slammed the door shut behind me and ran down the road to my car, tears streaming down my face, almost expecting to turn and see Katie running after me in her dressing gown.

I didn't see her for another year after that, and then it was only from the other side of a road. She was staring blankly ahead, even though I knew she'd seen me. As she'd marched past me on the opposite pavement, I'd noticed her hair was much shorter than I'd ever seen it. Almost elfin—pretty. It made her look delicate and slight. I'd wondered where she'd had it done and who'd persuaded her to do it. But I walked straight past her too, pretending she was a stranger. Neither of us was prepared to say anything at all.

No one around us would have guessed that once we were best friends.

If I could be that strong when it came to Katie, I can do it now with this Liz.

I simply have to find her and tell her to get out of my life. I'm not afraid of her. I have passed through the stage of overload now. In the past twenty-four hours, I have trashed my own house, lied to the police, tidied up, watched a film, read five texts that have made me angrier than I think I've ever been, broken Pete's phone on purpose and forced the uncomfortable image of Katie looking questioningly at me, an image that has swum around my head for hours now, out of my mind.

If I can do all of that, am I really prepared to be so meek and afraid that I am going to allow this girl to just shove me out of my own life? If he doesn't love me at all, why hasn't he left already? Why hasn't he just gone to her?

Everything that I have agonized over sleeplessly, cried about incessantly and thrown around recklessly has finally merged together to form one fluid stream of crystal-clear consciousness. I put the saucepan away carefully in the kitchen cupboard, dry my hands on a tea towel and hang it back up determinedly.

There is something to fight for, there has to be.

The only course of action now lies ahead.

I know what I have to do.

TWELVE

It is now time for me to go back upstairs to our room, get into bed and pretend that I have been there all night. Pete's alarm will be going off in twenty minutes. It's about to begin.

When it shrilly pierces the air, I am lying still, next to him, pretending to be deeply asleep, but I am practically holding my breath. He gets out of bed and goes straight to the bathroom. Within seconds I hear him switch on the shower. Then the loo flushes, the shower curtain is yanked back.

Nothing more for a moment or two until a metallic clash makes me jump. It's the sound of the showerhead dropping on to the floor of the bath. The handle has been loose for months and the shower bursts excitedly free when you least expect it. I hear Pete swear as he gets blasted by the uncontrollable spray whipping round the small room like a hosepipe on speed. It's nothing compared to the language I'm expecting when he goes downstairs in a minute and finds his very *broken* phone.

Much like a smoker discovering someone has thrown away a full packet of their fags, he will not be able to have his first text of the day with Liz.

I lie in wait, listening carefully.

I hear him thud down the stairs and into the kitchen. My breath slows . . . any minute now he's going to find it . . .

He starts shouting. Now it will be the countdown until he comes upstairs and bursts into the room for a rant. I wait nervously. After all, I have to act both surprised and cross on his behalf.

Sure enough, the door blasts open and rebounds violently off the wall.

"Look what that fucking dog has done!" he explodes, holding the two halves of his phone up, one in each hand.

"Oh no!" I pretend to look horrified and sit up in bed. "Is it broken?"

"Well, seeing as I found most of it in a puddle of piss, the battery in her basket and I think she's eaten the SIM, I'd say yes, wouldn't you?" He slings the phone on the floor in frustration.

"Urgh!" I wrinkle my nose. "Can we get it off the carpet if she weed on it?"

"FUCKING dog!" he shouts, then gathers up the phone and marches out.

Seconds later he marches back in. "What I can't work out is how she got into the sitting room. I know we shut her in last night."

"Oh, I'm so sorry." I roll my eyes. "It was probably me when I got up for a drink in the night. I must have left the kitchen door open. I was a bit afraid down there on my own after the burglary; it must have slipped my mind to shut the door."

He hesitates, and I can see he's really pissed off, but he can't shout about it because it was an accident and I'm all shook up after the break-in, aren't I?

He takes a deep breath and manages to say stiffly, "It's okay. Don't worry about it. I'll just have to get a new one later today. I'll have to get a new SIM too . . . and go into the office now and get all my numbers. I *so* don't need this . . . I would say I'll call you, but . . ."

He angrily kisses the top of my head and slams out. Five minutes later the front door shuts violently, reverberating through the house, and I hear his car squeal off.

My victory, though, is short-lived. I haven't stopped him for long. Also, I would have said his reaction to the phone being bust was irrational and over the top, but knowing what I *do* know, I'd say he is pretty desperate to talk to her and have her be able to reach him. That is an unbearable thought.

And now I don't have any way of knowing where he is either.

I deflate and sink down into the mustiness of our bed. The sheets need changing. I ought to do that, I suppose. No one else will. Oh, where is he going? Is he out there on his way to her right now?

I'm so tired, unsurprisingly after creeping around half the night, that in spite of my mind spinning, my eyes want desperately to shut . . . just for a moment. I don't want to get up yet . . . I want to stay in bed.

But I have to. I have stuff to do. I have to go and find her.

Thinking about her makes me start to tense. I feel my fists ball up and my jaw clench. I hate her. I really, really hate her. After last night I think I know exactly what kind of woman she is. The kind who thinks it doesn't matter if there's a girlfriend involved. I can see her now, flinging her hair over one shoulder defiantly, holding a cocktail at a bar with some other equally loose-moralled, drinks-too-much, floaty, flighty, useless actress-type.

They are both giggling conspiratorially. "What are you going to do about the girlfriend?" says the friend. *She*—IT—shrugs and sucks gently on the straw to her cocktail, with a sly half-smile. "He'll leave her for me . . . when I want him to," she says decidedly, and she and the friend giggle again—that's how much power over men they think they have.

Once, when I didn't leave quite enough time to get my train after work and was feeling really pissed off that I was going to have to wait an extra twenty minutes to get the next one—and it wasn't even the fast one, but the one that stopped at every bloody lamppost, I went to blast through the gate to let me out of the tube so I could gallop up to the station, but this stupid girl with a huge backpack was fiddling with her ticket. She fed it through TWICE even though it said *Seek Assistance*, so I tutted behind her, and she swung round and said piercingly, "I'm not doing it on purpose, I can't help it!"

I didn't even bother to say anything. I hadn't got time. I just shoved past her, expertly fed my ticket through, then grabbed it and stalked through the gate. I heard her shout, "Oh! Because you're sooooo important! You snotty bitch!" after me.

I didn't turn and yell back at her, I kept on marching . . . and she shouted something else too that I didn't hear properly and didn't much care about. But as I carried on walking, a charming little imaginary scene popped into my head where I reached calmly into my bag, pulled out a sawn-off shotgun, swung round and blew her head off before putting the gun back in my bag and continuing on my way.

That is how Liz makes me feel. I want her gone.

I accept that something has gone adrift with Pete and me that has made him vulnerable to someone else pursuing him, but I can't fix that with her in our lives. So she has to go. It's that simple. I won't lose him—I can't. It is as clear to me now as it was last night.

I am going to find her and get rid of her.

Sitting on the train about an hour later, I barely notice how different a journey this is to my usual morning hike into town. There are seats, fewer suits. Someone eating a sandwich, magazines rather than papers. As Canary Wharf comes into view, I wonder briefly if Spank Me is in one of the tall buildings, trying to persuade a large company to buy into a campaign they don't want or need and that I'll have to chase up. Probably. Scrabbling for my phone in the bottom of the Mulberry, I text Lottie to say I'm still ill and not coming in.

Her message comes straight back:

You poor thing. What you got?

Flu—urgh! is my response—which seems suitably vague and covers a multitude of symptoms.

Make sure you drink plenty of water and stay warm, she texts back. Give me ring if you fancy chat/get bored. Bit mental here on own. Get well soon!

I feel horribly guilty at that and text her that I probably won't call as I feel so rough. More lies. But then she'd guess in a second that something was up if I spoke to her.

I start to feel a little light-headed as we slide into the station, but once I'm looking at my reflection in the glass doors, I feel a sense of purpose tingle through me. Breathing a quick, nervous breath out, I pull my head up and grimly step through the doors as they jolt open.

Out of the station, into the surge of people on the street, I begin to make my way up toward the theater. Her theater. Well, probably Andrew Lloyd Webber or Cameron Mackintosh's theater, more accurately. My heart starts to thud as I march purposefully past a noisy road drill that people are glaring at and giving a wide berth to. I don't care that I bash into a couple of them, and ignore the *Big Issue* seller as well as the bloke who tries to sign me up to a charity.

Gathering pace, I determinedly swing round a corner. Not long now, starting to breathe quick, short breaths. What am I going to say? Am I going to try and get her on her own? God— I've never hit anyone in my life. Will I know what to do? Then I picture her hard, smiling little face and my lip curls. Yes, I'll know what to do—and if not, I'll make it up as I go along. All the same, I'm feeling a bit sick and a light sweat has broken out on my forehead. I can feel more sweat collecting damply at the base of my spine. Come on! You can do this. Picture Pete leaving you. Is that what you want? You want him to be with her?

"No!" I bleat to myself out loud, and earn myself a funny look from a builder drinking a coffee and leaning on some scaffolding. Don't care. Don't care what anyone thinks today. Just got to find *her*.

I march up a little side street that stinks of piss, stepping over a half-full beer bottle, round another corner, heart thumping against my rib cage now as I see the theater in front of me, but I keep on walking, get to the door, reach out a shaking hand to shove it open and DO this. Who cares who hears what I have to say? If I have to yell in front of other people, that's the way it is . . . if you fuck other people's boyfriends, you can't be choosy about where and how you get your comeuppance . . .

But the door just rattles against my hand. It's locked.

Disappointment wells up in me; my heart feels like it's sitting fatly at the back of my throat, taking up too much room. I don't let it floor me for long, though. I grit my teeth and peer through the glass into the foyer. She must be in there . . . but it's gloomy inside, and all I can see is a cleaner pushing a Hoover around who can barely be bothered to glance up at me as I knock. Finally, and without smiling, he motions me to go round the back of the building.

Stepping back, a little more uncertainly, I start to walk round the side of the theater. There's nothing but a small street, barely wide enough for cars, a big wheelie bin overflowing with knotted black sacks and a grubby sign on the wall that says *Stage Door*.

The door looks very heavily shut. There's no bell, and no one answers when I knock uncertainly. I'm not sure what to do next, so I just stand back and wait on the other side of the street. No one comes in and no one comes out.

Just as I'm starting to wonder what the hell I'm doing here, the door pushes open and a short, dark-haired, moody-looking bloke swings out.

"Can you hold the door, please?" a shaky voice says, and it's mine. He looks at me, running his eyes up and down before deciding I'm not worth bothering with, but he holds the door and I clatter across the street.

Once I'm in, the thick metal door jerks shut behind me and I'm in a long, wide corridor: harshly lit, with a floor like a hospital corridor. No plush velvet like the foyer and the inside of the theater. I see a noticeboard on one wall and another door at the far end. I start to walk toward it, my heels click-clacking, when a voice says, "Excuse me! Miss? You need to sign in. Who have you come to see?"

I turn and notice for the first time a small office. Peering through the glass, I'm looking into the face of an old bored man with sagging jowls like Deputy Dawg. He's enormous, with a strip of pasty flesh just visible above his waistband where his shirt isn't quite big enough to tuck into his trousers. I'm not sure how he squeezed into such a small space. Maybe he hasn't been out of there for years and years. What I can see of the walls behind him is lined with hanging keys. There is a phone sitting on his desk, and he has a big notebook in front of him. "Name?" he wheezes, reaching for his pen.

This makes me panic a bit. "Lottie Myer," I say finally. Sorry, Lottie.

"Who are you visiting? Marc's in. Come to see him?"

"No," I say truthfully. "I, er, work for a magazine that is interested in reviewing the show."

He snorts dismissively. "You do know how long this show has been running, don't you?"

I stand there mutely, and he sighs. "All right, then. Wait there and I'll see if the company manager is in. She can tell you who you need to contact." He reaches for the phone and I feel my heart speed up. Shit. Now what? What's a company manager? That sounds important. What do I do?

The door bangs again, making me jump. I turn around, and a delivery bloke looks over the top of my head like I'm not even there and says something crossly to the old boy about moving the truck that's just arrived and is blocking them in. He, in turn, hangs up the phone and a row ensues about what is whose responsibility, so I melt back and am wondering if I should wait or run when the door flings open again. A lanky man comes in with a cello or something on his back and I have to flatten myself against the noticeboard on the wall behind me to get out of the way. The old man is still arguing and there's a lot of finger-pointing going on. No one notices that I've got my hair caught on a pin on the board and have to turn to unhook it.

As I untwist it, I pull out a pin and a load of cards cascade to the floor. It's a very full noticeboard. Drinks for Sharon's birthday on Thursday. Tony and Tim are doing a concert in Wimbledon, Sunday night at eight on the 19th. A note from the company manager saying that this show has been designed around the concept of long hair for the men. Any further examples of haircuts, as noticed recently on CERTAIN cast members, will be deemed a breach of contract and they will be disciplined. A flyer for *A Night of a Thousand Voices!* in Hammersmith. A card for an accountant who is an expert in tax for those who act. A card with "For Sale! Vocal Scores for *Lion King, Grease, Full Monty, Billy Elliot, Anything Goes,*" and then . . . then . . . a card that says, "Girl wanted! Flatmate. One big double room, sunny, tube close. £500 pcm plus bills. Tell your friends! Call Lizzie or Debs on . . ."

Oh my God. It's her—it's her. One of the two numbers listed is definitely hers! I quickly rip the card off and shove it in my pocket. The old bloke and the delivery man are still arguing. I hover for a minute, guiltily, and then manage to slip out without being noticed.

Back on the street, I pull the card out and look at it like I'm holding the secret to eternal youth in my hands. Reaching for my mobile, not taking my eyes off the numbers, I bar my number and dial the one that is *not* hers.

It clicks straight on to voicemail, and a tinkly voice says:

"It's Debs here. Can't take your call, but you know what to do! Ciao for now!"

Then it bleeps, so I hang up quickly. Ciao for now? Who are these people?

Half an hour later, over a coffee, I'm still trying. Finally it rings, but then goes to voicemail. "It's Debs here. Can't take your call . . ." I fucking know. For God's sake . . .

I try again after another ten minutes, and this time a sleepy voice answers, which throws me completely.

"Oh hello," I stammer. "Is this Debs?"

"Yeah," says the voice boredly. "Who's this?"

I don't know what makes me say it, I hadn't planned to or anything, but my mouth suddenly and very assuredly says, "I'm phoning about the flat."

"Oh cool!" says the voice, brightening. "What's your name? Did you see the card?"

"Er, kind of . . . I'm a friend of Marc's?" I try cautiously. "Lottie?"

There's a pause while Debs searches her no doubt vacuous mind. "Oh God! Marc Banners! Oh fabs! And Lottie—didn't we meet you at Tyler's?"

"Yes?" I venture uncertainly. If you think we did, then we did. This girl is a fruit.

"Oh, how cool is this? Well, it's still up for grabs, Lotts." Lotts? We've known each other for under a minute. "Want to come and look at it? Marie's already moved out, so it could be yours ASAP."

"How about I come today?" I say brightly. Again, my mouth is acting on its own. If *I* were an actress, it would have its own contract. Come on, give me the address.

She pauses again. "Er, yeah? I suppose. I'm in this afternoon, be here by four, though, won't you, because I'm going in early tonight."

I promise I'll be there before four, then she gives me the address and I give her a false number to reach me on if there are any problems, and that, as they say, is that. It's that easy. I know where the bitch lives.

THIRTEEN

An hour later I am sitting in another café right across the street from the cut-price crockery shop Lizzie and Debs live above. Just sitting in the window on a high stool against a long bar flush to the glass, watching and feeling sick with nerves and anxiety. I'm actually shaking slightly (although that might be the coffee overload).

That's it. That's the place where she lives and where my boyfriend has probably had sex with another woman. She might be in there *right now*. I'm going to go over there in a minute and confront her . . . but what am I going to say? What will she do?

I've ordered another coffee, but it just sits in front of me going cold. I can't stop staring at her flat. It looks so . . . so *ordinary*. It doesn't look the house of a glamorous woman, more like a scrubby student flat. It's just a building, I know, but as I'm sitting looking at the place where she lives, its horrible realness overwhelms me and my face is suddenly wet with tears. How could he? How could he let this happen?

The café owner is eyeing me suspiciously, but wisely chooses not to get involved with the weird crying girl who has sat motionless staring at the crockery shop for about half an hour.

It's just so ordinary, so cheap. What was I expecting? Something sexy, opulent? I don't know.

What is worse is that I am actually going to go and knock on the door, and maybe she's going to come out and maybe I'm going to hit her. Oh, this is so fucked up! I have an overwhelming desire suddenly to phone my mum. My nice, almost normal mum, sitting at home in our kitchen. I wish I was there now. I wish *she* was there. A tear creeps down my cheek as I start to frantically look in my bag for my phone; I don't care that she's on a boat on the other side of the world, I need to hear her voice, I want to tell her everything . . . but I can feel my phone buzzing already. Someone is calling me. When I find it, a number I don't recognize is flashing on the screen. I don't answer. It's thrown me and I forget about ringing Mum. Who is it? Debs? Seconds later I get a text saying,

It's me! Got new mobile and number. Save it to phone. P xx

Pete. Dutifully I do as I'm told. I stare at his name on the phone and try to steady myself before slipping it back into my bag. Get a grip. Get a grip . . . I push the hair out of my face and wipe my eyes with the back of my hand before lifting my head.

What I see next, as I look through the window, makes my hand fly to my mouth and clamp over it, as a muffled gasp of shock slips through my fingers.

She—Liz—is standing just the other side of the glass, right outside the window, staring down at the screen of her phone and smiling. There in front of me, less than three feet away. She's wearing a long pillar-box-red coat and a floppy wide-brimmed

Biba-esque hat. Her long blonde hair curls out from under it.
On anyone else it would probably look totally stupid—on her it
looks both cutting edge and very little-girly at the same time.
Most importantly, though, she has a bag IDENTICAL to my
Mulberry one slung over her shoulder. Utterly inseparable. They
are one and the same.

It is partly this, I think, that renders me incapable of standing and running out into the street and ripping her head off, and
partly the sudden shock of seeing her there in front of me. I just
sit transfixed and stare at her as I wonder how much of a coincidence it can possibly be that we have identical bags, and yet she
lives above a crockery shop in a not so nice area . . . Could she,
would she really spend over £700 on a bag?

No . . . but I know a man who would. Equally, I seem to remember that that first text referred to him buying her another
something . . . same brown, I believe . . . Was my bag meant for
her?

If it was—that means he must have bought a replacement
yesterday and seen her yesterday morning too—all while he
thought I was ill at home in bed? Fucking, fucking hell.

I'm amazed that the waves of hate don't shatter the glass and
send deadly daggers slicing into her, or at the very least that she
doesn't sense someone staring at her with such loathing. Too
self-absorbed, I think savagely, as I watch her staring at her
mobile screen. I am frozen to my seat with shock and hatred.
Her face has lit up and she is now holding the phone to her ear,
waiting . . . totally oblivious to me . . . and now speaking. She
smiles, says something into the phone and starts to walk off
jauntily up the street in the direction of the tube. The thought
immediately occurs to me that Pete might have sent both of us

the same text with his new number . . . so is that him she's talking to now? I grab my phone and frantically dial him. Sure enough, it bleeps for a second and then goes to voicemail.

This fills me with a new, cold, clinical strength. I don't go running after her, I don't grab her in the street and shove her hard up against a wall, making her gasp with shock and pain as the back of her head smashes into the brickwork and her stupid fucking hat falls to the ground. I am suddenly icily calm and composed. Something enables me to stand up, stride out of the café, march across the street and ring the bell to the flat over and over. There's a frenzied yipping of a dog, but I keep ringing and ringing until I hear a voice shout, "Hang on, I'm coming!" and the door swings open.

FOURTEEN

The first thing I notice is some revolting little rat thing leaping around my ankles and yapping. It's wearing a collar with a sparkly medallion hanging off it that reads, *Mummy's Little Princess*. Resisting the urge to kick it away, I try to focus on the girl standing in front of me.

"Hi!" She grins with little white teeth. "You must be Marc's mate Lottie. I'm Debs."

She is tiny, very pretty and wearing a T-shirt that says *Future Diva* on it. She looks at me expectantly and beams vacantly. "Want to come in?" She stands to one side and I see a flight of stairs stretching out in front of me.

"*Please* stop barking, Pixie," she scolds the animal that apparently is a dog and is still springing around our ankles. "Sorry about her." She smiles at me. "She's my flatmate Lizzie's 'ickle baby. Yes you are! Yes you are!" She coos at the rat, which, exhausted at the exertion of coming downstairs, has collapsed pathetically on to the floor, probably as a result of being genetically engineered to have short enough legs to live in a handbag.

The sound of Liz's name being spoken out loud makes me

dig my nails sharply into the palm of my hand, but I don't say anything. I just want to get into that flat. I really don't know what I intend to do once I'm there, but I am now determined to get into this space that he has been in—see it with my own eyes, invade her life like she has mine. We go up the tiny narrow staircase, which has a door at the top, leading into the flat. It opens into the sitting room, and right away I get a good idea of what kind of girls Debs and Lizzie are.

There are helium balloons in the corner and a couple of empty wine bottles by the brightly colored sofas, one of which is orange, the other neon pink—both, I think, Ikea. The carpet could do with a hoover and *This Morning* is on TV, with the sound down. There are big montage frames of pictures on the walls. Glancing at one quickly, I see some pictures that look like dressing-room shots: lots of heavy makeup and people pulling faces, all trying to be the center of attention. Lizzie is in some and not in others. There is one shot of her hugging a very beautiful man and trying to look sultry. Debs starts to bang on about phone bills and council rates, but I'm not really listening. He has been in here. He's seen all of this.

The kitchen is tiny, but then looking at Debs I should think she last ate a full meal in 2001. There is a box of Special K on the side and a blender next to some tired, wizened fruit sitting lethargically in a fruit bowl.

"So you're a smoker?" Debs says.

I shake my head automatically and she looks appalled. "Really? God, how d'you manage that? What show did you say you were in?"

"Er, I'm not. Actually." I'm too overwhelmed to be quick enough to lie, and the words just stumble out uselessly.

"Oh bad luck," she says, barely listening. "Not many new

things at the mo, are there—just sodding revivals everywhere."
She rolls her eyes. "Still, something will come up, always does,
doesn't it? I've been in *Zippity!* for what feels like forever . . . I'm
soooo bored with it now. Anyway. This would be your room."

She walks ahead of me and I follow her uncertainly into the
most girly room I have ever seen. Pixie trots in after us and gets
into a little pink, sparkly bed that's sitting underneath a selection of glittery leads. As it stares balefully at me with oversized
gremlin eyes, I decide it really is the most vile, pointless excuse
for a pet.

"This is actually Lizzie's room at the moment," Debs chat-
ters away, "although she's going to move into the bigger one that
Marie's just left. All a bit complicated—Marie had some rather
light-fingered friends, if you know what I mean—but basically,
she's gone and this could be yours ASAP. Nice, isn't it?"

The walls of the room are a deep clotted cream and honey,
but there is a kind of chandelier thing, which has lots of pieces
of brightly colored glass attached to twisted wire that catches the
light shining in through the large window. Muslin curtains waft
and the bedspread looks crisp and clean. It smells faintly of a
heady, heavy perfume and there are lilies . . . actual real fresh
flowers in a vase.

"It's a beautiful room," I manage to say truthfully, gripping
the straps of my bag so fiercely my fingers are cramping up.
This is her room. Oh my God. What am I doing?

Debs looks around her. "Yeah, Lizzie has good taste."

I know. She's fucking my boyfriend.

I move slowly around the room and open the wardrobe. Her
clothes hang in front of me. I can see a long blonde hair on the
sleeve of a red jumper. Hers. How disgusting. "Good storage
space," I find myself saying. A lot of her clothes are cheap, high

fashion, disposable. She's a lot about image. Good shoes, though. Doesn't scrimp there. Shutting the door again, I turn, glance at the bed, see the bedside table and almost cry out loud.

There is a picture of Pete by her bed.

I am nearly sick on the floor. I swear I actually physically retch.

Luckily though, Debs, who is nattering away about storage under the stairs, has wandered out into the hall again and doesn't hear me. I'm frozen to the spot with the shock. It is him, isn't it? Yes, it is! He's wearing the Paul Smith shirt I got him for his birthday! Oh God oh God oh God. Breathe. Keep breathing.

"Lottie? Oh, you're still in here." Debs springs back into the room like a little lamb, all fresh and innocent. "So what do you think?" She smiles brightly.

I open my mouth but no sound comes out . . . Thankfully from somewhere in the sitting room the phone rings.

"Hang on," says Debs and dashes out.

This gives me enough time to leg it round the bed and stare at the photo more carefully—definitely Pete. He's smiling and holding his hand up as if he doesn't want his picture taken. I scan the background of the picture but it's impossible to tell where he was. Then I see a card resting behind the photo. It has a dancing girl on it. I open it.

Good luck, Lizzie, from your number one fan. All love always, Peter xxx

The words swim, or maybe it's me wobbling uncertainly, but I don't hang around. Before I even think about what I'm doing, I shove it in my bag. I grab a cheap-looking pair of earrings as well. Then my legs give way and I sit heavily on the bed.

Debs comes back in and looks a bit surprised to see me sitting down. "Sorry about that. So what do you think?"

"I . . ." Come on—get the words out.

"I have a boyfriend," I say. "Would he be able to come round whenever?"

"Oh yeah!" Debs smiles. "We're all seeing someone then, so it might get a bit crowded as we're all mostly around in the day and working at night, but it'll be a laugh. It'll be fine."

"Are your boyfriends in the theater too?"

"Hardly!" laughs Debs and gives me an odd look. "You know what boys in the biz are like. No, mine's a chef and Lizzie's is an architect."

Make it stop, please God, please . . .

"Well, if you want it, it's yours." Debs shrugs. "You seem great to me. You'll have to meet Lizzie too, though, but I'm sure you'll get on; after all, you've lots in common. Marc for one. How did you meet him? Was it on *Chicago*?"

God—I have to go . . . I have to . . . My phone rings. It's Pete.

"Excuse me," I say, and Debs nods and just hovers.

"Hi, its me," he says. "I've just tried you at work but the answer phone's on. Did you know?"

"Yeah. I'm not there at the moment." This is of course true. I haven't lied. I just don't mention I'm sitting on the bed he has shagged another woman in—looking at his picture.

"Are you okay?" I can tell he's frowning. "You sound weird."

"Do I?" I say, forcing a smile on to my face . . . Don't go to pieces—come on, hang on in there. "Well, everything is absolutely fine." I force the words out, trying to keep my voice level while still looking at his face smiling back at me. "I'll have to call you later. I can't talk properly now." Quite literally, actually. And I snap the phone shut. I just want to get out of here. The cloying smell of her perfume is making me feel truly sick.

I stand up, and take a deep breath.

"I'm going to need to think about this, Debs," I say lightly. "It's a bit smaller than I'd hoped for and I'm worried things might get a bit . . . crowded. Can I call you?"

"Absolutely!" Debs smiles happily at me. I'm not sure this girl has ever had a bad thing happen to her in her life. She couldn't care less if I took this flat or not.

In less than five minutes I'm back in the street, leaning on the closed door, gasping for air. If I didn't have the card and her earrings in my bag, I wouldn't have believed that just happened.

FIFTEEN

My feet find their way back to the station on their own, and before long I stumble on to the train, sitting down heavily. I feel a bit dizzy and thick-headed. What the hell did I just do? What happened there? Did I *really* see Pete's picture next to another woman's bed? It can't be real . . . but it is! I saw it with my own eyes. I saw her, her flat, her clothes, her *bed*. And him next to it.

As the doors jolt themselves shut to a mechanical bleeping, I get the card out of my bag. Looking at it, I trace the loop of his writing with my fingertips, before putting it back guiltily; which is ridiculous, because no one else knows that I stole it from another woman who my boyfriend seems to be sleeping with.

Once we get out of London, I have a couple of moments when silent tears of utter desolation course down my cheeks, and at one point I do a strange hiccup and sniff at the same time, which earns me a couple of darted glances from behind books and papers. I have to stare furiously out of the window and focus on familiar landmarks to stop myself losing it completely. Pretty much everybody does their best to ignore me, keeping their heads buried in the *Evening Standard*, not wanting to get involved. Only one girl stares curiously. I look back, hoping to shame her into looking away, but she continues to stare, chewing gum with her mouth open, completely unembarrassed. I break the gaze first and try to ignore her. I don't want a confrontation now. Reaching into my bag for my iPod, I fumble around with it and select shuffle. I don't care what it is; I just want something, anything to focus on, but, of course, every song it lands on is a slow ballad or love song that I can't listen to, as the words seem to relate to just me and Pete.

Eventually I can't bear it any more and I turn it off to sit in a silence that is punctuated only by other people's mobiles and coughing. When the rooftops of houses on the outskirts of our town finally begin to flick past the window, the sense of relief that I am nearly home is almost overwhelming.

Having hung around in town until the time that I would normally be home from work so Pete isn't suspicious, I'm knackered and should be hungry, but I'm not. In fact, have I eaten at all today? Can't remember. I don't want anything anyway, so what does it matter?

I feel flat, empty and shell-shocked. I went to confront her and I've been smacked in the face with the truth instead. Walking up to the front door, I try to fix a smile to my face, smooth my hair back, take a deep breath. Pete has obviously heard my key in the lock, because he appears at the top of the stairs straight away. I smile up at him and ask him if he's had a nice day, and he says not bad, but where have I been and am I okay? I look like I've been crying.

I look at him like he's mad, laugh and say of course I'm okay, and that I still feel under the weather, which probably explains why I look like I've been crying, and where does he think I've been? Work, of course!

He looks at me doubtfully. Big fat liars are always the hardest to fool . . . but he buys it and says as he comes down the stairs, "So why couldn't you talk to me earlier? And you didn't call back. I was waiting to speak to my lovely girl all afternoon."

I manage to fake a puzzled look, as if I'm trying to remember what he's talking about, then I laugh and say, "Oh, that. I was in the middle of something. I can't just stop for you!"

Then I pat his arm fondly and walk past him into the kitchen. It's incredibly difficult to do. I actually want to collapse on him and cry and cry and show him the card, tell him that today I saw his picture by the bed of another woman. That I know, I *know* he is lying to me . . . but I don't.

Just stay calm. Don't blow it. He'll think you're mad if you tell him what happened this afternoon. And it *was* mad. It was! What was I thinking? I just wanted to get rid of her. Get her out of our lives.

"You don't happen to know where my black gym shorts are, do you, babe?" He follows me in, slides his arms round my waist and kisses the back of my neck. "I looked for them earlier but I'm buggered if I know what I've done with them."

"They're in the ironing basket," I say automatically, managing not to stiffen and shove him away from me

"You little star," he says, releasing me and stretching. "What's for tea?"

I shrug and say I don't know. Has he any plans?

He looks blank. Like what?

Like calling Liz from the bathroom? Like taking Gloria out so you can phone Liz, like going to the gym so you can call her? I DON'T FUCKING KNOW!

"You look tired, sweetheart." I try to look concerned. "Why don't I do us a stir-fry—something quick—and then if you like, we could go out for a drink later. Perk you up a bit."

This is something we never, ever do. Our usual evening is, of course, food, TV, bed. Maybe with me talking on the phone to Amanda or Louise while he's upstairs doing a bit of work.

So he looks a bit surprised by my suggestion, but after thinking for a second says, better still, why don't we go out to dinner? This in turn surprises me . . . and actually I don't want to. I'm so tired I want to just curl up in a dark place and sleep for a thousand years. My dry, swollen brain needs a rest from thinking; but the girl who is tired and whingey doesn't get the man. So I smile and say that would be lovely, I'll just go and get changed.

I go upstairs and hide Liz's card and earrings in the bottom of my underwear drawer. They nestle up alongside the first card Pete ever sent me and a small box with a dried leaf in it from the first walk we had together. He picked it up, handed it to me and said, "This is my first ever present for you. It was *really* expensive, so don't throw it away."

So I didn't. In my mind all those years ago, I imagined me keeping it and then sticking it on a card that I would give him on our wedding day. So much for idle dreams.

I get changed into a dress that I know he particularly likes and put on enough makeup to look like I'm not actually wearing any. I make sure I'm quick so that he doesn't lose the urge to go out, and as I come downstairs, I see I am just in the nick of time. He's sitting on the arm of the sofa, remote in hand. When he sees me, he smiles. "You look very attractive," he says. Not beautiful, not sexy. Attractive. My heart breaks just a little more and Liz smiles smugly, alluringly blowing him a slow-motion kiss. I force her out of my head, and in silence we get into the car.

Over dinner, we start to talk about the break-in and he begins an unnerving line of conversation about how weird it was that they didn't take anything apart from my jewelry and he can't understand why they did so much reckless damage. I can feel my skin starting to prickle with worry and I'm immediately suspicious. Has he guessed it was me—*how* has he guessed? I must have been watching one too many cold and flu remedy adverts, because in the true spirit of attack being better than defense, words that surprise me more than him slide smoothly and effortlessly out of my mouth.

"I know," I agree, pouring myself a big glass of wine. "It was almost as if someone knew what they were doing."

"What?" He wrinkles his brow and looks confused.

"I mean, why did they do so much damage to your office in particular?" I say casually. "No forced entry . . . they didn't take anything of value. And why take the trouble to stab a picture of us? That's a bit . . . chilling."

He doesn't say anything, just jabs his fork into a bit of steak before reaching for the pepper. I'm searching around for something, anything to throw him off track.

"I don't mean this to sound odd," I say lightly, reaching over and pouring him some more wine, "but at first I wondered if you'd done it."

"ME?" He chokes slightly and reaches for a napkin. "Why on earth would you think that?"

"Don't get angry," I soothe. "It's just like the police officer said, it's so odd that they didn't take anything much . . . and how did they get in? I just got thinking about that and wondered if maybe you'd had a flip-out about something? Is everything okay with work?" I reach over and rest my hand on his arm.

"You've seemed a little *agitated* recently. I just put two and two together. You could tell me if anything was wrong."

He looks at me like I'm crazy. "What are you talking about? Nothing's wrong . . . I can't believe you think I'd trash our house. Have you gone *mad*?" He pulls his arm away from me.

"Sorry, sorry. You're right." I shake my head. "I shouldn't have asked if it was you . . . it was just so odd. Almost as if someone had a key or something . . . and let themselves right in!"

And I've hit on it. Completely by accident, but that taps right into a nerve. He stops chewing for the briefest of moments. If I wasn't looking for it, I'd have missed it, but I don't.

I realize he doesn't think it was me at all. He thinks it might have been her! My mind starts to race. Is she the kind of girl who might have "borrowed" a key? Is he now thinking she could have let herself in and for some reason gone crazy and smashed our house up?

We fall silent, presumably both dwelling on the ramifications of Liz being the kind of girl who might be . . . could be . . . a bit of a bunny-boiler.

As far as I'm concerned, it doesn't matter if she is or isn't. Clearly he thinks she could be, and that's all I need. I think I've seen the chink in the armor, and just to make sure, I carefully dig a little deeper.

"Maybe we should call the police back, get them to do some fingerprints or something? I might call them tomorrow."

He doesn't say anything at first, but then casually says, "I don't think we should bother. It'll only prolong the situation. I think we have to just put this behind us and move on. Anyway, I doubt they have the resources for that sort of thing. They're not the FBI, and it's hardly crime of the century."

Steady, Pete—you're babbling.

"Let's just leave it. I don't want to put you through anything more than you've already had to deal with. It really shook you up."

I take it I can assume from that little speech that her prints will be everywhere, then? So she has been in my house. Has she been in my bed too, with her disgusting perfume and cheap clothes? He has screwed someone in *our* bed. How can this be happening?

"Okay! You know best!" I manage to smile at him. "Still odd, though . . . just like they let themselves in and went mental . . . I'm just nipping to the loo. Won't be a minute."

Off I totter, leaving him with that indigestible little nugget. In the loo, I stare at my reflection as I apply another sweep of mascara, and then it occurs to me that I might have stumbled on a far more effective way of getting rid of her than going and finding her.

What if he was to start to believe that Liz was not all she seemed? That she was not in fact perfect—but very far from it? What would he do? Might he just decide that she wasn't worth it?

Could I be shot of her without reducing myself to little more than a fishwife, scrapping in the street? I might not have to lose Pete or my dignity after all. I am suddenly glad that I didn't come face to face with her earlier. Not because I couldn't have done it—I could have slapped her so hard my hand would have left the mark of each finger on her face—but because I know now that I can be much, much cleverer and smarter than that. This way, she really won't know what's hit her.

"Tell you what as well, I haven't been able to find some of my other stuff since the break-in," I say as I sit back down.

He stops chewing altogether now. "Like what?"

"Strange, really." I drop my voice, like I'm telling him a story. "I didn't like to say anything to you, but the bag you got me? It's missing."

He raises an eyebrow and then says quickly, "I'll get you another one."

Three bags in one month? You might want to think about opening an account at Mulberry, my darling.

"You don't have to," I say gallantly. "I did love that bag, though. Although I'd got an ink stain on the lining already." I pause and let that sink in. "Anyway, let's change the subject. Tell me how work is going."

So after a long, boring conversation about his work and a silent drive home during which I make a mental note to hide my bag the second we get in, we arrive back.

Under the pretense of needing the loo, I dash upstairs and kick the bag under our bed. He puts the dog out and is remarkably quick. Not texting tonight, it seems.

I'm in bed when he walks in, tired but wired. I've had a bit too much wine and am feeling very carried away with my own success. I want to giggle and confide in him, tell him what I've done today. I feel flushed and a little overexcited. I watch him strip off moodily—he's been very quiet since we left the restaurant. Then he climbs into bed and switches off the light.

And turns away from me.

It takes less than a second for my mood to switch from girlishness to tight misery. Why on earth has he done that? He never does that. Ever. What has this woman done to him?

I start to cry tipsily and he sighs and says, "What's the matter now?" I sob something about the burglary (I'm going to have to come up with another excuse soon—this one is wearing very thin), and will he give me a hug? And he does, although reluctantly.

I'm not wearing anything, and I press up against him and whisper that he makes me feel safe. Despite his pensive mood, the combination of wine, my soft naked flesh, maybe the thought that his lover might have gone temporarily and scarily nuts . . . possibly even feeling like the big brave man who is my protector . . . seems to do the trick and he starts to kiss me.

His hands slide over my trembling skin and his mouth crushes mine—it's urgent, deep, fucking kissing. There's no preamble—just straight to it.

I throw myself into the role, gasping little gasps, telling him he's amazing . . . and he starts to respond, getting a bit rougher and biting the skin on my shoulder, which actually I don't like, but I don't say anything, I just gasp a little louder and wiggle away from him so that he has to move after me. He says nothing throughout the whole thing apart from a hoarse "Oh my God, you're good!" as I lick and suck and stroke.

Strangely, I'm not actually feeling anything myself. When he's finally lying on top of me and saying my name and then, "Oh God, oh God, oh God," all I am feeling is like I'm having an out-of-body experience, as if I'm watching myself. My body feels limp, unresponsive and as if my limbs are made of Playdoh. I certainly don't feel like I couldn't be closer to anyone than him, or that I just experienced some deep spiritual connection.

Afterward, he doesn't kiss me gently as we lie there, stroke the hair off my face, look deep into my eyes or whisper in the dark that he loves me. He just rolls to his side of the bed and is silent.

By the time I have shut the bathroom door behind me, I am crying. This is not us. This is not how *we* are. I don't feel sexy and powerful any more, I just feel like shit . . . I didn't know it was possible to feel this bad about myself. How have things come to this?

I look at myself in the mirror and lean my forehead against the cool glass. That doesn't calm me either. Pulling away wretchedly, I feel as unhappy for myself as if I was standing opposite Clare watching her cry like I am now. I think this is how it might feel to watch my little sister's heart breaking in front of me. It's so strange, seeing myself like this and not being able to do anything to make it go away. I feel helpless and just want someone's kind, warm arms around me. And yet I have just been as intimate with another human being as you can be.

I hang my head eventually, all cried out—there are no more tears. He used to kiss me gently, tenderly. I didn't imagine it. I know I didn't . . . Why can't she just go away—just drop off the face of the earth? I'm not a bad person. I just want her to GO AWAY. Let me live my life with him. Like we always have done.

I look like crap. Blotchy red skin with scarlet patches on the cheeks and a livid nose. Small slivers of eyes buried in puffy lids. I can't look like shit when she's out there in her muslin bedroom with her lilies, busy being perfect.

Splashing water on my face, I blow my nose. At least he won't be able to see me in the dark.

I needn't have worried anyway. By the time I creep back into our room, he is so dozy he barely murmurs good night. In seconds he is asleep. I wonder who he's dreaming of.

SIXTEEN

When he wakes up, I am dressed for work with my coat on, standing over him.

"Bye," I say quickly. "Got to dash—bit late. See you tonight." I duck to kiss the top of his head, and then I'm gone.

I don't want to hang around, as I have in a carrier bag by the front door my Mulberry bag and the pieces of jewelry I reported as stolen.

Fifty minutes later I'm in town again, stopping before I descend into the tube to phone the office, knowing that Lottie won't be in yet. I leave a message saying I'm really sorry but I'm still ill. I'm off to the doctor's today, though, and I'll ring with a progress report later. I ask her to divert my phone to my mobile as soon as she gets in. That way if Pete calls, he'll still get hold of me and no one will be any the wiser.

I have far more important things to do today than go to work, and I'd be useless anyway. I can't think about anything else but Pete and her. It's occupying my thoughts every second of the day and has been since I found out. I hate her so much, I simply don't have room in my head to think about anything else at all. I even dreamed about her last night, for God's sake; as if it's not enough that she's polluting my life, she's now even stealing my dreams.

In between the fitful bursts of what could loosely be described as last night's sleep, but was more like me closing my eyes for twenty minutes here, an hour and a half there, as the hand on the clock wound slowly round and round, I thought about how shifty and uncomfortable Pete had looked over dinner, how he seemed seriously unnerved to think there might be a side to Liz he hadn't seen before.

If he believes she's becoming jealous, possessive, whiny, needy, tightening the reins . . . in fact all of the things I think every man hates . . . if it turns out that underneath that glossy exterior she's a gun-slinging, ball-busting, bunny-boiling neurotic mess and that actually he really doesn't know her AT ALL . . . will he still want to be with her? I'm certain he'll get cold feet and walk away. I know he loves me, I know it. He wouldn't still be here if he didn't. He'll walk away and then . . . then it will be just him and me again and we'll have a chance to fix everything and get back to when it was good between us.

I have a vague idea of what I'm going to do. I wouldn't call it a plan as such, it's not very sophisticated, but then neither is losing your boyfriend to a slut.

My feet clatter down the steps to the tube barriers and soon I'm bouncing up and down in my seat as the train chunters through tunnels, weaving me underground toward Liz's flat. As I stare at my reflection in the window, I realize I look tired. I should sort that out. I need to be looking good right now, making an effort, looking better than her.

I actually wind up at my destination, the coffee shop opposite her flat, far too early, leaving me time to kill. At eleven a.m., three coffees, one tea and a Danish later (no wonder detectives wear stomach-concealing overcoats and macs), I see the door open and Liz walks out. The now familiar surge of hot acid in my stomach heaves as she strides purposefully toward the tube.

Where's she going? To meet my boyfriend? Or is he genuinely working today? I almost reach for my phone to call him, but I don't, I'm too busy watching her. Today she is wearing soft caramel-colored boots with a denim micro-mini that looks suitably retro, rather than eighties throwback; a thin scarf and long strings of brightly colored beads around her neck. No hat today, and her long hair catches on the wind. She looks like an effortlessly elegant but slightly arty student; all legs and innocent doe eyes, like a foal. How does she do it? She's a chameleon. A man walking past her turns and looks over his shoulder admiringly as she passes. Bitch.

I wait another half an hour until I'm certain she's not coming back. Getting up, I cross the busy street, bag in tow. Having rung the bell, I wait for Debs to answer, but there is nothing. I ring again and again. Still nothing.

Fucking hell, Debs, you stupid cow! Where are you? I was banking on her being in. She's an actress, for God's sake. I thought they were supposed to be all nocturnal if they're in a show. Come on! It's me, Lottie, here for a second look at the flat . . . I walk back round the front and peer up at the window above the shop. No signs of life. Then a movement catches my eye and I see in the crockery shop a man beckoning to me.

Cautiously, I open the door and walk in. He's smiling and holding up a key.

"You must be here to look at the flat," he says. "Lizzie said someone was coming this morning."

I look at him blankly.

"Well, go on then," he says, holding out the key. "Just bring it down when you're done. They've got another girl coming after you, so if you want it . . ." He taps the side of his nose and nods tellingly.

Seriously? I just get handed a key on a plate? It's that easy? Someone up there must love me a little bit after all. I'm still too skeptical to reach forward and take it, though, so we lapse into silence. Before long he feels compelled to fill it. "I'll miss them, I really will. They're great girls. Always say hello to me. Today's my last day, you see." He points to the closing-down sale sign. "No market really round here any more. Not enough for a living, anyway. It's all the big chains on the industrial estates."

I nod sympathetically, not really taking in what he's saying, and he leans on his desk, settling in for a chat. "So you an actress too?"

I smile apologetically. "Look, I ought to get on and—"

He holds up a hand and says "Quite right, off you go." He throws the key and it arcs through the air, catching the light as it twists and turns before landing heavily in my palm. "Just drop it back down when you're done. Nice to meet you. Hope you get the flat, love."

I nod dumbly, unsure quite what to do with this unexpected gift. Holding it tightly, I smile good-bye and close the shop door behind me, before wandering round to the flat to nervously let myself in. As I'm slowly and silently clicking the front door shut behind me, I think about how very, very stupid Liz and Debs are. Fancy leaving a key with some bloke downstairs. Who lets a perfect stranger into their house when they're not there? They're just asking for trouble. I tiptoe up the stairs, almost expecting someone to jump out, to catch me in the act. I move so slowly the steps creak under my feet, echoing in the stillness.

There is a rustle and a small movement upstairs that makes me stop dead in my tracks. Oh my Christ. Is someone there? "Hello?" I stammer. What the hell am I going to say? I should have thought this through!

But no one answers. Uncertainly, I creep to the top of the stairs and find myself staring down at the thin, straggly, hairy face and watery eyes of her repellent dog. It is utterly silent and totally still. Not so brave without Debs around. No yipping today.

"Hello, Pixie," I say softly and crouch down. I don't want it to suddenly go for my ankles, although I doubt it even has teeth—it's probably just fed liquidized truffles and champagne. The dog just stares at me, its name tag twisting and catching the light. Reaching my fingers out I start to coo: "Come on, Pixie, come here. Good girl!" I deliberately make my voice a little higher. The rat looks at me and doubtfully moves closer. I let her sniff my hand but she rubs the side of her face on my wrist like I'm no better than a rag, leaving a trail of eye goo behind.

Feeling utterly revolted, I stand up and look in disgust at my arm, then stride into the kitchen to rinse the eye snot off in the sink. Pixie trots after me and just stands there, watching as I scrub myself and dry off on a tea towel.

"Oh go away!" I hiss at her, and after staring malevolently at me for a second, she turns tail (although she barely has one) and flashes me her disgusting puckered arse before trotting boredly off.

Reaching for a glass on the draining board, I fill it with a little water and sip slowly—my mouth feels dry. Then it occurs to me I might be drinking from something that has touched her lips. I spit the water out quickly and put the glass back where I found it.

I go back into the sitting room. It all looks just as it did be-fore, except the balloons are not as perky. I look more closely at some of the pictures. Liz stares glassily back at me, sultry smile fixed on her face. Her eyes are hypnotic, like a snake. Some of the pictures look like studio shots—she's posing heavily; the wind machine is going, she has smoky, smudged half-closed eyes and appears to be laughing.

The phone rings shrilly, shattering my concentration and making me leap about ten feet into the air. I freeze as it echoes around the flat.

A girl's voice fills the room, I think it's Debs but it's hard to tell. "This is the voicemail for Elizabeth Andersen and Deborah Wills. We can't take your call right now, but please leave a mes-sage after the tone." There's a bleep, then the breathy voice of someone walking and talking cuts in.

"Debs? Honey? Pick up if you are . . . No? Okay, just me. Wondered if you might be popping home before you come in. If you are, can you bring in my patent slingbacks? I forgot them and I'm meeting Peter in between shows. Ta, bitch. Byyyyyyeee!" It clicks off and there is silence.

I wobble slightly with the shock and horror, her picture star-ing back at me, laughing, and then jump violently as the phone begins to ring again.

"This is the voicemail for Elizabeth Andersen and Deborah Wills. We can't take your call right now, but please leave a mes-sage after the tone."

"Me again . . . forgot to say, if you do go home, I left my key like you said so that girl can view, so don't leave yours as well otherwise we're fucked later. Remember, hon—two weeks till rent day, so if you are there when she comes round, sell it to her! And can you chase up that dull friend of Marc's, the one with the bad coat who bounced on my bed yesterday? Fuck . . . what's her name . . . oh, can't remember! Anyway. I'm totally past caring now who moves in—we just need someone! Okay, slag—see ya later at work. Love ya!"

Her eyes in the picture seem to narrow and her laugh seems bigger as the click signaling the end of the message reverberates around the flat. Shaking slightly in my "bad coat," it's all I can do not to grab the photos and bring them crashing to the floor. Bitch . . . BITCH. Marching into her room, trying not to look at the picture of Pete, I throw open her wardrobe door. Right at the back of it, in a deep, dark, dusty corner, I shove my Mulberry and bits of jewelry out of sight, buried under some carrier bags. They are now utterly invisible. Straightening up, I look around the room and move sharply toward her chest of drawers. Opening the top one, a load of bras and knickers burst out. I hide a lacy pair of peach knickers in my own, old handbag. I choose them because they look nothing like anything I own. She's meeting him later . . . she's meeting him later.

I'm so angry and fired up as I crash blindly around her room that I'm not quite sure at first what the piercing ringing is. Halting uncertainly, I listen again carefully and realize that someone is ringing the doorbell—and very persistently too. My heart starts to hammer . . . I should have been quicker.

I stay rooted to the spot with no idea what to do. Pixie begins to yap and growl, making a surprising amount of noise for such a small bag rat.

Shit, shit, shit! I hear the letter box open and someone call up, "Hello? I've come to look at the flat?"

I have no choice but to answer it. Any second now, Mr. Nosy Git from the shop is going to hear her and come and investigate.

Biting my lip, I go quickly to the door and swing it open. A small but sexy girl is standing there, chewing gum and wearing a tiny skirt that barely covers her bum. Her huge, fluffy coat, on the other hand, gives the disconcerting impression that she's killed Big Bird's little sister and is now wearing the result. She's absurdly pretty and smiles disarmingly at me. "You must be Debs?" She sticks a hand out. "I heard about your ad? We spoke on the phone?"

Everything she says goes up at the end. It's very affected and I find myself not liking her very much already, despite her perkiness. Still, very helpful of her to let it slip that she has never met Debs and is clearly not a friend of hers. My tracks will at least be covered. Debs will think that she came and left without wanting the flat, and as for the prospective tenant in front of me . . . Well, she doesn't get a new place to live today, that's true, but she's been useful, if annoying.

"Oh!" I pretend to look gutted. "I'm so sorry! The flat went this morning! I should have phoned you . . . I'm really sorry!"

She looks a little crestfallen for a moment and then forces a smile, shrugs and says, "Okay, well, let me know if anything changes."

"I've got your number," I say firmly. As she's saying, "Nice to meet y—" I'm already shutting the door. She is in and out of my life in less than two minutes. If only I could say the same for Liz.

Having her ring the bell, though, has *really* unnerved me— and I don't want to be here any more. If I got caught . . . Fear speeds me up. Closing the front door quietly behind me, I slip back out on to the street.

Once I have dropped the key back to the crockery man, we have wished each other a fond farewell and he has assured me he will tell Debs that I said it was a lovely flat, but not quite right, I am whistling away on the tube.

Back in the West End, I reach into my bag and pull out my mobile. I call our landline at home and it rings and rings. He's out.

So then I ring his mobile.

"Pete? Hi, babe, it's me. Are you working at home? You are? Oh thank goodness. I just had an awful thought—when I put the dog out this morning I forgot to lock the back door . . . I know, I know. But you're at home so you can just nip down and lock it now, can't you? Oh, and listen, I'm coming home early. I feel dreadful . . . What? No, just a really awful headache. Sort of sinus. Okay, I'll be home in an hour."

Then I hang up. I hate it that he has just lied to me so smoothly about being at home and I hate it that I have just managed to outmaneuver him so easily. It makes him look a fool and doesn't make me feel smart or clever—just very, very sad.

The only good thing to come out of it is that he won't now be able to see her today.

I look at my watch—he must already have been on his way, but now he'll be seriously worried about the house being unsecured and vulnerable, to say nothing of needing to beat me back home. He'll have to turn back.

Frustratingly, I miss a train by minutes and there isn't another one for three-quarters of an hour. With such an unhealthy amount of adrenaline running around my system, I'm anxious and agitated, and although I pace around Jigsaw while I'm waiting, to try and take my mind off what I've just done, I don't notice a single thing; I could be looking at hammers and keyrings. Lottie unnerves me horribly by ringing and I have to leave it, earning myself dirty looks from other shoppers who don't understand why I'm not answering my own phone.

So I step out into the crisp air of Trafalgar Square and the hum of the traffic. There is a female tourist who is actually letting the pigeons sit on her head, her hands and shoulders. They flap around her face as her boyfriend films it all in delight. She is squealing excitedly but nervously, her shoulders have gone rigid and she's closing her eyes tightly. It makes me shudder to see them beating their wings so close to her that her hair is lifting. How can she? Suppose one shits on her head or scratches her hand? Has she never watched them hobbling around with one stub where a foot used to be, beady little eyes glinting and heads bobbing?

Revolted, I pull my coat around me tightly and jump guiltily as my phone rings again. This time it's Clare. I let it go to answer phone but she immediately starts to ring again. This is our code for "pick up—it's urgent."

I don't want to talk to her now, I'm too stressed out . . . but she's ringing back to back . . . Shit. What if it's an emergency to do with Mum? I have no choice but to pick up.

"Ah. Bonjour!" she says delightedly.

"What's up?" I say quickly. "Urgh!" A pigeon flies too close to me and I have to duck out of the way, almost dropping the phone.

"Where the hell are you?" she says instantly. "What just happened?"

"A pigeon," I say faintly. "Right in my face."

"That's gross." I can hear her shudder down the phone. "And I already feel sick. Amy's grandparents got her a chocolate tool kit for her birthday and I've eaten the pliers and the screwdriver today, plus I drank so much vodka last night my face nearly fell off and now I think I'm going into renal failure."

I hear a laugh in the background and she says to someone else, "I am actually, Amy! What? No—I'm telling you—she was right next to the heater . . . sorry, Mi, I was halfway through telling Amy about this still-life class I did where this model had underarm hair so long you could plait it and the smell kicking out from her—"

"Clare!" I interrupt. "I'm at work. Do you actually have something urgent to tell me or not?"

"All right," she says, needled. "Although since when did you have actual real-life pigeons in your office? Fine, I'll be *quick* since you're obviously up to something. I've been invited to go to Barcelona in a couple of weeks but I can't go unless you lend me the money and everyone wants to book it today. This bloke Adam's going. He's a sexual being, Mi—I'm going to get him drunk on ouzo."

"That's Greece," I say automatically, checking my watch. I'm going to miss my second train if I'm not careful. I start walking.

"What? Barcelona's in Spain, you tit."

"No . . ." I close my eyes tiredly for a moment and discover I can't be bothered. I want to get home. "Look . . . I'll lend you the money." Anything to get her off the phone, I don't want to talk. I just need to get back.

"Also," she pauses dramatically, playing her trump card, "Jack and I are no more."

Immediately I feel dreadful for hurrying her. "Oh, Clare— I'm so sorry. He's a stupid little twat to let you go. Are you okay?"

"No—I've been sitting in my room listening to Daniel Beddingfield, crying and stroking a picture of him," she scoffs. "Of course I am. I did it. *I* dumped *him*."

Oh.

"The little shit has already got another girlfriend, which is just bloody rude."

How does she do it? How can she be so strong? So blasé?

"Do you want him back then?" I say faintly; this is all too close to home. I can't do this now.

She snorts. "No—he's got the smallest knob in the world."

"Okay," I say hastily. "Well, there you go. Just pity this new girl—doesn't sound like it's going to be a whole lot of fun for her."

"She's a dick anyway," she says. "She gave this bloke a blow job in a club—not even in the toilets—in a booth under a table. And she drinks pints. I just would have rather I met someone first before him, but . . . enter Adam in Barcelona. *Hola!*"

It takes another three minutes of listening to her overexcited plans before I can get her off the phone without arousing any more suspicion on her part as to why I'm not at work. Finally I'm hurrying back on to the station concourse toward the ticket barriers. Once I'm actually on the train, however, the journey goes so slowly I feel like I'm being dragged backward or dream running and, perversely, I almost want to phone Clare back to help kill the horribly slow journey. By quarter to six I'm practically galloping up our garden path.

I find Pete in the kitchen, as if he's been there all day, boiling the kettle. When I walk in, he smiles and then yawns. Keeping his arms up in the air he says, "Hello, sick note. Come and give me a hug."

I don't need to be asked twice.

Later, we're eating our tea on our laps in silence, staring at the TV, Gloria at our feet.

Although he's been perfectly pleasant, asking me if I'm okay and making tea, Pete is being a little vague, as if there is something on his mind. I don't push it, I don't ask what is wrong.

We watch more TV, and then the phone goes.

"Darling? It's me."

"Mum!" In contrast to Clare earlier, I am immediately happy to hear her and yet my throat goes tight with tears. For God's sake—I've got to get a grip! "Where are you?" My voice wobbles.

"We've been to St. Lucia today. Honestly, it's so beautiful. I swam with turtles. How are you? Have you . . . over the weekend . . . Clare . . ." The line starts to break up.

"Mum? Can you hear me? Mum?" I say desperately.

"Hello? Oooh. I'm back again. Anyway—yes. It's all lovely here. I can't tell you how relaxed I feel. It's amazing, isn't it? You just don't realize until you get away how much you needed some time off. I just tried Clare but it's on answer phone. Will you tell her I rang? And you're okay?"

Pete's sitting right there, looking at the TV and scratching his foot. I can't say anything even if I wanted to—and I wouldn't anyway, she'd worry herself sick. She needs this break so much.

"I'm fine." I close my eyes briefly. "Fine."

"Are you sure? You don't sound like you."

I do a strange barklike laugh and Pete glances at me in surprise. "I don't feel like me." I smile sadly and tears well up. "Just ignore me." I reach for a tissue from my sleeve and wipe my eyes. "I haven't been very well. That's all."

"Poor little bunny," she says kindly. "Try to get a good

night's sleep and drink plenty of water. Get Pete to give you a big hug from me. I'd better go, darling, this'll be costing a fortune. Love you billions."

"Love you too," I say, and then she's gone.

"You all right?" Pete looks at me curiously.

"Just miss her." I blow my nose noisily. "I would have liked to have told her about the break-in . . . but I don't want to worry her." He reaches out and pats my arm.

"She's only gone for three weeks! She'll be back before you know it, and I'm sure she's having a rare old time. Knowing your mum, it won't be long before she's in charge of the ship. Come on, you're just tired and ill. Time for bed for you, I think."

I nod wordlessly, still clutching my tissue like a bloody five-year-old.

"Go on. Shoo," he says gently. "I'll be right up."

I brush my teeth, clamber into bed, pick up my book and wait for him.

Ten minutes later he pads into our room, pulls his jumper off over his head and lets it drop to the floor.

"Did you put the dog out?" I look like I've been reading for hours, but in fact I have been on page eight the whole time. I don't think I've taken in a single word.

"Yeah, I put her out *and* locked the door, which *wasn't* unlocked earlier—nutter." He leans over as he gets under the duvet and ruffles my hair affectionately. "Seriously, Mi, you've got to chill. I know the robbery was horrible, but there's nothing to worry about. It's not like you to be so stressed out and teary just because your mum rang. Don't give it any more thought, okay?"

I nod, and satisfied, he turns over, having given my leg a friendly squeeze.

Half an hour later, when his breathing has slowed down and

he's started to snore, I roll away from him and slip out of bed and nip downstairs.

His phone is in his jacket pocket, which is hanging on the banister post. It's still on and is showing one new message: Liz.

Is he getting sloppy, or do I now just know to look?

I open it and read:

> If u didn't want to cum 2day u should just say so. Pls don't ever lie to me. The back door was unlocked?... Wot do u take me 4?

This makes me thrill all over—like I've got four lottery numbers and just need one more. And as I know that she will be out there waiting for him to text her back with an apology once he reads what I've just read, I delete the text, so he can't.

Then I click on his inbox. There is one message from her, sent at 5:15 p.m.:

> WHY wld I trash ur house? Am so upset u cld THINK that never mind ask... and if u think it WAS me, why did u need to go home and lock door? Am not stupid.

He tackled her about it! He actually did it! She's out there all upset and he's up in our bed asleep . . .

I carefully place the phone back where I found it, then I go back upstairs to bed and fall asleep surprisingly quickly.

SEVENTEEN

I can't come out," I say carefully into the phone, aware that Pete might be able to hear me. "I've been off work ill for the last two days and I just don't feel like it." Sure enough, Pete wanders into the room seconds later and sits down heavily on the sofa. He's been in an inexplicably vile mood all day.

"Well, your boss isn't likely to be in a bar in our local high street having a drink, is he?" Patrick says reasonably.

"No," I sigh. "He isn't."

"Who is it?" Pete mouths to me, and when I mouth "Patrick" back, he rolls his eyes and disappears behind a glossy magazine called *Best Barns*.

"Look, you're not trailing a limb or anything. It's Friday night, you've already said you and Pete have no plans, I haven't seen you in ages and I'm talking about one drink. I'll come and get you in an hour—no," his voice becomes insistent as I try and protest, "decision made. No further discussion required."

And then he hangs up.

I genuinely am tired, it's been a knackering couple of days. As far as Pete is concerned I've had a relapse of illness—so I can be at home and be around him. He's got a really big quote coming up and so although he's been in his office a lot of the time, I do know he hasn't been to see her. Which is good. I think. I am, however, very stressed about next week. Although Pete thinks I was at work on Tuesday and Wednesday, I now haven't been in for a full week. Lottie texted me again today to ask when I'm coming back—I can't just keep delaying things.

I feel suspended in mid-air, permanently twisting. One minute I'm fixated with his phone and unable to think about anything else but getting rid of her, then the next I'm appalled and horrified that I was in her flat and thinking that there has to be some other way for this to turn out right. When I'm at home with him, it doesn't feel like it's real anyway, that he can have another woman out there. But then I stand in our bedroom holding her earrings in my hand—proof that I haven't imagined the whole thing—and I know I can't pretend she doesn't exist. Last night I sat in the bath until it went cold and just cried, not knowing which way to turn or what to do.

I even thought about purposefully stopping taking the pill, but the very idea scared me rigid. I love Pete very much and I don't want to lose him, but I want more than anything for that to happen with him the right way, through love, not desperation. How could I ever look my child in the eye otherwise?

"Mia. Woo-hoo!" I look up and Pete is smiling at me. "You're a million miles away."

"Sorry. What's up?"

"What did Patrick want?" he says with the slight edge to his voice that he always has when he says Patrick's name, but it gives me a cheap idea as I sit there on the sofa. It's the equivalent of a carton of long-life milk or a tiny white loaf that has all the nutritional value of cardboard and couldn't satisfy anyone—but

I bite in anyway. After all, it's not deliberately not taking the pill or ramming my car into the back of another one, forcing Pete to realize how much he loves me as he hangs over my bedside where I'm rigged up to tubes and beeping machines.

Because I've been there too over the last few days. When I'm calmer and sitting on my sofa, I know it's an utterly sick thing to think. I can't defend it and it's very far from all right and normal, but when I heard the answer-phone message in her flat announcing smugly that she was meeting him and I heard her say it again in my head when I was stuck in traffic this morning coming back from Sainsbury's, I stared dully at the back of the car in front through the windscreen and wondered what would happen if I slammed into it . . . I thought about him dashing to my bedside, clasping my hand in anguish, saying, "She's going to be all right, isn't she, Doctor? Promise me?"

And so somehow, what I decide to do next doesn't, in the grand scheme of things, seem so bad. In comparison with where my mind *has* been, it feels positively rational.

"I'm going out for a drink. You don't mind, do you?" I say decisively and stand up, stretching.

Pete looks up in surprise. "But you're ill!"

I shrug. "I feel a bit better tonight. I managed a food shop earlier. I'll be back by nine-ish."

I know there is every possibility that the second I'm out of the door he'll be on the phone to her. And . . . making your boyfriend jealous? Am I really resorting to the tactics of a fifteen-year-old? But he doesn't look thrilled at the prospect, and that's better than nothing.

He looks even less thrilled when I come back downstairs three-quarters of an hour later in a short shift dress showing a lot of leg.

"Shouldn't you wrap up warm?" he says, and in spite of myself I laugh a little at his prudish tone.

"Would you rather I wore dungarees?" I tease.

"Seriously, Mia. You know why I want you to change." He shifts irritably. "I don't want him perving over you all night then going home for a wank."

His gaze drops back to his magazine and I'm slightly stunned at such an unnecessarily graphic remark. The doorbell rings again. "That'll be him. I don't have time to change."

He says nothing.

"I'll be home later," I say softly.

He nods without looking up and I let myself out.

EIGHTEEN

S o, my new flat has an added extra I didn't bargain on," Patrick says as we sit down with our drinks.

I do my best to look interested.

"Mice!" he says dryly, and then laughs at my wrinkled nose.

"Oh come on, what's not to love? Mouse shit everywhere, chewed bread packets, not knowing if girls I bring home are screaming at me naked or a small rodent scuttling past the end of the bed." He takes a swig of his beer. "It's awesome."

"Have you put traps down?"

"Yeah. Caught two this morning. Although I've had some interesting suggestions for alternatives. One of the girls at work said, 'What you need to do, right . . .'" he mimics a chav accent, although not unkindly, "'is put daan a little bowl of water and a little bowl of cement powder mixed with sugar. Then, right, the little mouse walks up and first he smells the sugar so he eats the powder and then, right, he's really firsty so he goes to the water bowl, has a little drink and then it all goes off in its belly and . . . he turns into a brick!'"

For the first time in a week, I manage a genuine laugh.

"I know!" he grins. "Brilliant, isn't it?"

"But mice notwithstanding, you like it?"

He shrugs. "It's okay. I can be at the station in under ten minutes, I've got the TV working now and the shower's not a dribble. Don't need much more than that."

Patrick has always been easy-going to a fault. At school, he was the one who used to make everyone laugh in class. Just sporty enough not to be a geek, but not good enough (to his huge frustration) to be on school teams, he was a jack-of-all-groups, which was what drew a lot of girls—including Katie—to him. She relentlessly pursued him at several parties, until at one, to Nirvana's "Smells Like Teen Spirit," he caved in and they snogged passionately in a dark corner of the living room. Later, in the bathroom, she breathlessly told me that he was the best snog she'd ever had, which was why it surprised me *and* Patrick when the following week she was discovered snogging Adam Stebbings in his mum and dad's bedroom at *his* party.

"Sorry." I shrugged helplessly to Patrick. "She did say she really liked you, but . . ."

"She just likes Adam more," Patrick said ruefully.

"I think he's a dick. If it helps," I said.

"Not really, but I'll survive. Do you want a drink . . . Mia, isn't it?" he said.

And so began a friendship that lasted through Katie's resulting strop. She'd snogged him and dumped him—it was inconvenient to have him still hanging around getting in the way, as she grumpily put it. Why couldn't I be friends with some other boy instead? But I liked Patrick. He made me laugh.

In the end, he and Katie not getting on was simply never an issue. They were coolly polite if they were ever forced to speak at school, she'd melt away if he came over to talk to me; and when Katie and I finally fell out at university, he was fantastic. I leaned on him a lot.

The brief time when I did have feelings for Patrick only lasted for about three months, just before I met Pete, and I didn't let on to Patrick. It was after we'd been out on a Friday night and I went back to his afterward, like I'd done a hundred times, to call a cab. We were both pretty pissed, and while we were waiting for the taxi we collapsed on the sofa and put late-night TV on.

I don't know what made that night different to any of the others, but I was all cosied up to him and suddenly realized that it felt nice. Patrick is really tall, but works out loads and has this fab upper body—not too big, just blokey.

His arm was resting lightly round me and I could smell his aftershave. I remember looking up at him and for the first time ever wondering what it would be like to kiss him, which was a really disturbing thought. He must have felt me looking at him, because he looked down at me and there was this God-awful pause where it suddenly felt like we *were* about to kiss. He moved slightly closer and I felt my eyes close, but then there was a knock at the door and the cab was there. I've never sobered up so fast in my whole life. We just sort of looked at each other and then both jumped up and it was all awkward "Ooooh, where are my shoes?" and "God, I feel *wrecked*!" and "Shit, I can't believe what time it is!"

I got to the front door and turned back to say good-bye, but for the first time ever didn't know what to do next. Everything that had nearly happened a second ago was drifting in the air round us. Normally I'd have kissed him on the cheek to say good-bye or punched him on the arm or something, but suddenly I felt shy of touching him, which was ridiculous.

We just sort of stood there for what felt like forever. Finally the cab driver said impatiently from his window, "Where is it you're off to, love?" and his voice broke the tension. The atmosphere changed; we both snuck another look at each other and laughed in a sort of relieved "Phew, that was close!" sort of way. Patrick said, "Come here, you!" and gave me a friendly bear hug, and I lightly pretended to punch him in the stomach. Then I legged it into the taxi feeling totally confused.

We didn't talk the next morning and about three days passed before I saw him again, by which point I wasn't sure if I'd been more drunk than I thought and imagined it all. I certainly didn't want to ask him if he'd been more sober than me and have to have that horrible "Er, about the other night . . ." conversation.

So we didn't discuss it and things went back to normal, which is to say I started to think about him in this new and very confusing way for a few weeks. I wrestled with myself and couldn't work out if I fancied him or not, or was just mixing up friendship and feelings that weren't real. Just as I finally decided yes, I did fancy him, he got himself a really gorgeous girlfriend.

Once my heart had plummeted down a well when he walked into the pub on the Friday night holding her hand and smiling happily (I had thought I *might* tell him how I felt that night), I got my breath back, smiled a beaming, welcoming smile and thanked God I hadn't said anything. I stumbled through the evening okay, had a little cry that night at home and got on with it, as you do.

It all worked out for the best anyway, because I met Pete not long after that. I started seeing him, and was blissfully happy, just about the same time as Patrick and Mel, I think her name was, split up.

"So what's new with you then?" Patrick glances up as a girl brushes past him and then turns his attention back to me.

I manage not to laugh hysterically and for a brief moment I picture myself sitting there saying, "Not much. Found out Pete's cheating on me, staged a burglary, went looking for this girl to tell her to fuck off, ended up in her flat and saw Pete's picture by her bed. Same old same old."

"Well, I've been ill pretty much all week, so everything's been quiet. You?"

"Rubbish really," he says dismissively. "Work's pretty pedestrian and I'm here with you on a Friday night which tells you everything you need to know about the current state of my love life. Bumped into a blast from the past recently, though . . ."

I try to look interested but I'm thinking about how long I've been away and if he'll have phoned her yet. I can't leave it too much longer.

". . . It was really weird. I was at the station and she just walked up to me and said hi. I can't remember the last time I saw her. Probably before you and her had your falling-out, I expect."

"Sorry." My attention snaps back. "Who's this?"

"Katie," he says, looking over my shoulder. "Do you want another drink while the bar's quiet?"

"No thanks, I'm okay," I say quickly. "What did she have to say, anything interesting? What's she up to these days?"

Patrick looks at me curiously. "That's a lot of sudden questions."

I shrug, trying to look nonchalant. "Just nosy, that's all. How did she look?"

He ponders for a moment. "A bit too thin, actually," he says thoughtfully. "Sort of—angular. Not massively different, though. Older."

"What did you talk about?"

He thinks again. "Not much, really . . . she's going traveling."

I frown, glass on the way to my mouth. "Traveling? Where?"

He shrugs. "I dunno, one of these save a disadvantaged yak programs somewhere. Did I tell you I saw Reuben too—d'you remember? That kid who set the science lab on fire? He's running a division of JP's now in—"

"Did she say when she was going?" I cut in insistently. He looks surprised. "I didn't ask. We didn't speak for that long."

"Did she . . . did she mention me?" I say, and hate myself for asking.

He looks awkward and shifts in his seat. "Honestly, it was like a five-second conversation and—"

"So she didn't?"

"No. 'Fraid not." He reaches out and pats my hand affectionately. "Sorry."

I don't say anything, just shrug and try a smile.

"But not being funny—why would she, and why would you care anyway? She was a total cow to you!"

I hesitate. Was she? Or was she telling me the truth?

"To risk a friendship over a bloke is bad enough once—but twice?" He shakes his head. "I'm sorry to say, Mia, I don't think she lost much sleep over it. Did you think she might still want to set things right?"

"Maybe." I don't look at him directly.

"But perhaps it isn't unfinished business for her," he says gently. "Perhaps it just is for you."

We go a bit quiet then.

"Don't take it to heart," he says eventually. "You know what she's like, she didn't ask me anything about myself either—Katie is only interested in Katie."

I don't say anything, as I know he will always be slightly biased on that front. Funny how a kiss at the age of fourteen will stay with you for years afterward.

"All she did was gabble on about herself, say that we must meet up to catch up properly, gave me her mobile number and that was it."

My eyes widen. "She gave you her mobile number?"

"Yes," he says, exasperated, "but I'm not going to call because a) she's totally self-absorbed, b) she was horrible to you, and c) she's going traveling. The only thing more boring than listening to someone else's travel plans is listening to their dreams. I dreamed I got married to Mel the other night. Remember her?" He shudders.

"Well, they say that whatever you dream, the opposite comes true in real life."

Patrick frowns. "Well—while I hope that's certainly true in the marrying Mel case, that sounds like total guff to me. I dreamed I was walking to work the other day—but last time I checked, I still can't actually fly."

"You dreamed you were walking to work?" I look at him perplexed. "How crap are your dreams? And since when is flying the opposite of walking, you daft sod? I mean things like if you dream you die, you're going to have a long and happy life."

"D'you think you and Pete will get married?" Patrick says suddenly.

I manage to smile, then shrug and squint up at him. "Hope so. He hasn't asked me."

"He will." Patrick takes a swig of beer. "He'd be crazy not

to." He glances to his left as a short fat bloke punches the air with his fist and goes, "Yesssss!" loudly as he hits the jackpot on the fruit machine and it begins to pump coins into the tray. "Lucky bastard."

I dart a glance at him, and my heart inexplicably does a little thump-thump. Who is? Pete or Tubby Fatso over there shoveling pound coins into his pocket? But then my phone, which has been lying on the table, lights up, starts flashing Pete's name and begins to vibrate itself into a puddle of spilled Diet Coke.

"Hi, it's me," says Pete smoothly. "Can you come home?"

"What, right now?" I look at my watch as Patrick mouths "Another drink?" and grins cheerfully at me. The moment has passed, if it was even ever there.

"Clare's here."

"What—at our house?" I'm confused and shake my head at Patrick. "What's she doing there?"

"Hang on—I'll pass her over."

There's a fumbling sound. "Yo, chick," says Clare. "Where the bloody hell are you?"

"I'm at the pub. What are you doing at mine?"

"Well, *someone*, aka our mother, phoned me and said she was worried about you and could I come down and make sure you were all right. She said you were weird on the phone to her."

"I've been ill, actually," I say quickly.

"Evidently. Nice pub, is it? I *told* Mum you were all right. Anyway, I thought I'd come and surprise you since you were on your sick bed. I've got Lucozade and magazines and everything. And I've sacrificed a Friday night."

"Well, you should have called first."

"Er, except then it's not much of a surprise, is it? And since when are you ever out on a Friday these days anyway? What pub are you at? I'll come and find you."

"The Bottle House, but don't worry—I'm coming back in—" But the line has already gone dead. Great, now I have to wait until she gets here and I want to go home!

"My sister is coming to join us," I say to Patrick.

He frowns. "Isn't she about fifteen?"

"Yes, seven years ago. Has it been that long since you saw her?"

He looks nonplussed. "Maybe. It's been a while. I don't really remember. Shall I get some more drinks in? What'll she have? Lemonade?"

I snort. "If you put about four vodkas in it, yes, she probably will."

He's still at the bar when Clare puffs up to the table, all rosy-cheeked from being outside, and slings her bag down on the floor.

"Hiya." She leans in to kiss me. "Oh yeah, I can see what Mum meant—you look *really* ill. You're such a wanker—I could be out getting some bunty tonight, but Mum was like, 'Stop being so selfish and get on a train.' Where's your pal, or did you make him up too?"

"At the bar," I begin. "Look, Clare, I don't want to stay that long . . ."

"Oh great." She rolls her eyes. "Is he a tit?"

"No! It's Patrick. You've met him before."

She looks blank. "Must be a gooch, I don't remember him at all."

"I just don't want to leave Pete on his own all night, and—"

"Why?" She makes a face. "He was in a right stomp when I

arrived. I could hear him shouting as I came up the garden path. I'd leave him to it."

"Who was he shouting at?" My heart freezes.

She shrugs. "Dunno. He was holding the phone when he answered the door and said he'd call them back. I thought it was you, I was going to kick him in the nads. Oh, hello."

Her voice suddenly becomes a little smaller and shyer as Patrick appears by the table clutching three drinks.

"Hello." He clears his throat, smiles and remembers his manners. "Er, let me put these down. Sorry, my hands are all wet. Um, hi, I'm Patrick. I don't think we've met."

But Clare is gazing at him like the rest of the world has just frozen and they are the only two people in it. I'm almost embarrassed and turn apologetically to Patrick, but then I realize that he is looking at her pretty intensely too.

Oh no . . . no, no, no.

"Yes you have," I say quickly. "This is Clare, my *little* sister. Clare, this is Patrick."

Patrick's eyebrows shoot up into his hairline. "Jesus! Sorry! I thought you were . . . well, my God, you've certainly changed."

Clare actually flushes a little pinker. "Well, thank you . . . Patrick." She says his name slowly, like she's trying it out for size. "It's good to see you again."

Patrick sits down and passes over our drinks. "And you . . . and you . . . Well, um, so what have you been doing for the last seven years?"

"A-levels, getting pissed, nicking my clothes and going to uni," I interject sharply, and Clare frowns. "Look, Clare, are you sure you don't know who he was shouting at?"

Clare laughs lightly in a "No I don't and shall we talk about this later?" sort of way and then says firmly, "I've no idea. Sorry, sis." She turns back to Patrick and smiles as she pushes her hair off her face, saying brightly, "So, Patrick. Do you work around here?"

Half an hour later, they're getting on like a house on fire and I have the sinking feeling that something significant is not so much brewing as bubbling up madly. I'm also chewing my nails down to the quick, desperate to get home, but not seeing how I can without being blatantly rude and letting on that something is up.

"Wings or gills?" says Clare.

"Easy. Gills. Maybe I'll hook up with the Little Mermaid," Patrick says flirtily. God, no wonder he's single.

"What?" They both look at me.

"Sorry?" I say innocently. "Did I just say that out loud? Look, Clare, we really have to—"

"Okay," says Clare thoughtfully, completely ignoring me. "Would you rather be completely covered in fur or scales?"

"Fur," says Patrick, "because at least then I can shave it all off and look slightly normal."

"Five o'clock shadow over your *whole body* is normal?" teases Clare.

"Good point," he concedes. "Would you rather . . . shave your tongue or . . ."

". . . eat a pizza topped with Dot Cotton's pubes," Clare finishes.

Patrick gags on a mouthful of drink. "I'd cut my tongue *out* rather than do that."

"Okay, would you rather . . . French kiss a dog—"

"Been there, done that," Patrick says. "Come on—test me."

"A *real* dog . . . or go down on Ann Widdecombe?"

"Clare!" I put my glass down. "Please!"

But Patrick is laughing. "Definitely the dog."

Clare, who is now on a roll, shoots me a mischievous grin. "Oh, I'm sorry. I seem to be lowering the tone. Let's talk politics. Would you rather teabag John Prescott or stick your fingers up Tony Blair's arse—no gloves?"

"Er, would there be any room, what with George Bush's whole hand already being up there?"

"Well," Clare says admiringly. "Not just a pretty face, a satirist too." And Patrick actually blushes. For God's sake.

"Right—that's enough," I say firmly. "I'd like to remind you I am actually ill already without having to think about John Prescott."

"Bollocks," coughs Clare as she takes a sip of her drink.

"I am!" I say, widening my eyes at her and standing up. "And I really need to go home now."

"Well, go on then," says Clare. "No one's stopping you."

"But I need you to come with me!"

"Why?" says Clare simply. "Ring Pete, he'll come and get you." I can't think of anything to say to that, so slightly foolishly I just stand there for a moment. Clare sips her drink innocently and Patrick stares at the table, struggling with the obvious desire to stay in the pub and chat up my sister, and his innate good manners that mean he should see me home. My sister wins.

"Okay, fine," I say wearily. "Patrick, can you make sure Clare gets back to mine safely, please. I assume you're staying with us tonight and not going back to uni?" She nods.

Patrick stands up. "You're sure you don't mind . . ." He trails off awkwardly.

"No, I don't mind." I do actually. I can see what is happening here—you'd have to be blind not to. But I need to get home.

I can't sort Pete and me, and deal with Clare and Patrick flirting like crazy, *and* think about Katie. It's too bloody much.

Pete barely says hello when I get in the car.

"Thanks for coming out," I say tiredly.

"Welcome." He looks over his shoulder as he pulls out. "Told you you should have stayed in."

"I know." I hold my buzzing head. "Sorry about Clare landing on us. Is it okay if she stays at ours tonight?"

"She's still here? Where?" he says in surprise.

"Still in the pub, with Patrick," I say.

"Oh!" he says and then a slow smile spreads across his face and he chuckles. "Oh dear!"

"Just don't," I say, closing my eyes. So much for making him jealous.

"Are you sure she'll be staying at ours tonight?" he teases.

"Yes! I'm absolutely sure," I snap back, slightly more sharply than I intended.

"Okay, calm down." He looks surprised. "I was only joking."

"Sorry." I try and make my tone more conciliatory. He doesn't need a row with me—I'm supposed to be the one he's getting on with, it's her he should be rowing with. "How's your evening been?"

"Quiet."

I glance at him sideways and I just can't help myself. "Oh? Clare said she heard you shouting at someone on the phone."

"Get out of the bloody road! Jesus, they'll get themselves killed!" He slows down as some kids decide to cross, mistakenly believing in their drunken haze that our car is much further away than it actually is. "I ordered an Indian after you left.

They said half an hour and it was seriously late. I did lose my rag a bit at that."

"That must have been it then," I say doubtfully.

After I've made up the spare room, we watch some TV and then he says he's going to bed. I say I'll wait up for Clare and he kisses me briefly and goes upstairs. Then something occurs to me. I go into the kitchen and look in the bin. There are no take-away trays in it. Another lie.

I look for his mobile, but I can't find it anywhere.Pausing only to send Clare a text telling her where I'm leaving the key, I give up and go to bed.

NINETEEN

I wake up to the sound of laughing and chatting downstairs. Pulling on my dressing gown, I wander into the kitchen to find Clare, in last night's clothes, munching her way through a bowl of cereal and Pete putting some drying-up away.

"Top of the morning to you," says Clare. "Like your new mugs. When d'you get them?"

"After the burglary," I say, without thinking.

Her chewing slows. "What burglary? You never said anything about that!"

I wave a hand quickly. "Let's not talk about it, it was nothing really—I don't want to go into it now. How was last night after I left?"

She looks smug; I have successfully diverted her. "Well, I'm afraid I had a rather controversial snog . . ."

". . . with Patrick! And she stayed there!" says Pete delightedly.

Clare gives him a look. "Not like that. Honestly, Mia, your boyfriend's mind. I came back, but some twat had forgotten to leave the key out." She looks pointedly at me.

"I bloody did leave it out," I say indignantly. "I can't help it if you were too pissed to find it."

"*Luckily* Patrick had come back in the cab with me," she ignores me, "and being a gentleman had waited to see me get inside. Only I couldn't, so I went to his. And he slept on the sofa."

"Yeah, yeah!" Pete crows.

I sit down at the table. "So you snogged, then?"

"Yes, we did." She sighs happily and pours some more milk into the bowl. "He's fit. And well funny."

"Are you going to see him again?"

She shrugs. "Nah. Shouldn't think so. Maybe. I don't know. I'm at uni and he works . . ."

I know what this means. This is faked indifference, just in case he doesn't call her. She likes him. She likes him a lot.

"You're only an hour away," says Pete reasonably, putting some glasses in the cupboard. "That's no distance at all, and he works in London." I stare at him. Remarkable how quickly he's become captain of Team Patrick since it means he can no longer be even vaguely interested in me.

"You don't mind that I snogged him, do you?" Clare says, looking at me carefully.

"Mind? Why should I mind?" I laugh. "I'm totally cool with it." Reaching for a spare bit of toast, I start to butter it carefully. "Did he ask for your number?"

Clare looks smug. "Of course. And I've got his. He's under McFittie." She waits but I say nothing. "His surname is McDonald?" she says patiently. "Jesus, Pete, good luck with this one today."

"What about that trip to Barcelona you're going on? Aren't you after some bloke called Adam?" I say hopefully.

"Who?" she says blankly. "Oh him. I'm not so sure I'll go

now. Think I might like to stay . . . a little closer to home. If you know what I mean." And she grins naughtily.

By lunchtime she is on the train, and when I get back from dropping her off at the station, the house feels empty and lonely without her. Pete is working on his quote upstairs and I just wander around, feeling a little lost and unsure what to do. My friend and my sister . . . As if on cue, my phone bleeps with a message from Patrick.

> Are we ok with what happened last night? As in me and you? Don't want to mess anything up but would really like to call Clare. Is that ok?

What can I say to that? I text back that it's fine. And on some level it is. I couldn't love Clare more than I do, and if a guy as lovely as Patrick wants to be in her life—well, how great is that? She's right, he is fit, and funny; but he's also kind, loyal, thoughtful, generous. Everything I could want in a man for my sister.

I think about them flirting last night and wistfully gaze up the stairs. Pete and I used to be like that. I know we did.

Later, I'm still thinking about how Pete just needs to be reminded of how great we have always been—me and him—while he's still arguing with *her*. So I make a phone call . . . which, on Sunday lunchtime, sees us driving out of the town. We've been going for a little over half an hour when he twigs.

"Are we going to the Brown Trout?" he says, looking over at me. I nod shyly.

The last time we went to the Brown Trout was about a year and a half ago. The food was amazing and we ate on the terrace overlooking a stunning spread of shimmering summer fields.

We went for a walk afterward clutching each other's hand and a glass of Pimm's, with the ice chinking in the glasses. All we could hear was fat woodpigeons cooing and leaves rustling as the breeze tickled them. Because it's in the middle of nowhere, we might just stand a chance of having some peace and quiet; some time just for us.

Sadly, it seems that things have changed a little since we were last here. The terrace is firmly closed up when we arrive, piles of wet leaves everywhere, and the umbrellas I last saw flapping lazily in the summer breeze are folded away. Not that that matters really—it's too cold to sit outside, and they have a cozy fire in the bar anyway.

But my heart sinks as we go inside. New management seem to have taken over, and what used to be warm, comfortable and traditional—beams and intimate nooks and crannies—has been replaced by edgy tables, a cocktail menu and a slick black and gray bar.

Where the fire used to be, there's a spiky arrangement of red-hot pokers and austere lilies, and instead of the warming, hearty roast I'd hoped for, we end up with pesto cannelloni for Pete and Thai salmon on a bed of seared honey parsnips and leeks for me. When they arrive, Pete's is so hot—fresh from the microwave—that it resembles a bowl of lava, and yet mine is tepid with floppy, waxy vegetables. I try gamely to keep the conversation going, but Pete is distant. He's still perfectly pleasant, but doesn't seem entirely there. He's just not trying. At all.

Afterward, I suggest a walk. We trudge down to the gate at the bottom of the car park and Pete looks doubtfully at the bog that is just about passing for a field. "I don't want to get my trainers muddy."

"Oh, you'll be fine!" I try to sound convincing. "We'll stick to the edges. Come on!"

"Do you remember that walk we had here in the summer?" I venture fifteen minutes later, my arm looped through his as we carefully pick our way through the less squelchy bits.

"I remember it was a lot warmer—and drier." Pete shivers, pulling away from me and zipping his coat right up. "I think we should go back. It's getting daft now."

"Just a bit further," I say, more confidently than I feel. "Let's just get to the trees."

"Okay." Pete slips a little as he tries to step over a large muddy stick, avoiding a puddle the other side. "Thank God we didn't bring the dog—she'd be filthy. Oh SHIT!"

I look up in alarm from where I'm negotiating a tricky bit myself and see Pete, one leg completely submerged in the puddle, looking crossly back at me. "THIS is why I didn't think this was a good idea," he says through gritted teeth. He starts to try and pull his foot free, and finally it pops out with a big farting sound. I can't help it, I laugh. He looks so silly standing there with one enormous mud clubfoot.

"It's not funny, Mia! My bloody trainer is completely ruined—look!" He lifts it up to show me and wobbles slightly with the weight of it. "Shiiiiit," he says in alarm, as he slips and plunges the other foot into the mud bath.

We both fall silent.

"Well, at least they match now," I say helpfully.

We look at each other, look at his feet, and then we both laugh.

"Sorry!" I wheeze. "You just look so funny!" Out of nowhere, I find myself laughing so much tears spring to my eyes.

"Yes, okay," he says patiently. "I am actually getting pretty cold now. When you've stopped wetting yourself, can you come and help heave me out?"

In the car on the way back—with his socks drying on the dashboard—he turns to me.

"Thanks for lunch and the walk," he says. "It was actually really nice." Then he squeezes my hand and my heart fills with love.

Later, when the house is still and he is asleep, I am again creeping downstairs, past his drying-out trainers, which make me smile, in my now nightly ritual to find his phone. I am already so used to doing it, I almost don't expect to find anything worse than I already have. So it comes as a huge, ugly, horrible shock that makes me catch my breath, like being plunged into a bath of icy water, when the screen lights up as I open his inbox and read:

Ha ha! Bet you looked funny. We'll have to get you some new trainers. Time you updated anyway! And thanx for saying sorry. I love you! xxx"

The little flame of hope lit earlier in the afternoon blows out suddenly, and I stand immobile in the darkness.

TWENTY

At nine o'clock sharp on Monday morning in London, having called work and left another message saying— surprise surprise—that I'm still ill, I march into the post office and buy an envelope and a stamp. Taking the card that I stole last week from Liz's bedroom out of my handbag, I cut the top half of it off, so her name has gone, but so that it still says "All love always, Peter xxx."

Then, disguising my writing, I scrawl my name and address on the front of the envelope, stuff the half-card in, seal it and post it. The top half of the card goes back in my handbag for later. Then I stride grimly off to the tube station. I'm not messing about any more.

Four hours later, Debs is holding the end of a tape measure for me as I pretend to make a note of what curtain size I need.

"I'm sorry Lizzie isn't here *again*." She rolls her eyes. "You don't have much luck with her, do you?"

"It's no problem." I let the measure go and it whizzes back, snapping shut. "You said when I rang this morning that she definitely wouldn't be here and I *know* I'm going to meet her soon."

"Of course you will," Debs beams. "I'm so glad you called back. I couldn't believe it when that number you gave me didn't work—I'm *such* a blonde, I must have copied it down wrong—and of course Marc's in San Fran so I had no way of tracking you down!"

Thank God for Marc and his big gay holiday.

"Anyway, you're here now." Debs smiles confidently at me. "So you definitely want the room then?"

I hesitate. Then I say softly, "Yes, I think I do. Can I move in straight away?"

Debs squeals theatrically and gives me a quick, insincere hug. "Of course. Yay us!" she says. "We're going to have so much fun." Then, without missing a beat, she looks me square in the eye and says, "I'll need a check for the deposit today, though."

"No problem," I say smoothly.

"Then I'll go and get you a key, roomie!" she giggles, practically skipping out into the hall.

Left alone, looking around the room I have agreed to rent, I can't believe what I am about to do, and feel my heart thump against my rib cage. I close my eyes briefly. This is crazy.

Debs comes back in and holds out a key. "Here you go."

I look at it and then I tentatively reach out and my fingers curl round it. "Thank you," I say, slipping it into my bag. She looks at me expectantly and I realize she is waiting for the check.

"Oh, of course." I start to scrabble in my bag, and just as my hand closes round my checkbook, my heart stops. I realize that my real name is printed on the check, and that Debs thinks I'm Lottie . . . Shit.

I play for time, pretending I can't find it, and root around some more. "Where the hell . . ." I mutter. "I swear I had it this morning . . ."

Debs is looking bored.

"I'll have to give it to you next time." I look her straight in the eye.

But Debs is not quite *that* green.

"Riiight," she says uncertainly. "Well, I don't mean to be rude, but could I have the key back then? I'm not saying I don't trust you or anything . . ."

We have a stand-off moment. Neither of us really moves, and suddenly a mobile goes off in Debs' pocket.

"Excuse me, Lotts." She pulls it out. "Hello? Yeah, why? What? FUCK! I'd completely forgotten! Oh shit! Tell them I'm leaving now. Oh, I'm so sorry! Yeah, yeah, I KNOW, yes, right now, bye!"

She snaps it shut and looks wildly at me. "I've forgotten a wig fitting. I'm really sorry, I've got to go." She holds out her hand for the key.

"Well, tell you what," I say slowly. "Why don't I finish up my measuring and then I'll stick the key back through the letter box when I'm done? I totally see that you can't let me just take it with no deposit. I could pop it over tomorrow morning . . . in cash."

Debs' eyes gleam greedily. "That sounds perfect! You're a star, Lotts. Hey—and that way you can meet Liz too. She'll be in then. Oh, I've got to go—I'm so *late*! They're going to *hate* me!" She giggles like she couldn't care less if that was the case, grabs a coat and her bag and squeaks over her shoulder as she gallops down the stairs, "See you tomorrow, roomie!"

"Will do, roomie!" I call back, smile fixed glassily to my face until the door slams behind her. I wait for a moment or two, then I let out a deep breath.

Looking at my watch, I realize I don't have much time to get over to the theater myself now, but I'm going to have to wait another five minutes. It won't do to arrive at the same time as Debs, but then neither do I want to be late. I am going to see the show again: a matinee performance.

When I arrive, I am unamused to discover that a ticket will cost me thirty quid. Thirty quid! Pushing my tenners under the glass window of the box office actually hurts. I'm paying to see her in the show, effectively almost paying her wages. Jesus. And I'm at the back!

Once the lights go down and the band start up, I tense. The curtain rises and I scan the stage for her as the big opening number begins. Finally I see her, all eyelashes and teeth, loose limbs and sparkly costume. My whole body tautens with the stress. I can't seem to take my eyes off her—it's like a car crash: I don't want to look, it's making me feel sick, but still my eyes are irresistibly drawn to her.

I watch her dance and move with mounting jealousy. She's good, even I can see that. She moves gracefully but with a sexy sharpness when required. Effortlessly she lifts a leg, drapes it over her male partner's shoulder and throws her head back as he slides his hand down her breastbone. It's a sexy, intimate move, slow and languorous. Next minute she's up again and he's hoisted her on to his shoulder. She's smiling out at the audience. Out at me. The lights catch the shimmer and glitter of her costume, making her look luminous. And she is in love with my boyfriend.

Next to her, I feel drab, boring and flat. I'm suddenly aware of the safe shades I always go for in my hair, the fact that the roots could do with a touch-up. The ordinariness of my outfit. I whinge bland; she whispers allure.

This was a bad idea. She exudes sex on the stage, offers it on a plate. Why did I not see this before? Why didn't I notice her when we came to see the show? How could I have missed it?

I sit there, my nails digging into the seat, thankfully with no one either side of me, staring at her, wondering intently what would happen if I stood up right now and yelled BITCH! at the stage. In assembly at school, I remember sitting cross-legged on the floor with the other bored children, wondering what everyone would do if I stood up and swore.

I'm seething and writhing on the inside with hatred and jealousy, as if I have a stomach full of squirming snakes. I don't think anyone can tell just by looking at me, though. Anyway, they're all looking at the stage.

I don't shout after all. I watch her fling and be flung, my eyes follow her every move. I see Debs too—she obviously made the fitting on time. She's giving it all she's got, but it's Liz that I really hunt with my eyes. We get to the end of Act 1 and the moment when they all freeze, waiting for the curtain. She is motionless, staring out into the auditorium, smile fixed to her face, and I'm staring, staring at her, and for a minute I think I see her eyes flicker in my direction and narrow slightly, but that's ridiculous. She couldn't see me, right at the back, with all those lights shining on her. Could she?

I slip out when the safety cloth has dropped. It's started to rain outside, a light, fizzly rain. I've seen enough glitz and glamor and I want to get back—I've got stuff to do now I've checked they are both definitely at work and not going anywhere near the flat.

The key takes a bit of wiggling in the front door, but finally it swings open and I go upstairs. Pixie doesn't even bother to yip when I walk into the sitting room, just eyes me disdainfully and settles back down on the floor without making another sound.

Watched over by Pete's fixed, grinning face, still there on the bedside table, I'm rummaging through Liz's wardrobe in minutes. The bag is still there. Good. I have a better look through her stuff this time and find in her bedside table a half-full packet of condoms, which makes me feel sick, and a vibrator—which makes me feel even sicker. It's like finding my boyfriend is addicted to a real-life porn channel; a walking, talking, fucking, doll-like, proper girl, with a flat, sex toys and his picture. It's just unreal and it's the whole separateness that I can't get my head round. I knew nothing about this. I still don't know when or how they met, how long it's been going on. Is this what he sees in her? Sex? I'd rather that than love.

I go over to the bed and pick up a pillow. Sniffing it, I decide I can't smell his aftershave. I pull back the covers and look in the bed. I know it's sick but I can't help myself. It's just crisp and clean. Tucking it carefully back in, I smooth the duvet down, and then it's over to her pine dressing table, which is festooned with strings of bright beads and glittering costume jewelry. I read through some of the cards she has in the small drawer, but it's boring stuff. Then I notice her credit card, just left there. Sitting on the table.

Picking it up, I stalk through to the living room, and when I see the deflated balloons hanging forlornly there, it seems obvious. I am so angry with her that I don't know where to put myself. I just want to hurt her, like she has me, and I know that this will be better than doing anything to her physically.

This will make her look like a total nutter.

A quick call locates me a company who do boxed balloon gifts. A nice man goes a little bit quiet when I tell him what I want, but laughs, relieved, when I explain it's for a party.

I decline an accompanying message. Then I give the address that the balloons need to be delivered to, a week from today, read them my credit card number and give my name as it appears on my card: "Miss E. Andersen." I ask that they don't send me a receipt, and he wishes me a nice day.

Then I pop the card back where I found it so that she'll be none the wiser. Having used the bathroom and taken a brief unplanned moment to wipe both of their toothbrushes around the inside of the lavatory bowl (a little harsh on Debs, but that's a price I'm willing to pay), it's time to go. I pull the front door shut quietly and then post the key back through the letter box.

It's when I get to the tube station that what I've just done hits me. I glance back at the flat and my head starts to swim. Leaning against the wall, I gasp for air, reach my hand up to push the hair out of my face and find that I have broken into a light sweat. A couple of people are staring curiously as they walk past me—an old woman in a tea-cozy hat dragging a tartan shopping trolley, and a middle-aged man in thick glasses and a stained zip-up jacket—but, this being London, no one says anything.

I try to slow my breathing down, feeling my pulse fluttering at my wrist. Just calm down. Take a deep breath. I look at the flat where I've just been, busily trying to make her look like a lunatic, and I know that the person who is behaving really irrationally is me. But I can't stop myself. I'm so frightened, and she *loves* him, for fuck's sake. Has he told her he loves her too? What if he does? I don't want him to leave me. I . . . I can't do this any more, I can't. I have to talk to someone. This is sending me crazy.

I reach for my phone.

"Hi, it's me," I say. "Look, I know it's short notice but can you come and meet me for a quick coffee and a bite to eat? . . . Please? . . . Oh, thank you." I close my eyes. "I'll see you in an hour."

I feel sick with relief. Thank God. Oh thank God. Feeling a bit better already, I straighten my coat, smooth my hair down and descend to the underground.

TWENTY-ONE

I'm waiting in the window, fiddling with the menu, when the door pushes open. Amanda walks in, scans the restaurant and then smiles widely as she sees me.

"Hello, you!" she says as she leans in to kiss me. Although it's cold outside, her cheek is warm and rosy. She straightens up, unwinds her scarf and slips her coat off before sinking into the chair opposite me.

"Well, this is a nice surprise," she says. "And you know what? I'm really glad you called. I've got something to talk to you about. But you first. What's up? You sounded a bit funny on the phone."

I take a deep breath, but as I'm trying to find the words, the waiter arrives with a bottle of red that I've pre-ordered, pours a little into my glass and waits for me to taste it.

"I'm sure it's lovely, thank you." I look up at him and he inclines his head modestly as if he crushed the grapes himself. He pours us both a glass expertly.

I take a big sip of my wine to steady my nerves.

Amanda looks curiously at me. "Not like you to indulge in lunchtime drinking."

"Not like you not to!" I nod at her untouched glass.

She reaches out and wraps her fingers round the stem, but then hesitates. She looks at me uncertainly from under her eyelashes and I notice for the first time that her eyes are positively dancing with excitement.

"There's something I've got to tell you," she says slowly. "It's really early days and you've got to keep it a secret because I haven't told *anyone*—well, except Nick and our parents, obviously—but I'm nine weeks pregnant!"

I freeze to the spot, mouth open. "You're what? But you can't be!" I say. "When we met up, you said you and Nick hadn't . . . and you were drinking!"

"I know, I know!" she laughs. "I had no idea I was, but I asked my doctor and she says it won't have harmed the baby and I've stopped now. And smoking. Which, FYI, is killing me." She rolls her eyes. "I'm going to turn into a beached whale—stopping smoking and eating for two."

"I . . . I don't know what to say." I'm completely stunned. "But . . . but I didn't even know you were trying," I blurt.

"We weren't!" she admits. "God knows how it happened. Nick's over the moon. Keeps going on about how strong his swimmers must be considering, as you quite rightly said, we've hardly been in the same bloody room for more than ten minutes over the last three months. Must have been a dodgy condom or something."

"Wow. This is just . . . just such a surprise and . . . my God. Congratulations!" I finally manage to smile and do a little cheer. We both half stand up and I hug her. I *am* happy for her, I really am. Keep smiling.

We sit down and I just stare at her.

"What?" she says, laughing.

"I just . . . I just thought you didn't want children yet, for ages. I never thought . . ." I tail off as I'm not sure what I'm trying to say.

"I know!" she agrees, sitting back. "I swear, I was as surprised as you are. I mean we're not married; we have a fucking third-floor flat, for God's sake. It's going to utterly bugger up my chances of promotion, and that little shit Gavin who's been after my job for ages is going to come in his pants when he finds out I'm going on maternity leave. And that's before we even start on everything we'll have to buy for this . . ." She points at her tummy accusingly, but then her hand relaxes and she rests it there protectively. Her face softens. "But, Mia, I think I love it already. Is that possible? Can you love someone before you can even see them?"

She looks at me earnestly and I feel a lump in my throat.

"Because I know Nick is a complete twat sometimes, and I swear, if this child winds up with his nose I'll pay for the surgery myself, but we were in bed last night and he was kissing my tummy, stupid arse, which is ridiculous," she rolls her eyes, "because there is nothing to see *at all* and I just thought, oh my God, we're going to be a *family*. And it didn't scare me at all! I'm just so excited!" A huge grin spreads across her face and she looks totally incandescent. "I mean, obviously, I know that you're not in the safe period until you get to twelve weeks, so we're not telling anyone till then, but I knew you'd guess! Can you believe it? I mean, *can you fucking believe it?* But listen, if I ever turn into Lou and start telling baby stories and farting in public, you've got to promise you'll tell me. You will, won't you?"

I smile faintly and nod. "I promise."

"I've been so tired over the last few days! I didn't know it would be such hard work, but Nick has started calling me

Moggie because I'm like an old cat when I get home, I just want to curl up, sleep and be stroked."

"Well, you're building fingers and toes—it's no wonder you're tired."

"Actually, toes aren't till much later. At the moment it looks like a gross bony-backed tadpole thing. Nick's bought me this book with actual pictures of each stage. They're incredible . . . honestly, it really is amazing; I'll show you when you next come round. Nick's so into it—I've been really surprised. D'you know, I reckon Pete will be like that when it's you two. It's incredible, Mi, you just start looking at them and realizing, shit, I'm bound to him forever. There goes the father of my child . . ." She shakes her head in disbelief. "It just changes everything. I said to Nick . . . Hey! Hon?" She suddenly looks at me, her face knotted up with concern. "You okay? You look like you're about to cry."

I look at her through my swimming eyes and I do a little gulp and laugh. "I'm just so happy for you!" I reach up and wipe my eyes fiercely. "I really am." I grab her hand and she squeezes back, her eyes welling up too.

"I know, it's insane, isn't it?" she says softly. "We're growing up! Who'd have thought it?"

Later that afternoon, I am walking slowly up the South Bank with my hands buried in my pockets, hair catching on the fresh breeze, looking up the Thames, wondering what the fuck I am going to do.

A couple walk past me, arm in arm, and he plants a kiss on the top of her head. She gazes up at him with a heady mixture of love, pride and comfort—it's all there. He looks down at her and squeezes her to him a little more tightly, and they walk past me, oblivious to anyone but each other.

That's all I want. I don't need babies, I don't even need weddings.

I think back to the wedding reception I went to alone. What would it be like doing things like that all the time if I really *was* single? It'd be like living inside one of those mechanical claw games you see at fairs and amusement arcades. Me, stuffed into a glass case with a load of couples, waiting to be rescued by the big claw over my head.

I don't want to be standing at parties with one of my friends' boyfriends being sent off to get me a drink and the friend in question waiting until we're alone and then saying sympathetically, "So how are you *really*?" followed by the assured philosophy (while they twist their engagement and wedding rings idly) that I am better off without him and there are plenty more fish in the sea.

It's easy for them to say. I don't know any single girls I could hang out with, and the only single bloke I knew is now having a thing with my sister, and anyway, lovely as he is, he is not Pete.

Now there are two things that are scaring me. One is that I am going to lose Pete. I am so, so frightened of losing him. The other is that I don't want to be this person; I don't feel like I know who I am any more. Everything is shifting so fast I can't put my feet anywhere safe . . . I am desperately trying to hang on to the threads that are holding my life together but they keep slipping from my fingers. I can feel myself grasping at them madly, but it's falling apart around me and I can't keep up. I simply don't recognize myself or how I got here.

Diving into my bag, I fumble around desperately for my phone.

"What do you want that for?" Patrick says doubtfully,

moments later. "And where the hell are you? You sound like you're in a wind tunnel."

"I'm in town. Just, please—text it to me?" I wobble slightly as a particularly strong gust of wind blows. It really is a perfect day—the skies are bright, bright blue and the chill in the air is making my fingers turn red.

"Is everything all right, Mia?" he says.

"It's fine—promise. You all right? How's Clare?"

There's a pause and then he says uncertainly, "I'm going up to see her tonight actually."

I wondered why I hadn't heard from her in the last couple of days. "That's nice." I smile faintly. "Say hi from me."

"I will," he says, sounding relieved. "I really do like her, Mi, I think this could be the start of something . . . Well, anyway . . ." He peters out, embarrassed. "I promise I won't mess her around."

"Good. You will text me that number right now, won't you? Lots of love." Then I hang up.

A few seconds later, my phone buzzes and there it is. I dial carefully, not allowing myself to stop and think about this in case I lose the nerve. She will understand. She's the one person who will *really* understand.

Staring at a small boat chugging determinedly through the choppy water, all I can hear is the ringing tone, and I start to feel slightly faint and light-headed.

"Helloooo?" says a voice cheerily. Oh God—she doesn't sound different at all. Exactly the same.

"It's me." My voice cracks.

The pause seems to go on forever. "Me who?" she says eventually; her tone has changed.

"It's Mia—please don't hang up!" I beg.

Again there is silence. "How did you get this number?" she says, her voice suddenly flat and expressionless.

"Patrick gave it to me. I hear you're going traveling."

She says nothing.

"So when are you off?" I try again.

"The end of the month. What do you want?" She's blunt and direct.

"Look, Katie, I need to speak to you. I think . . . I think Pete's having an affair." The words rush out of me. "I just . . ." And then I falter. I just what? "Oh God, I'm sorry!" My voice hiccups as I try to steady it. "I'm so sorry. I just don't know what to do and I thought about that day, when we rowed and . . ."

"And what?" she says.

"I . . . I don't know," I stammer. "I just want to see if . . ."

"See if I *was* telling the truth? Start things up again? Sorry, Mia, not interested."

"Oh, Katie, please!" I start to cry. "I don't know what to do . . ."

"You made your choice, Mia. You're on your own."

"But you have to—" I begin.

"I don't 'have to' anything." She talks over me.

"Please," I beg. "Please at least just tell me if it was you or if—"

"Don't call me again."

And then she hangs up.

TWENTY-TWO

Patrick came up last night to see me. Was nice. I think I like him more each time I see him. How you?

I'm reading Clare's happy little text over breakfast as Pete comes in and finds me at the kitchen table. "What are you still doing here?" he says, surprised.

"Got a meeting at ten thirty," I manage through a mouthful of cereal. Which is crap, because I phoned Spank Me yesterday and asked for the rest of the week off as holiday. I asked him not to tell Lottie, but just to say I was still ill. He wasn't happy, but reluctantly agreed when I said I wouldn't ask if it wasn't absolutely vital. "It's not worth going all the way over to the office and then back to Covent Garden again. I'm off in a bit, though. How about you? Busy day?"

"You could say that." He sinks down tiredly on to a chair and yawns as he runs his hands through his hair. "God, I'm shattered."

We sit in silence, just the clink of my spoon on my bowl as he reaches for the cereal packet. Then the letter box rattles and Gloria barks importantly, rushing into the hall.

"That'll be the post," I say matter-of-factly. "I'll get it." And before he can do anything, I'm smartly up and striding out of the kitchen.

The letters are sitting on the mat. Is it there? Has it arrived?

Picking them up and sorting through, my heart skips a beat as I see that it has. I look at my disguised writing on the envelope I posted yesterday and walk back to the kitchen.

"A handwritten one for me." I try to sound absent and tear it open.

Pete doesn't look up, just pushes his muesli around his bowl. I pause for dramatic effect.

"Eh?" I say, all pretend confused. "Why have you sent me half a card? And why have you signed it *Peter*?"

Pete glances at me with a frown on his face, and I toss it over to him. It lands on the table in front of him and the color drains from his face as he recognizes it. He goes very, very still.

"I don't get it," I say. "What's that about?"

"I, er . . ." He is lost for words, completely lost for words. Pete! You can do better than this. Think, think! I know it's early in the morning, but come on! What are you going to say? How do you explain half a card you sent to another woman arriving at our house when you don't even get it yourself?

"I don't understand," I pretend to puzzle. "Why have you sent me *half* a card with weird writing on the envelope. Is it a joke or something? Am I being thick and not getting it?"

He just stares at it. God knows what must be running through his mind right now. He obviously recognizes it, knows where it's from. He's turning it over and over in his hands as if the answer to my questions is written somewhere on it.

"OOOOHH!" I squeal excitedly. "Is it part of a game? Are you going to send me the top half and all will be revealed?"

It's lame, and he knows it . . . but it's the best option he has. So he seizes it with both hands.

"There's no getting anything past you, is there?" He forces a smile up at me. "Yup, all will be revealed. Ask me no questions and I'll tell you no lies."

Oh Pete . . .

"Well," I say slowly, "I'll do as I'm told! Right, I'm going to brush my teeth then I better get going,"

He smiles again and I blow him a passing kiss as I walk out of the room.

I sneak back downstairs when I'm done. He doesn't see me as I peer round the edge of the door; he is out of the chair and examining the envelope that I left on the side. I cough loudly as I come back in and he jumps guiltily, stepping away as if he wasn't even looking at it. "So are we going somewhere, for this surprise? What's it in aid of?" I say as I go and pick up my handbag.

He taps the side of his nose and murmurs, "I know nuzzing!" in a mock-French accent.

And the sad thing is, he's right. He has no bloody idea.

I laugh dutifully and he says he'd better get in the shower. I say I'm off anyway now and I'll see him tonight. We kiss each other briefly and I bang the front door shut loudly as I step outside. I wait for a minute or two on the doorstep before silently slipping my key in the lock and easing back into the house.

I creep into the hall, leaving the door open behind me. I can hear him talking. God, he just couldn't wait, could he?

"Hi, it's Peter. I thought you'd be up but you must be still asleep . . ." He pauses as if he's not sure what to say next and I stand very, very still. "I'm at home but I'm going soon so don't call back. I just don't know what to say, I really don't. First the house, and now this morning your card arrived." He's gathering pace now and it's almost like he's having a conversation rather than leaving a voicemail. "It's not funny, Liz, it's not funny at all. And why the fuck did you cut the card in half? Is that supposed to be some crap dig? What are you trying to say? You're cutting me out of your life? You don't want to share me? I thought we'd sorted this, Lizzie. I thought you knew the score. You say you're fine with it and then you go and do something mental like this! I just don't know what to . . . Oh, look, I'll call you later."

Quickly, so that he doesn't come into the hall and realize I've just heard every word, I slam the door and shout loudly, "Only me! Forgot my umbrella!" I wait for a second, then add a "Bye, darling!"

"Bye! Have a good day!" he calls back. He must have wet himself when he heard me come back in then.

Outside in the fresh air, marching down toward the station to get on a train that will take me into London and then a tube that will take me to her flat, I feel grimly determined. On the one hand I can't quite believe I have just heard him leaving a message for some other woman with such familiarity, as if they speak all the time. But on the other hand he was really angry. I see Liz in my mind as I saw her yesterday, all glassy, glossy and shiny and grinning widely from the stage.

Who's laughing now?

TWENTY-THREE

"Hi. It's Lottie here." I am standing outside the tube station, leaning on the wall and watching a flower seller eyeing me hopefully. "I'm about five minutes away and just wanted to check I wasn't too early."

Mobile clamped to my ear, I look up the street that I know will lead me to her front door. "No, that's fine. I'll be right there."

Hanging up and putting the phone back in my handbag I take a deep breath and close my eyes briefly. I can't believe I am finally about to meet the woman who is sleeping with my boyfriend, *and* give her money. Four hundred pounds in cash is sitting in my handbag, ready to be swapped for a key to her house.

Someone bashes into me, making my eyes snap open again as they shoot me a filthy look. It's fair enough—it is a bit stupid to be standing in front of the tube entrance with your eyes shut. Come on. Only you can do this. You're on your own.

Gathering myself, I clench my jaw, set my shoulders and start to walk purposefully. This is it. I'm going to do it.

The strap of my bag is digging into my shoulder, but I barely notice. Is it going to be her that answers the door, or Debs? I'm confident she isn't going to recognize me. She's only seen me once—at the theater—and for all I know Pete didn't tell her who I was or even that I was there. I could have been a stranger, just someone sitting next to him. My heart is starting to thump and my breath is nervous and shallow. I am aware of the noise of cars around me, the siren of a police car shrieking past and the clicking of my heels on the pavement.

I'm fucking going to do it. I can do this. She's not getting him. I know what I'm doing is working, I heard him say so this morning. I just have to keep focused. And anyway, what have I got to lose?

My shoes are rubbing where I have the remains of a blister but my eyes are fixed ahead. As I turn the corner, the flat comes into view and my pulse quickens, my breathing coming in fits and starts.

The front door gets closer and closer. *Is* it going to be her that answers, or Debs?

Then I'm right outside and I'm shaking, actually shaking. I close my eyes briefly and exhale deeply. Oh my God. It's going to happen. I imagine it's like being in a plane and looking down at tiny fields through an open hatch: the deafening roar of the wind and the engines, the light-headed rush and the prickle of adrenaline at my fingertips.

I hold my breath for what feels like forever, and then I jump.

My finger shoves the bell and it rings shrilly.

Footsteps start to thud down the stairs.

This is it.

The latch turns in what feels like slow motion. I straighten up, determined. The door swings open and everything goes still. In under a second I have gained complete control of my-self.

I look into the face of the woman standing in front of me, and my icy calm betrays nothing, not even a flicker.

"Hello," I say. "I think you've been expecting me."

TWENTY-FOUR

ebs smiles at me and says, "Certainly have! Come on up! You know the way by now!"

Indeed I do.

She turns and walks ahead of me; I shut the front door and follow her up.

"How was your wig fitting yesterday?" I ask conversationally as we go into the sitting room. I'm trying not to look around. Where is she? In her room? In the bathroom? "Did you make it on time?"

Debs wrinkles her nose and snorts. "Yes thanks, it was all fine. Bloody wardrobe. Think they own the place. You know what it's like. Want a cuppa while we wait for Lizzie? She stayed at a friend's house last night but she knows you're coming over and she's on her way back."

"Tea would be lovely." I slip my coat off and lay it carefully on the arm of the sofa.

"Cool." She smiles and wanders off into the kitchen.

I exhale deeply and stare at one of the photos of Liz. Deep breath. She's not here yet. Compose yourself.

Debs wanders back in with two mugs and hands one to me before sitting down on the orange sofa and curling her legs underneath her like a cat.

Just as we both open our mouths to say something, the phone goes. Debs shakes her head in disbelief. "That phone! God, it just never stops—I'm so sorry, Lottie. You know what? I'm just going to leave it. Now, tell me about you. Where did you say your last flat was?"

"Well, I—"

Just as I begin, a woman's voice feeds tinnily through the answer phone. "Hi, it's me! I'm really sorry . . . I'm running about fifteen minutes late—decided to take a bloody cab and we're stuck now. I'm guessing Lottie is there already. Say sorry for me and I'll be back ASAP. Love ya!"

Debs laughs and then groans. "Typical Lizzie. Sorry, Lotts. Anyway. You were saying?"

"I actually live with my—" I start, and then the phone goes *again*.

"I don't believe it! *Bloody* thing!" Debs glares at it. "Just ignore it. You live with your . . ." She looks at me expectantly.

"Boyfriend," I say firmly. "And—"

"Hi, it's Peter." A very familiar voice fills the room and I nearly drop my cup of tea in shock all over the carpet. "Lizzie, I'm on my way over—sorry, I'm on the car phone and the reception is a bit dodgy. I know you said you were going to be in this morning and I really think we need to sort this all out. See you in a minute."

My eyes widen in shock and I can barely breathe. He's what? Oh fuck! FUCK! I have to go—how close is he? And why's he coming to see her, why? What the hell do I do now?

Debs sighs and is busy setting her mug down on the carpet,

so she doesn't notice me having a moment of terror and panic in the corner. "Excuse me, Lottie, I have to make a quick call."

She gets up and stalks to the phone. "Hi, it's me. Peter's just phoned. He's on his way over . . . I don't know, hon . . . Yeah, she is." She glances at me. "Yeah, I think so too. It might be wise."

All I can think is, get off the fucking phone—I don't have much time!

She hangs up and turns to me. "Look, Lottie, this is really awkward and I'm SO unbelievably sorry but, well, there's a bit of a situation developing that Lizzie needs to defuse and I think it might be better if we do this another day. Do you mind? I promise it's not always like this!" She laughs awkwardly. "I'm so sorry."

I just don't care. All I want is to get away from here before he arrives.

"It's okay." I gather my bag and coat up quickly. "Look, I'll be in touch."

"Thank you," she says. "You've been really good about this, I appreciate it." Once we get to the bottom of the stairs, she holds the door open for me.

"Please don't worry, Debs." I smile brightly, my guts churning. I have to go! He could be here any second! "I'll give you a ring."

"Thanks!" she beams. "You're a star, Lotts! See you soon."

The door closes behind me. I let out a whimper and scan the street. He's driving. Should I make a dash for the tube? Oh, where's a cab when you need one! I stumble to the edge of the pavement. If he sees me here . . . Oh God, what was I thinking, coming back here again? It wasn't worth it! I shouldn't have taken the risk—I was getting too sure of myself. If I lose him . . .

Then I see a bus approaching a stop on the other side of the road. That'll do. I look urgently left and right, before hurtling across. It doesn't matter where it's going; I just have to get out of here.

I throw myself on, show my travel card and lurch over to a seat as we start to pull away.

Oh, thank God. I look back over my shoulder as the flat begins to disappear out of sight. I feel ill with the relief.

It's short-lived, though. He's going over there—he, *they*, might both be there right this second. Together. What's he going to say or do? Has he gone there to finish it? Or maybe just to tell her to start taking more care . . . I stare miserably out of the window.

I *wish* I knew what was happening. I wonder what he's doing right now.

TWENTY-FIVE

When he gets in later, he is not in a good mood at all. I jump when I hear the front door bang shut, and shortly after that he slams out to the gym.

He seems a little calmer when he gets back and flops down on to the sofa beside me.

"Sorry," he says shortly.

I shoot a glance at him. "What for?"

"I've been a bit stressed this evening. I'll just grab a shower, and then do you fancy a glass of wine?"

I nod, and he looks pleased. "Good, won't be long."

Later, on the sofa, I'm resting my legs on his lap affectionately, but being careful not to be too clingy. He's relaxed and comfy and stroking my leg idly. "This is nice," I say quietly.

He glances over and flashes a smile. "Yeah, it is." He turns back to the TV.

Then I feel his phone vibrate in his pocket. He ignores it, and minutes later it vibrates again. Another text message. He shifts carefully. Then it starts to vibrate properly. She's ringing him.

He swears under his breath and slides a hand into his pocket to switch it off. "Probably just Mum. No concept of the time difference whatsoever, that woman."

But then we both jump as the house phone rings shrilly. No! She can't be calling him here! Oh my God!

He pushes my legs off his lap, jumps to his feet and snatches the phone up. He doesn't say anything, no hello, nothing, just listens for a second and then says clearly with his back to me, "No, I'm sorry, no one has ordered a taxi to this address."

My eyes narrow. Either that was an utter, amazing coincidence or he really, really thought on his feet.

He hangs up and turns back to me, smiling. "Come on, it's late—let's get to bed."

I don't protest, and once I'm in bed I only say in amazement that he must have read my mind, when he offers to zip downstairs for my glass of water. He makes sure he's not gone too long and kisses me good night a little absently. I'm not surprised, with what must be on his mind.

Once the lights are off, and he's asleep, I slip noiselessly out of bed and downstairs. His phone is under a cushion on the sofa. I switch it on and look first at the call list. It *was* her who phoned him.

Then I look in his sent messages. Just as I thought, he sent one to her about twenty minutes later, while he was getting my water. It is short and to the point:

What you playing at? Don't ever call house again. Will speak to you tomorrow. Go to bed.

I switch the phone off and creep quietly back upstairs.

TWENTY-SIX

The following day, I am standing in a very upmarket underwear store in a part of London where most of the shops have doormen, and if not, doorbells.

The colors and textures surrounding me overload my senses. Sweetly innocent sugar-icing pink and yellow balconettes here, rich plum and damson push-ups and thongs over there. Black satin and bordello-green silk bras and French knickers. Antique pale lace baby dolls. I just don't know what to get. Thankfully, an assistant has clearly seen women like me many times before, and before I know where I am, we are both standing in a changing room admiring a plunging cleavage I never knew I had, she is telling me how much more flattering a high-cut line is, and don't my legs look longer?

"He'll love it!" she twinkles at me conspiratorially as she takes the items to wrap in tissue paper. God, I hope she's right. I can only assume that the tissue paper must be laced with diamond thread and spun by angels, as the total bill for one underwear set (two pairs of knickers) is £370.

That leaves me £30 change from my cash. Dear God.

I feel faint and almost lose my nerve, but then I remember Liz on stage. I have no choice but to do this.

After all, I used to dress a little more like that when I first knew him; it's just over time that I began to tone things down. We started not going out to clubs as much, so there was no need to buy tiny little sparkly tops. Then because I wasn't wearing that sort of thing I didn't need to watch what I ate quite so carefully. Loose jumpers and tops can be very forgiving. But now I can see that was where I started to go wrong. I took my eye off the pan and it boiled over badly.

Next, I go and have my hair washed and styled in an expensive salon that luckily for me has had a last-minute cancelation. When the very camp but very beautiful stylist called Bernardo finishes and with a flourish whips out a mirror, smiling smugly at my exclamations of delight, I could cry, but this time with relief. I look, well—quite pretty! My hair is glossy and bouncy, full of life. Just what I want Pete to associate me with.

I go and have my nails done too. Subtle attention there, though, no long Essex-wife talons; I'm going for effortlessly gorgeous. Tottering past the counter of a makeup brand I have seen in lots of glossy magazines, for once I stop. Normally I have no time for this sort of thing, but today I ask the girl's advice and she's not thick or caked in foundation at all. She's actually very sweet and makes me up artfully.

It pays off for her, though, when I buy a handful of products that cost so much, I almost gasp in shock. She sees my look of alarm, pats my arm reassuringly and tells me it will be worth every penny and that I look amazing. I half smile and say she probably has to say that to everyone. She looks earnestly back at me and says, well yes, she is supposed to, but with me *she really means it*.

Finally I take a cab over to a small boutique that I have always walked past before because it looks horribly expensive and places like that scare me. I tend to assume, probably not wrongly, that the shop assistants are going to know, as soon as I walk in, that the bag I am carrying on my shoulder was thirty quid in Monsoon and that my trousers are French Connection, not Prada. This therefore makes me a fake and not of their world. I've always imagined a *Pretty Woman* scenario where they won't serve me. But wrong again! It turns out, once I plunge in through the door before I lose my nerve, that they too are actually lovely. Honestly, there are so many really nice people in the world when you're spending money.

The sales girl is very chatty as I'm twirling this way and that, looking at myself in the mirror. She tells me that they have some new stock coming in next week and she knows there are a couple of items that would look simply stunning on me. She starts to tell me about them, and I'm being seduced by her descriptions of chocolate and raspberry silks when she suddenly breaks off and lets out an ear-piercing shriek while batting at her head. I can see something fluttering confusedly about and she flaps her arms wildly. It drops to the floor as she hits it, and without pausing for a moment she shoves an immaculately heeled shoe on to it and grinds.

She gingerly peels her foot away, and we both peer at the floor and see a butterfly crushed on the cold glassy tile. Its body is still twitching and pulsing; wings in a pulped tangle.

"Urgh!" She grimaces graphically. "What a disgusting mess. Excuse me, madam." She clicks off to the desk and curling her lip in distaste uses a tissue to wipe up the remains, throwing the balled-up result in the bin.

"Fancy that this time of year!" she muses, peering at the floor to make sure all traces of wing have gone. "Now, where were we?" She switches back on the smile. "Ahh, that's right! Beautiful clothes for you!"

The dress I finally settle on fits me so well and looks so lovely I know I have to have it. I will regret it forever if I don't make it mine. I want to wear it out straight away but I don't. I'm saving it for later. It is so stupidly expensive, it actually doesn't feel real as I pass my card over to the girl. But as I walk to the station, swinging glossy bags with expensive names on them, I know they are the genuine article. They just better be worth it. New underwear and getting my hair done to seduce my man. What a cliché . . .

Sitting on the train home, willing it to move faster with every fiber of my being, I become aware of a few admiring glances. At me!

My phone rings and it's Clare. She's wheezing with laughter before she even speaks and the sound of it is so infectious that in spite of everything it makes a huge grin spread across my face.

"Guess what?" she just about manages to say. "I've started this new discussion group on Facebook called 'I don't need a shag when uni fucks me every day' and . . . ha ha ha . . . oh sorry . . ." She gulps and tries to get herself back under control. "And me and the girls posted the topic 'Would you rather have a vagina where your belly button is or . . .'" she giggles uncontrollably again, "'a cock on your shoulder?' And Amy said . . . he he he . . . Amy said she'd rather have the cock, because then she could dress it up as a parrot and it would be less weird! HA HA HA!"

I laugh out loud and a man looks up from his paper and

smiles before glancing back down. Clare wheezes again. "Oh
God . . . my tummy hurts so much!" she gasps. "I mean, who . . ."
But then we go through a tunnel and I lose her.

The man looks up again and I glance shyly away as I catch
his eye. But then I spot the twinkle of a wedding band on his
finger and it tarnishes the moment for me. I think of his wife,
probably at the station with their kids in the back of the car,
waiting tiredly for his train to get in . . . So I don't meet his eye
again and he gets the message, turning back to his paper. I am
not the sort of girl who would do that to another woman, thank
you very much.

My phone goes again and it's a text. Lottie.

Please don't die. Is very boring without you. Saw Spank Me
pick nose AND EAT IT earlier. HATE him.

I decide not to text her back in case she rings and hears that
I'm blatantly on a train. She thinks I'm practically on my death-
bed by the sound of it. Instead I count down the stops and
almost break into a run when I get off at the station, I'm so desperate to get back, but I don't. I don't want to be all hot and
sweaty with running makeup. That would defeat the whole object of my plan.

Once the front door shuts behind me and I'm in the stillness
of the house, I race upstairs, strip off and put on my new underwear. I touch up my makeup, get the new dress out of the bag
and carefully lay it on the bed. Sitting down next to it, I wait for
Pete to get back.

I don't have to wait long. I hear the door slam, which is
my cue.

I start to pad around upstairs and hear him bounding up the

stairs two at a time. He comes into the room to find me applying some lipstick in my new underwear, looking like I'm getting ready to go out, and gratifyingly gives a low whistle.

"Bloody hell," he says. "Is that new?"

I look down at myself and shrug. "Don't think so, why?"

He raises an eyebrow at my pneumatic chest and says, "I think I'd have noticed, don't you?"

Well, yes, you would think so.

"How was your day?" I ask, reaching for my earrings.

He grimaces. "Shit. But it's picking up now." He smiles at me and I feel my heart flutter. Keep it cool—don't blow it. Then I notice he's holding something in his hand: an envelope. "What's that?" I ask as I walk past him to get the dress.

He stretches out his hand.

On the front in a crappy attempt to copy my fake writing is my name and our address. He has drawn a pretend stamp on it, which has a smiley-faced stick-head wearing a crown.

I open it and see that I'm not the only one who has been shopping. In the envelope is a top half to the card I received yesterday.

It is a new, sanitized top half, which says my name in it instead of hers. How lucky for him that he obviously remembered where he bought it. Although that stings . . . she's that special that he can remember where he bought cards for her?

It also says, *This card entitles you to a night at the ballet with me . . . who loves you very much.* All in pen the same color. He has, I'll admit, paid attention to detail, but as for the content? Is that really the best he can do? For the man who bumped me out of the way with a massage so he could fuck his lover two floors up in the same hotel, it's a little disappointing, really.

Instead of saying that, though, I go, "Ahhhh! How sweet!"

and "Ooohhh! You're so thoughtful!" And then I say that I still don't understand why he cut it in half and sent it separately . . . but whatever. I've always wanted to go to the ballet, and how clever he is to have chosen a card with a dancer on the front as well!

He has the grace to at least look at the floor. I put the card down and pretend to carry on getting ready. I don't kiss him or hug him. I just return to what I was doing.

"Are we going somewhere?" he asks as I loop the dress around me. "Nice frock, by the way."

"Thanks." I smile. "I am, you're not."

He looks surprised. "Oh."

"I won't be late, though. I bumped into an old school friend—we're meeting for a drink."

"Not Katie?" He looks dismayed.

My heart tightens uncomfortably as I think of her. "No, not Katie."

I go to walk past him and he catches my wrist. Pulling me toward him, he kisses me lightly on the mouth. I hesitate, then I kiss him back, just as lightly.

He kisses me again—a little more firmly. He presses me up against the bedroom wall and then his hands are moving inside my dress.

"I've got to go," I try protesting. Although this is not true, I've not arranged to meet anyone at all. But he doesn't know that.

"Not yet," he murmurs.

He opens the front of the dress. Tracing a finger lightly over the lace of my new bra, he pushes it up, stroking and teasing, making me gasp and bite my lip. Then he undoes it and pushes the dress from my shoulders. It and the bra fall silently to the floor. His fingers slide down, then he's undoing his trousers and moving my expensive, pretty knickers to one side. We've never done it up against the wall before, and as the weight of his chest presses against me, I just feel crushed and squashed rather than turned on. My back hurts and I don't think my legs are strong enough for this.

But just as I'm thinking that, he picks me up and I wrap my legs round him. It suddenly becomes much, much better. I catch sight of us over his shoulder in the mirror. We're moving together instinctively now, no clumsiness, no jolting and jarring. We look beautiful. The muscles in his back move as he holds my legs up and I watch as I coil them tighter around him, feeling delighted as he groans in response. We move perfectly together, becoming louder and louder—until we both finally stop.

I feel like I'm shimmering—there must be some kind of ethereal glow around me, I swear to God. I put my legs down. He pulls his trousers up and we just stand there for a moment. He rests his lips on my forehead and whispers in disbelief, "You're incredible."

And I feel it. I actually feel it. Just for a minute, as I tip my head up and look searchingly into his eyes, I *feel* incredible . . . loved, where I'm meant to be and that she does not exist. I can pretend that it is just me and him and he has not betrayed me and that everything I want for us can still happen. It's possible; it still could be real.

She is no threat to *us*. We are too strong, too much in love. He could ask me anything right now and I'd do it. I'd tell him any secrets I knew, I'd go to the ends of the earth and back again for him. I love him. I really, really love him.

I stroke the side of his face and whisper, "I could never love anyone like I love you, Pete." And I look at him pleadingly, begging him silently to say it back.

He hesitates and says nothing . . . just looks desperately into my eyes.

We stand there in silence. Me naked accept for my knickers, shivering slightly as the wind blows violently outside and rattles the window, but afraid to move in case the moment is lost. He is looking at me as if he's seeing me for the first time again, and just for a second I know he's my Pete. The man he was when I met him—desperate to tell me what he's done, wanting to be honest. I'm sure of it.

But he says nothing, just drops his head and pulls me tightly to him, hugging me with a fierceness and intensity that makes it hard for me to breathe. I hear him say, "I love you so much," somewhere over my left shoulder, but I can't see his face. I push gently away from his chest and say slowly as I try and force him to meet my eyes, "You could tell me, Pete, if there was something bothering you . . . There's nothing so bad that you couldn't tell me." Although this is not true, of course; it is already so bad it has made me act in a more deranged way than I ever thought possible. But I will still forgive him.

He lifts his head slowly. I'm holding my breath, waiting . . .

But his eyes meet mine, and whatever it was I saw a moment ago isn't there any more. It has flickered away. He looks blankly back at me and says, "There's nothing to tell. You should get dressed. You'll be late."

He walks out of the room, and I sink to the floor.

TWENTY-SEVEN

I want to cry, I really do, but there's just nothing there. No tears, no fight, no spark. Just me in a crumpled heap on the floor, in knickers that I've spent more than a week's food shop on, next to a dress that doesn't feel special any more.

I don't sit there for long; it's cold apart from anything else. Once I've realized that Pete has gone downstairs and isn't coming back up, there is nothing for me to do but get to my feet, go to the bathroom, clean myself up and get dressed again. My makeup has smudged, so I touch it up.

I take a deep breath, lift my head and walk back into our room. I'm not done yet.

Reaching my hand into my underwear drawer, I fish Liz's earrings out. They twinkle merrily and I hold them out in front of me with distaste, as if they are diseased. They are beyond tacky; glass and paste gems. Clearly she is not refined enough to be allergic to cheap metals.

"Pete!" I yell at the top of my voice.

I hear him amble upstairs, and as he appears in the doorway, I rush over and throw my arms round him, exclaiming, "They're

beautiful!" He smiles, all pleased and surprised, hugs me back
and says, "What are?"

"The earrings."

He looks a little confused—as well he might—and I say, "I
found them on the top of the chest of drawers. That's such a
lovely surprise. Thank you!" Then I slide one of Liz's earrings
in my ear. I hate doing it. I hate putting something in my flesh
that has belonged to her. It's like sticking myself with a con-
taminated needle.

I let the earring drop and turn my head so he can see it. He
goes as white as a sheet. He really is the crappest person at hiding things, I've come to realize, but then I guess if you think
your bit on the side has somehow got into your house and left
her earrings for your live-in girlfriend to deliberately find . . .
well, it would be a tad worrying.

They are very distinctive earrings, to put it mildly. Not the
sort of things a modest wallflower would wear. They're theatri-
cal, over-the-top vintage-esque chandelier jobs, deep-green
glass, cut to look like fat emeralds. It is clearly very obvious to
him who they belong to.

I shake my head and the jewels glisten and gleam, casting
shadows on my cheekbones. "I'll wear them when we go to the
ballet." I smile at him. "All these presents. I'm a lucky girl.
What have I done to deserve this?" I pretend to look back in the
mirror, but sneak a glance at him instead.

He looks very worried. "Nothing," he says quietly. "You
haven't done anything to deserve this." He says it under his
breath, but I hear him. I look at him inquiringly and he smooths
a smile over his face and comes over to me. "On second
thoughts," he says, easing the hooks out of the lobes gently, "I
don't really like them. They look a bit cheap. You're more of a

diamond girl. I'll take these back, swap them for something else." He slips the earrings into his pocket.

"You know what?" I say lightly. "I'm going to call my friend, tell her we'll meet up another night. I'd rather stay in with you instead. Give me five and I'll be right down."

He nods and clatters off downstairs.

Through a chink in the bedroom curtain, I watch him stride into the garden, illuminated by the kitchen light. He has his phone clamped to his ear. I would kill to hear what he's saying. I get the picture, though, because whoever he is speaking to . . . and God I hope it's her . . . he is very, very angry with. At first he shrugs his shoulders in a melodramatic way. I imagine him saying something along the lines of "Well, *you* tell *me* how they got there."

He starts to frown and the finger-pointing begins. He listens for a bit, rolling his eyes, then closes them, running a tired hand over his forehead. Suddenly he snaps them open again, and says something very short and final as he clicks the phone off and pulls it sharply away from his ear. I watch him just stand there, looking exhausted. Then his phone lights up merrily again. She's calling him back. Without pausing, he switches it off and shoves it in his pocket.

I let the curtain drop, smiling in the darkness.

TWENTY-EIGHT

On Saturday morning, Pete's cousin's wedding, I wake up in our bed alone. Out of the corner of my eye, I see a note on his pillow, which terrifies me at first because I think it's the "I don't know how to say this, but I've met someone . . ." letter, but actually it just says he's gone to the gym.

Sitting up makes my head swim. Catching a glance in the mirror at the end of the bed, I see a panda-eyed, gray-faced old woman, with skin like tired dough and hair that looks like two squirrels had a punch-up in it, staring back at me.

I look like shit. Shuffling through to the bathroom, I try to ignore Gloria howling downstairs, although the noise pierces through my delicate wine-soaked brain like hot knitting needles sliding into suet. The second bottle of wine Pete and I opened in front of the TV last night, both of us drinking silently while staring at the screen, has come back to haunt me. I feel foul.

My mood is not improved by discovering it looks cold and damp outside as opposed to the fresh crisp day I'm sure the bride prayed for. I wish we didn't have to go.

As I'm applying some makeup in our bedroom—which

curiously is not actually improving things, as it should be, but making me look like a transvestite—my phone goes next to me.

"Hello," says Clare solemnly. "How are you?"

I think about that for a second. "On balance I think I'm hanging on in there," I say lightly. "How are you?"

"Well," says Clare, sounding like she's settling in for a long one, "I have an actual true story to tell you."

"Okay," I say, glancing at my watch. "Just keep it snappy. I've got a wedding to go to."

She sighs huffily. "Fine. Here's the short version. Patrick came up last night and told me he's falling in love with me, and I think I love him too. Bye."

"What? Oh fuck it!" I drop my mascara wand into my lap in shock. Dammit! I've got the reflexes of a turd today and now I've got a black stripe down my dress. "What are you talking about?" I say crossly, rubbing furiously at the stripe and watching in dismay as it spreads like an oil slick. "You've known each other less than a week! Don't be so ridiculous!"

There is a pause, and then she says dryly, "Not *quite* the reaction I was hoping for, but better than 'He's *my* friend,' I suppose."

"You're not serious! Clare, you're at uni, you're a student. You're supposed to be getting pissed and spending your loan in Topshop."

"Yeah? And?"

"But Patrick works, and he's not a student, and—"

"Shit, you're right!" she says, mock afraid, "and he *doesn't* shop at Topshop. What was I thinking . . . it'll *never* work." She tuts in disgust. "Why is it that everyone thinks that just because you're a student, you're some kind of sub-species that just shuffles around trying to get a shag and the rest of the time watches *Neighbors*? For your information, I work bloody hard, I spend what little money I have on rent and food and I am capable of genuine feeling. Wasn't it you who told me I'd know when I met the right one?"

"Well, yes," I begin. "But . . . Clare, it's been one week and—"

"Doesn't matter—I just know," she cuts in bluntly.

"And it's Patrick, and—"

"I still just know," she says, a little more softly. "And I *know* he does too, Mi. It feels just amazing."

I hold the phone to my ear for a moment and just listen.

"And I'm so, so glad I listened to you and never settled for second best. Before, with Jack and other boys, I'd be like constantly looking over my shoulder thinking that this felt good—but what if there was something better out there? Someone who could give me more? But I know I couldn't better what I have with Patrick."

Oh, please. "Clare—you're so young," I plead. "You've got so much time!"

"To do what?" she says in surprise. "I can still do it all—only with him too. How much fun will that be?"

"And he said he's falling in love with you?" I say doubtfully.

She laughs. "Yes, and I didn't imagine it and I know he meant it. I just know. I don't know how to describe it, Mia—and it's not just lust."

Please, no details, I think to myself. Spare me that at least. "You can't possibly know you love each other!"

"Why?" she insists. "Why can't I know I love him?"

I don't have an answer for that.

"I'm so happy, I can't tell you. Can you just be happy for me too?"

I soften. "Of course I can."

"Well, yay!" she says, and then she shouts, "I'm in love! Hurrah!"

In the church a couple of hours later, in a second-choice dress, I am pondering the unsettling possibility that now maybe even my little sister is going to make it up the aisle faster than me, and I'm starting to feel like it's never going to happen to me. Ever.

However, I'm sure that none of the other congregation can tell, just by looking at me, that I'm dying slowly from the inside out because my boyfriend has another woman on the side. Sitting in the cold, dusty church, waiting for the bride to arrive, with Pete irritably pulling at his tie and saying that he's sure we'll get a parking ticket where we've left the car and me hissing at him to stop fidgeting, we look like any other normal couple.

I look around the pews, and variations on the theme are happening everywhere. The women are craning their necks to see who is wearing what and then ducking down excitedly to bitch to their bored-looking husbands. Some of the men are doing the jolly handshake and booming laugh bit . . . and next to them sit nervous wives, like little birds. Not all of them look miserable, of course—it's a happy occasion, for goodness' sake—but now, with the benefit of the last two weeks behind me, I can see that not everything is how it seems at first glance.

When the march begins, we all clamber to our feet and turn to watch the bride start her walk down the aisle. She's this slender, wobbling, nervous girl whose dress is already slightly too loose around her shoulders, trying to keep in time with the music and busily hauling back her dad, who is intent on getting this first nerve-racking bit over as quickly as possible. She glances shyly around the church and bites her bottom lip nervously . . . but as soon as she sees the back of her fiancé's head, she lets out a visible sigh of relief and a very sweet, gentle smile starts to creep across her face. Her whole body releases and she transforms from this uneasy slip of thing into a serene, calm, elegant, willowy girl as she glides toward him.

Clutching my bag and the order of service, I watch her. Pete is standing with his hands behind his back. There is a gap of a good foot between us. Very suddenly I am reminded of a wedding we went to together, early on in our relationship. As the bride and groom were exchanging their vows, stumbling over the words in their sincerity, Pete and I clasped one another's hands tightly, leaned against each other and shared a shy, meaningful look that said that one day, that might be us, saying we wanted to be always together until death parted us.

So I listen to this couple being married, making promises I hope they can keep and vowing to be true and kind to each other. I feel the space between me and Pete, and I find myself suddenly wondering sadly if I could, now, actually marry him, knowing what has happened. Closing my eyes briefly, I suddenly see in my head me standing next to him in a wedding dress. Our backs are to the congregation as the doors to the church are flung open in slow motion, and Liz—framed in an ethereal light—is poised, ready to hurl herself down the aisle screaming, "Nooooooo!" wildly—like a scene from a bad film.

I sway slightly and Pete, frowning, puts out a hand to steady me. He gives me a funny look and mouths, "Are you okay?" I nod and bow my head down.

The rest of the wedding is actually very lovely, although the vicar nearly gives the bride's mother a heart attack as he delivers a sermon that requires a pair of garden shears and a nearby flower arrangement to illustrate the point that two halves pulling together make a formidable whole. This is said as an innocent and probably very expensive severed dahlia head drops to the floor. Thankfully, just as the bride's mother looks like she's about to throw up, he stops and puts the shears away. He then cracks a joke that isn't that funny, but gets a big fat relieved laugh all the same.

After the service is over, the newly married couple walk up the aisle, him grinning broadly and her with her arm looped through his, one self-conscious hand already twisting her wedding band. I watch them, thinking wistfully how lucky they are.

Then Pete leans in and says can we bloody get going to the reception because he's not fannying around with car parking there too.

On arrival, we squidge through the mud of the country hotel gardens with the other guests. It's way too cold to stand outside, so everyone dutifully makes small talk in the foyer while the photographs are done. We watch the bride's mother stoutly puff after two tiny bridesmaids who would rather chase each other round the muddy lawn squealing like piglets, trailing their flower headdresses behind them, than pose for the camera.

Then it's on to the reception line, and finally we are all seated at our tables so the painful business of introducing ourselves to other people and asking how they know the bride and groom can begin. I am sitting next to a man who inexplicably introduces himself to me as Fish. Pete is next to Fish's other half, a stacked blonde in an outfit that barely contains yards of rather crêpey mahogany-tanned bosom. She nudges Pete and says, "I can tell you and I are gonna get on like a house on fire." Pete smiles politely but sends me a pained look, a silent plea across the table that makes me giggle into my glass of warm champagne. I feel my doubts and tension from the church lift as he smiles back at me, and suddenly the afternoon seems like it might be fun after all.

Unfortunately, as the meal gets under way, it turns out that the booze is the only thing that is warm. We all pick at our tepid beef and clammy potatoes as the flustered waitresses dispense with formalities and just dump the veg on our plates. At the other end of the room, some tables are already on their puddings—so we, as the last one on the circuit, are playing catch-up.

Fish, however, is determined to get utterly hammered and take us all with him. "Come on, girl," he blusters as he tops up my glass. "Get some more of this down your neck. Well, it's free, innit? You might as well." His cheeks are beginning to glow; he's getting a little friskier and sitting just a bit closer to me than he needs to. Mrs. Fish is likewise shrieking with laughter at something Pete has said, and he's looking a little alarmed at her OTT reaction.

Despite Fish, his cackling and his totally inappropriate story about what he did to a bloke who owed him £250 for a telly, I am tentatively enjoying myself. People are starting to get up and wander about in the lull between coffee and the speeches, and an aunt of Pete's who I have never met before comes waddling over to the table and envelops Pete in a lilac-silk hug. She's very jolly and powdery, asking Pete with a nudge and a twinkle when he's going to make an honest woman of me; surely wedding bells ought to be chiming for us soon? I am more than a little disconcerted to find both me and Pete hurriedly clearing our throats and saying, "Oh, plenty of time for that yet!"

All the fun fizzes out of me like someone letting go of a balloon, and quietly I shrink back into my seat, barely noticing as the aunt whitters on about what a shame it is that Pete's mum and dad weren't able to make it, and when are they back from their safari holiday?

A glass is tapped and the speeches start. They are painfully long, the bride's father having drunk a little too much wine and thus adding anecdotes he hasn't practiced, which consequently are about as funny as discovering someone has shat in both your shoes. Just as we're all drifting off to sleep, a mobile rings and everyone jolts awake. It's Pete's. He scrabbles to turn it off, but in his haste can't find the button, so grabs it and holds it to his ear and makes his way out of the room to jeers, holding up an apologetic hand as someone, wittily, shouts, "I'M AT A WEDDING— NO, IT'S SHIT!" making the bride's mother purse her lips crossly like a cat's bum.

I can't concentrate on the rest of the speeches, as all I can think is, who is he talking to? *Who's he talking to?* Is it her? They must have made it up . . . Feeling sick, I peer anxiously out of the window into the garden, but I can't see him. I take a big slug of wine and it makes me cough and splutter. Fish helpfully whacks me on the back and a bit of red wine spit flies out of my mouth, which is nice.

Pete sidles back in as we are all on our feet for the final toast. The best man announces that the tables will now be cleared for dancing and we all sit down heavily, silently thanking our stars that we survived the speeches. Fish spies that Pete has returned and says, "Look who's back! Your other bird all right, then?" He winks at Pete and chortles. Pete freezes for a second, forces a laugh and then jokes, "Oh, she's good, thanks for asking." Fish retorts quickly with, "Steady on, mate! I don't want to know what she's like in the sack—not with Princess here." He elbows me, then he leans in and, tapping his nose, murmurs, "Tell me later!" before letting rip with another cackle.

I can't take any more of this, so I get up and weave my way unsteadily through the tables. Pete doesn't come after me; probably thinks I've had too much to drink and need the loo. Outside in the chill air, the sun is dipping low and the sky has gone a magnificent red. It's by far the best weather of the day, but the photographer has long since packed up and gone home.

The cold air rushes into my lungs and I can smell wood smoke from nearby houses and a mushroom-like dampness from the surrounding trees. Two skinny young waiters, all spiky hair and hunched shoulders, are having a crafty fag by some French windows, shuffling from foot to foot to keep warm in their thin white shirts. The smell of their cigarettes carries over to me, making my head swim a bit. I feel giddy and light-headed, and my pulse starts to quicken slightly. I'm a woman on a mission again, I think, as I totter off toward the car park in my high heels.

A stealth mission, but I'm going to come out of it all guns blazing. I have Pete's keys in my handbag, and something else too; I'm almost giggling naughtily to myself as I reach the car. But as I slide into the driving seat and click the door shut behind me, I sober up a little and remember why I'm there, what I'm about to do, and that actually it isn't funny at all really. Looking over my shoulder to check he hasn't followed me, I reach into my bag and carefully pull out the wisp of peach knickers that I stole from Liz's flat. Shoving them under the passenger seat, I make sure they're completely hidden before getting out of the car and locking it up again.

I'm back in the hot fug of the room within five minutes.

The floor has been cleared, and the band are just doing their final "one two, one two" to test the mics, while a pageboy who is turning in faster and faster circles in the middle of the dance floor makes himself dizzy and happily falls over.

Then the first dance is announced to cheers and whistles and the happy couple take to the floor. They are a little hesitant at first, with everyone's eyes on them, but as the band start to croon

"Something Stupid" they clutch each other tightly, her looking up at him dreamily and whispering something, him looking proudly down at her, arms protectively round her waist. They look so happy that it makes me want to cry. I'm standing there watching them, feeling more alone than I think I ever have, when I feel arms slide around my own waist, and Pete is there.

I'm looking at the couple on the dance floor in front of me and trying to picture us instead of them . . . but I can't. I'm staring at them so hard they are going blurry in front of my eyes. Suddenly I don't want to be here . . . I just want to go home.

I tell Pete I want to leave, and he seizes the opportunity gratefully, getting my coat and ushering me back to the car. We are on our way and he's saying what a twat that bloke I was sat next to was and how he's still hungry and have we got anything to eat at home?

I'm thinking, when shall I pull the knickers out from under the seat?

I wait until we are back home and he's turning the engine off; then I pretend to reach down to get my bag. I feel my fingers grasp the wispy material. Here goes.

"Ooohh!" I squeal. "There's something furry under the seat! What the hell is that?" I pretend to look. "Oh, hang on, it's a tissue or something." I pull out the carefully folded knickers and then I say, "No it's not . . . I think it's material. What *is* this? . . . Put the light on, Pete."

He sighs tiredly and switches it on, saying something about just wanting to get in. The words die on his lips as I carefully and deliberately unfold the knickers. I let the information sink in and then I say, ominously quietly, "Would you like to tell me why you have a pair of women's knickers in your car?"

TWENTY-NINE

He is just gaping like a guppy trying to find water, and for a brief second I almost feel sorry for him. But I don't stop.

"Whose are these, Pete? They're not mine . . . Oh my God!" I clamp a hand to my face, like it's just dawned on me. "Are you . . . have you . . . have you got another woman?"

Staring at the knickers, he bleats, "I . . . I . . . no, of course not!"

You bloody liar.

I reach for the door handle, I scrabble out of the car and run up the path, trying to fit the key in the lock to get into the house.

I hear him going, "Shit!" as he gets out of the car, and then he shouts, "Wait!"

I kick my shoes off and run upstairs to the sound of Gloria barking, before slamming into the bathroom and locking the door. Then I wait. Come on, Pete. This is the bit where you run upstairs and deny everything.

He comes pounding up the stairs and rattles the door. "Sweetheart, let me in!" he pleads. "I don't know how they got there! I've never seen them before!"

I don't have to force a laugh, but I do make my voice sound deliberately wobbly. "Don't try that one!" I explode, all high-pitched. "Knickers in a car? Bit of a fucking cliché, isn't it? What were you doing? Off for a quick shag? She left her KNICK-ERS there? Oh my God!"

Now when I need tears, where the hell are they? I've cried enough to float the Ark recently . . . and when I could really use them? Nothing. Fucking hell!

He's still rattling the door. "Come on, Mia—that's ridiculous! Me? Have an affair? Don't be so stupid!"

That just makes me even angrier. I feel ragingly mad. I could happily go out there and punch his face in. He must think I'm some kind of idiot. Not having an affair? The lying bastard!

Tears are now so far away that I have to rub a bit of soap on my finger and dab it briefly on my hot, dry eyes. It does the trick, making them sting and water immediately. Quick check in the mirror—yes, I look like I've been crying now, so I fling the door open. "How did they get there, then?" I shout accusingly.

The question hangs in the air, and he paces about a bit and then says, "Look. I'll tell you the truth. But don't go mental, okay?"

This ought to be good, seeing as I know I put them there under two hours ago.

"There's this girl I met . . ." he begins, and I feel faint as the words reach me. My heart crashes ten floors in two seconds and then suddenly the tears are there for real. It's finally hearing him say it that does it. I whimper and move a step away from him.

He says earnestly, "No, no, sweetheart—it's not what you think. Let me explain." He takes a deep breath. "I met this girl, an actress, at a bar when we were having a work do."

Oh my God, he's actually going to tell me the truth. I try to catch my breath and wobble slightly, looking at him with scared, wide eyes.

"It was nothing—we just chatted, that was all, about my work, her work. Most of my lot were pissed and I was driving, it was just a relief to have someone sober to talk to. Toward the end of the night, she said she really liked me, and could we meet up again? I said I was flattered, but that I had a girlfriend . . . then I left. She must have hung around and managed to get my mobile number out of one of the lads, though, because she called me the day afterward. I should have told her not to call again, but it felt rude to do that—and she just seemed normal, a nice chatty girl who knew I had a girlfriend. She called the next day too and we talked again, but pretty soon it went from one or two calls to her starting to, well, bug me.

"I realized she'd got a lot of problems—and I mean *a lot*— but she just wanted someone to talk to. She said she needed a friend and that I was real and not as self-absorbed as people she worked with, who weren't really her friends. She told me a lot of stuff about her . . . pretty fucked-up stuff . . . and then when I said I didn't think I could be the friend she needed, she started crying and said how she always bored people and how she didn't know how she could cope any more, and hung up on me. So I called her back, talked to her . . . I mean, she made it pretty clear she was talking about topping herself." He pauses to let the words sink in.

"I just got too involved. I think she liked the attention and everything revolving around her. Then she got this part in a show in town and I was really pleased for her. We met up for a coffee, I got her a card and stuff—even said I'd come up to see it. In fact we did, it was that show I took you to in town?"

I don't say anything, I just nod, but I'm starting to feel a little worried. This actually is starting to sound . . . well, almost believable.

Pete sinks to the floor and holds his head. "But it all backfired. She thought I'd come up with the intention of seeing her. I'd mentioned what hotel I'd booked into. I don't think she realized I was bringing you, and when we got there, while you were having your massage, I got a call from her room—she'd booked into the hotel too! I think she thought that I wanted to . . . well, you know." He looks at me, very embarrassed. "Or maybe she thought she could persuade me to . . . Anyway, I went up to her room to tell her to leave, and this champagne arrived and everything . . . so I finally went mad and told her it was never going to happen and the calls were to stop. She got really apologetic and said it was cool and that she was sorry she'd misread the signs and that she wouldn't bother me again if I didn't want her to, but we could stay friends, couldn't we? I was so relieved, I just said of course we could still be friends and stuff . . ." He looks at me pleadingly. "But I didn't really mean it. It's just what you say, isn't it? She stopped calling for about a day, but then it started again. She called me in tears because she got robbed . . ."

I raise an eyebrow. "She got robbed?"

He looks shamefacedly at the floor. "Oh God, I've been such a prat. She got robbed and rang me in tears saying that she couldn't pay for this bag she'd been waiting for, for like EVER, because all her cards had been nicked, and why did bad stuff only happen to her? And I felt so sorry for her that I went and bought it for her. I phoned her and said I had it and that she could pay me back when she got the money. I felt like I'd done a really nice thing, and she was really happy, only you went and found it under the bed." He smiles at me ruefully. "So I had to give you that one and say I'd pay her for another. Bloody expensive gesture."

My legs start to give way, and I sit down heavily. I stare at him transfixed, and in a hoarse whisper say, "Carry on." But I don't want him to. This can't be true, it can't be!

"I thought about what you said about the burglary not ringing true, and that it looked like it had been done just to wreck the place. It all seemed to add up and point to her. So I went nuts and called her. Phone calls is one thing, but breaking into our house? That's just weird freaky shit." He shakes his head. "She denied it totally, but I said I was calling the police. She said she'd top herself if I did that, and that I was the mad one, not her. How could I be so nice to her one minute and then turn on her and accuse her of something she'd never done and would never do? She cried and said that she'd fallen for me," he flushes red, "and that it really hurt that I could say something like that to her, and that she thought we were friends. I didn't know what to say to that, so I just hung up and didn't do anything—I just hoped she'd go away, I suppose. I don't think she wants to hurt me or you, she's just obsessed with me."

I don't say anything. I can't.

"As if that wasn't weird enough, that card arrived for you. Well, that was half the good-luck card I sent her . . . I can only assume it was designed to make you ask if there was something going on you should know about, or that she was trying to say I was hers, not yours. I dunno." He looks tiredly at me. "She's mental, totally mental. Once I'd managed to get out of that one with you . . . well, then the *earrings* happened. I didn't leave them out for you, babe . . . I think she broke in and left them there on purpose for you to find."

He looks at me, his face haunted and screwed up with misery. "And now the knickers . . . She just wants to have me to herself! She's intent on breaking us up . . . and it's only because you're so innocent and have such a trusting heart that I've managed to hide it from you up until now. I've pleaded with her, begged her to leave us alone, and all she keeps saying is it's not her, she's not doing anything, and *I'm* the mad one. But it keeps happening . . . I don't know what to do any more. I think I'm going to have to call the police."

Oh God. Oh my God, what have I done? What the hell have I done? I'm truly horrified, and feel sick to the pit of my stomach. I can feel the acid starting to swirl and bilge. So he hasn't been having an affair? And everything I've done has made an innocent girl with a schoolkid crush look mad . . . and has in fact driven him to speak to her more than he would have done if I'd just left everything alone? Oh, Jesus! He's not having an affair . . . I don't know what to say. I just sit there trying to take it all in. "Why didn't you tell me what was going on?"

He looks at me challengingly and directly. "Would you have believed me?"

I stop and think about this. Would I?

Do I?

I think about the picture I saw by her bed. It could have been him reluctantly having it taken . . . could it have been in a bar? She is young, I suppose . . . I used to have pictures in my room of boys that I had a crush on that I'd never even kissed, but surely I was fifteen or something then; she's in her twenties!

Maybe she is just an innocent girl who although she has her problems (and don't we all?) fell in love with Pete, and now has him calling her all the time and wrongly having a go at her, accusing her of things she hasn't done and knows absolutely nothing about. I mean, obviously I know she's not mad and didn't do all those things, because I did them.

I don't know what to believe . . . it all sounds so plausible, and everything fits. Is he telling me the truth? But what about Debs, and her assured "Lizzie's boyfriend is an architect . . ."

Maybe Liz is just nuts; maybe she *told* Debs that Pete is her bloke and Debs just took it as read . . . If only I'd had the chance to speak to her properly yesterday. If only he hadn't rung and said he was on his way over . . . Hang on. He went over to see her! But I can't ask him directly about it. How would I know about that?

"So how many times have you told her to back off?" I say directly. "Have you just said it over the phone?"

"Oh no," he says grimly. "Believe me, I've told her to her face too. Nothing seems to sink in. She's unhinged."

Okay, so that fits, and Debs was there when he went to the flat. That would suggest he was going there to have it out with her. Oh my God. What's going to happen when those balloons arrive on Monday?

"She even called me today at the wedding . . ." He shakes his head. "Still bleating on about how she didn't do it, any of it. Then this goes and happens. I don't know how she's doing it all . . . How the fuck did she get into my car?" He bites his lip. "It's getting scary now. I'm so, so sorry I didn't tell you. I was just so worried you'd leave me. But I think maybe we have to do something serious about it now. Phone calls are one thing, but these two weeks have gone way beyond that—the break-in, the freaky stuff she's sending . . . What do you think, should we call the police?"

Nooo! That's the last thing I want! All of a sudden I realize how weird *I* would look if it all came out: "The thing is, Officer, I thought my boyfriend was having an affair and I was so deranged with grief that I went mad and trashed our house, then I went looking for the woman in question at her place of work. I gained entry into her flat by deception. Once there, I stole items of hers, and among other things I posted an item to myself and bought some balloons on her credit card to make her look like a nutter."

Why, WHY didn't I just ask him what was going on when I found the texts? What would have happened? It seems he would have told me the truth and I would have saved myself two weeks of absolute hell. I wouldn't have upended the house and told those lies, I wouldn't have gone steaming off to find her and behaved like a lunatic. I wouldn't have nearly broken my heart . . . And God . . . I wouldn't have raked up all that stuff with Katie—wouldn't have *rung* her and wouldn't have given her the chance to shit all over me yet again from such a great height.

I should have just asked him about the texts, but I was so scared of losing him . . . and if he finds out what I've done, he'll leave me for certain. *I'd* leave me . . . I have no choice but to carry this on now.

I take a deep breath and then I say, "Okay, I believe you. If she's that much of a nutter, though, you need to change your number right now and you need to report her to your network for harassing you."

He hesitates for a second, and then says, "But that might tip her over the edge."

Um, I think I might have done that already.

"Not your responsibility," I say firmly. "Do it right now. This stops here."

So he does it. I listen to him change his number . . . I listen to him report her . . . and I start to feel very, very guilty indeed for the campaign I've waged against her.

Once he's hung up, he turns to me. "Should we call the police too, do you think?"

Very carefully I pretend to consider this. "No, I don't think so. We've got no proof that it was her that broke in . . . and so what if she sent me some silly little bits and pieces in the post? She's just a girl playing games. I bet now that you've changed your number and she can't get hold of you, it'll all stop . . . and anyway, what can she do to make it worse? I already know, so she has nothing to threaten you with any more. Best leave it, I think . . . it'll die a death."

He nods and says, "Maybe you're right," looking exhausted. "I just want it to stop. I wish I'd never bloody met her. I'm so sorry, I should have told you." He reaches for me and I sink gratefully into his arms. We sit there and hug each other—not saying a word.

That night, in bed, I can't fall asleep. Not because I need to get up and check his phone any more, but because I am thinking of Liz out there in her white bedroom . . . having fallen in love with a man who then starts accusing her of things she knows she hasn't done, but somehow he has proof that she can't explain. I think it must be driving her mad and she must be wondering how the hell her things are winding up in my hands. No wonder she's feeling a bit crazed.

I think of her sad, small messages to him and I feel a little pang of guilt. I remember what it feels like to have a crush on someone so badly that you think you love them, an infatuation that you confuse with love but that isn't really. After all, how can it be when you don't even really know them? Love isn't having to call someone obsessively all the time; it's being able to do mundane things like pick up their cups from by the sofa time after time, even though you're bored with saying they won't walk to the dishwasher on their own; it's doing things like that and loving them *in spite* of it.

I glance at Pete, who is floating deeply in untroubled sleep. His brow is unfurrowed, his breathing deep and relaxed. He doesn't look like a man who nearly lost his girlfriend tonight and is being stalked by a nutter.

The tiniest of doubts creeps into my mind. If he's lying to me, if that was one very careful story he told me earlier, constructed for just such a moment, then he is a very, very devious man and I do not know him at all.

What if he *has* been having an affair, my plan has simply worked and he thinks she is actually crazy? Wouldn't he just tell me something to cover his tracks, thus getting her out of the picture while still enabling him to hang on to his convenient life with me?

Oh, this is sending me mad, utterly, utterly mad.

I don't know what to think any more, but I do know that somehow I'm going to have to intercept those balloons on Monday, because if he is telling the truth, when those turn up and he sees the message on them, he's going to call the police. That I know for sure.

THIRTY

Sunday passes very, very slowly. All I can do is think about how I can stop those balloons before tomorrow. I'm a nervous wreck, biting my lip, running over the last two weeks in my mind. When he sees them, he's going to go mental himself.

But for now, he is blissfully unaware. He is nothing but sweet to me, fussing around all day like a mother hen, as if I'm ill or something, saying what a relief it is to have everything out in the open at last, how he can finally relax, how he's hated hiding this from me, how beautiful I looked at the wedding yesterday . . . Maybe we should start thinking about when *we* might like to, as he says, "formalize" things.

This of course should make me feel happier than I've ever been; he has as good as said we will get married. Strangely, however, I haven't gone weak with delight, neither do I feel relief that my life is back on track and not thudding into the sidings. I'm getting what I wanted, but all I can do is move around the place like a ghost, thinking about *her*.

Although Pete has changed his number, I am still watching,

waiting, through habit now, but his mobile does not ring all day. I am still unable to shake the doubt. Is he telling me the truth? Surely he is? Everything fitted, didn't it? And why shouldn't I believe my boyfriend of so many years over some actress?

When I get five minutes to myself, I call the balloon company to see if I can cancel my order, only to get a recorded message giving me the office opening hours Monday to Friday. I'm going to need to be here tomorrow to get to them before Pete does . . . great. So I call Spank Me to try and get the day off work tomorrow. He is unamused to be called on a Sunday at home, which is fair enough.

I tell him that although I know I've been off work for two weeks now and that they've been flat out, I'm still having problems and am not quite up to the commute, so could I work at home tomorrow instead? He is not a happy man. He tells me, in no uncertain terms, that if I am not sitting in the office tomorrow morning when he gets in at 9:30, he will expect to either see the absence of a limb when I do return, or at the very least a letter from my consultant confirming the hideous and terminal disease that I have.

After he has forced me to confirm that no one has died or is about to die, and that I am not involved in the extradition of a family member from a politically unstable country, he says that while no one could be more sympathetic than him, he is nonetheless trying to run a business—and a small one at that.

My final pathetic attempt is that I didn't like to say before, but I have "women's problems." He says briskly that so does he—me—and can I please shut up, get off the phone and let him get back to his day off? Finally he concedes that he will, if I would like, give me an week of unpaid leave and get a temp in, to which I grumpily say no thank you. He *knows* I can't afford a week of unpaid leave. So I have no choice. I will not be home when the balloons arrive.

Monday morning sees me coming out of Old Street tube station and dialing a number on my mobile as I walk to the office. Still there is no answer—just a recorded voice saying the office is not open yet, would I like to leave a message? Yes I would—get into work and answer your bloody phones. It shouldn't be this hard to stop a delivery of balloons.

I am, thanks to the trains, running a little late, and when I finally pant up the stairs and into the office, Spank Me is already ensconced behind his desk, brisk in pinstripe. Lottie's eyes light up and she opens her mouth to welcome me back, but Spank Me gets in there first, acidly remarking how relieved he is to see I've survived my epic trek into work, and that Lottie will fill me in on my duties for this week. Oh dear.

Luckily he has back-to-back meetings all day and is on his way out again by 10:15, barking orders at us as he hurriedly collects his things, unaware of the finger I have stuck up at his retreating back.

Once the door slams behind him, Lottie pushes her chair away and says, "Oh my God—you're back! I've been so worried about you, you poor ill thing—you've lost so much weight! Right, brew up, and when I get back from the loo I want to hear all about it. Get the biscuits too."

But I'm already reaching for the phone. I've been waiting for an hour and a quarter now to make this call, getting more and more anxious. Dialing hurriedly, I wait for it to connect . . . but all I get is an engaged signal.

"Shit!" I explode. "Get off the fucking phone!"

I dial again frantically and wait . . . Still busy. Angrily I slam the phone back down and stare at it. Give it a minute and I'll try again. I have to get through—I can't believe this is taking so long. "Come on, come on!" I mutter under my breath. Then I have an idea. I snatch the phone back up, dial again, hit ring-back and it's accepted. Now all I have to do is wait.

I look up and see that Lottie has not moved, she's just staring at me. "Okay," she says slowly. "What the hell is going on?"

What feels like hours later, because I'm still waiting for the ring-back, Lottie is sitting in her chair, wide-eyed and open-mouthed with disbelief. Strangely, I don't feel much better for having confessed everything, and I am too tired to even feel embarrassed.

"So now you pretty much have no idea if Pete's telling you the truth or not?"

"That's about the long and the short of it." I manage half a smile.

"And you even called Katie, that's how desperate you got?"

"Yup."

"But she refused to say whether she'd been telling the truth about him and her . . . and basically told you to fuck off?"

I shrug and try to smile again. "Pretty much."

"Oh, Mia."

We both sit there in silence for a moment.

"Sucks really, doesn't it?" I do a weird little laugh that sounds a bit like a bark. "And I've still got these bloody balloons to sort. They could be there by now. He won't open them, but he'll definitely be wondering what it is."

"Shit," Lottie says simply. "Shit."

"Yes," I agree tiredly. "That about sums it up."

Then Lottie does something very unexpected. She gets up

and she walks around the side of my desk, reaches out her arms and hugs me.

Now Lottie and I are close—we've worked together for ages. We're part of the fabric of each other's day-to-day lives, but I wouldn't call her a best friend. I haven't met her mum, for example, or Jake for that matter. We don't hang out with each other at weekends, we've never been on holiday together. We certainly don't hug or kiss hello and good-bye. So to feel her arms round me is weird and a bit awkward.

"You poor thing," she says quietly. "You poor, poor messed-up thing."

And that does it. Her hug is so genuine, so kind and so unexpected that I burst into tears. Only they are not the tears that I *have* been crying, the frightened, hurt, heartbreaking tears—they're deep, dam-busting, release-of-pent-up-stress, coming-from-the-pit-of-your-being tears. I think even Lottie is a bit surprised.

"I'm sorry!" I blub, scrabbling on my desk for something to blow my nose on. "It's just been so shit . . . and now not knowing what to think . . . not talking to anyone about it . . . Oh. I'm sorry!" I dab at my eyes and look at her desperately. "I should be happy! I've got what I want, haven't I? She's as good as out of the picture. She certainly will be by tonight. Does it matter how? Surely the important thing is that she's gone, and now we have a chance to really get everything sorted. I mean, he even said he thinks we should think about formalizing things after we went to that wedding." I look at her eagerly. "That's how sorted this almost is."

"Formalize things?" Lottie frowns, moving back round to her desk and passing me a clean tissue. "I don't understand."

"He meant get married."

She raises an eyebrow and sits down. "Oh, I see," she says slowly. "How very romantic."

When she says it like that, it sounds anything but. There is a pregnant pause while we both try and think of something positive to say, which is broken by the ring-back. Thank God.

I grab at the phone and at last hear a ringing tone. A youngish-sounding bloke answers with a cheery, "Hello, can I help you?" I am almost gibbering with relief when he tells me he can't see it will be a problem at all to stop the delivery, and that he, Max, will personally sort it out for me.

"Oh, thank you so much," I breathe, and Lottie smiles at me gently, getting the gist.

I hang up, sink back into my chair and close my eyes, totally silent.

"Well, thank goodness for that," says Lottie. "Time for a cup of tea, I think."

Later that afternoon, we are for once working. It's been a very odd day. Lottie has been quiet and I have been so relieved and so tired, I haven't felt much like talking.

I'm staring at my computer screen, frowning at the database and just wanting to go home, when Lottie suddenly says, "I don't think I've ever really told you about my mate Leah, have I?"

I try to remember if she has or not, but it's not ringing any bells.

Lottie pushes her chair back.

"She got married to this bloke she had a thing with in sixth form. They'd sort of stayed together through uni—on and off—although we all told her to dump him. Well, basically, they'd been married for about three years and surprise, surprise, it started to go wrong. She knew it too, but couldn't quite find the guts or will to tackle it, so didn't do anything. She just waited for something to change, trying to put off the evil moment. And not just for her own sake either, to be fair—she desperately wanted to stop him being hurt and would have given anything for it to work out. I really think if she'd had a magic wand she would have waved it to mend the cracks.

"But do you know what she said to me afterward? That dead time, where nothing was happening—they weren't going forward or back, or changing at all; waiting without seeing logically how it *could* change was what slowly killed her."

She looks at me steadily and I look back at her, saying nothing.

"Finally, when she had gone beyond unhappy and was just wilting in a relationship that while wasn't exactly hurting her, wasn't letting her grow either, her husband took the reins. You see, she was so busy trying to protect him, she hadn't noticed *he'd* been watching her. He had seen how unhappy she'd become and how suffocated she was.

"There can't be many things more soul-destroying than knowing you're not enough for the person you love, even though they want you to be, very badly indeed. So when he realized she didn't love him as she should, and he couldn't bear it, he left her. Just walked out on her one day.

"She totally fell apart when she realized he had gone. I think she'd known all along that their love, for lots of reasons, hadn't quite become what they had both hoped it would be, and what that inevitably would mean, although she would have given anything for it to be otherwise, because she loved him.

"But even stumbling through the pain of missing him dreadfully, wondering where he was, what he was doing and who he was doing it with . . . even all that wasn't as bad as being still stuck in it; trying to make herself into something she wasn't. That bit, she said, was like dying a little death every day.

"And do you know what? She's totally okay now." Lottie still stares at me, and still I say nothing. There is a long pause and then she clears her throat.

"I suppose what I'm trying to say is that she had a choice. Even though she didn't realize it, she was making choices all the way through—it wasn't just happening to her; she *chose* to let it happen."

She stops, looks at me earnestly and waits. Waits for me to say something, but I don't. I can't.

"Would being on your own again really be so bad?" she says gently, and begins to scoot her chair round the desk, closer to me. "Wouldn't it be better than this? You'd have all the promise of something really good and beautiful coming into your life again. And it would come into it; it really would. But it won't all the time you're . . . you're *letting* yourself be stuck like this. You have so many people who love you and we'd—"

"Oh please don't give me the 'you don't need a man' speech," I interrupt with a laugh that is clouded by tears gathering at the back of my throat and eyes. "I know I don't. I know I could be okay if I wanted to be—without him. But I'm not like your friend, I really love Pete."

"But you don't even know if he's telling you the truth about this girl! Okay—so it sounds like it all fits, but what if he's lying? Are you really sure you want to choose—because you do have choices here, Mia, you're not just stuck in this with no other way out. Are you sure you want to *choose* to be with a man you can't trust? Can that really be love?"

"I think he's telling me the truth."

"But you can't do! Why did you call Katie if you had no doubts at all?"

"Oh, I called her before he explained everything to me." I reach for a tissue and blow my nose violently. "That was just stupid, I was in a state—I think I just wanted to talk to someone who really knew me, and yes, if I'm being honest, I suppose I wanted her to say that it had all been her fault—that he hadn't tried it on with her all those years ago, that I had nothing to worry about now with this girl—but that was never going to happen. I mean, what the fuck was I *thinking*, phoning her?" I look at Lottie despairingly. "How stupid can you get? What positive outcome did I think could have come from it?"

Lottie shrugs and shakes her head. "I don't know."

"What was I expecting her to say? 'Oh, Mia, I'm so glad you called so I could confess my dark secret to you. Three and a half years ago, I came back into your life and having already stolen your childhood sweetheart, I decided to kiss the man you'd managed to subsequently meet and fall desperately in love with. I don't know why and it was very wrong of me. I should have told you the truth but I wanted you to still be my friend, so I lied and said it was all his fault. But hey ho—you're not my friend any more anyway, so I might as well come clean.'"

Pausing, I reach for another tissue, yanking it out of the box and blowing my nose again.

"'It *was* all my fault,'" I continue with my high-pitched mimic. "'Pete never tried to kiss me; I wickedly tried to seduce him because I was unhappy at the time and wanted what you had.'" I ball up the tissue and throw it toward the bin, but miss. "'He simply can't be having an affair now with this Liz. You are the only woman for him. I'm so sorry. I'm going traveling and I know you will never forgive me, but at least we've made our peace now and you know you have a good man there. Hang on to him . . .' Yeah, like that was ever going to happen."

Lottie sighs. "A touch unrealistic, perhaps. You said it yourself. What good outcome could there possibly have been? So what . . . you made a mistake. Don't beat yourself up about it. What matters is here and now. She really has nothing to do with you and Pete."

I inhale deeply and try to calm down.

"Look, you'll never really know what happened in that room between them—who did what, whose fault it was, who betrayed you. You made the decision you thought was right at the time, and that's all we can ever do. All you had to go on was what you knew for certain about her, and you saw her with your own eyes in bed with Dan. So what that you were only twenty-one?"

"Twenty," I say matter-of-factly.

"Whatever. She still did it. Would you have done that to her?"

"No. She was my best friend." My voice cracks and wobbles slightly and I close my eyes as I try to get a grip on myself. "I know you're right . . . it's just, the fucking stupid thing is . . ." I open my eyes and look Lottie square in the face, "the thing that I could still punch myself for is that even now, all these years on, I still went back for more. I didn't stop to think about who had done what to who and when. What it really comes down to is that I still hoped there was enough of our friendship there to help me through what has definitely been one of the worst times of my life. And there wasn't. There isn't. And there isn't ever going to be again. We're never going to sit down and set it right. I'll never really know why she didn't try to get in touch with me again after that night, how it slipped so badly into nothing when it used to be everything. And one day, when I'm old, someone is going to tell me in passing that she's died, and I know, I know that I'll wish with all my heart that it could have been different. I just keep thinking of those two little girls we once were, dancing madly round around her living room, giggling like crazy." Tears well up in my eyes again, to my immense frustration. "God, I wish I could stop crying!" I blink them back fiercely.

"Maybe there are friendships that are just never supposed to last into adulthood and that simply don't stand up to scrutiny," Lottie says gently and reaches out for my hand.

"Maybe," I concede. "Or maybe she just didn't like me as much as I thought she did. I'll never know. Such is life."

Lottie takes a deep breath. "I think you just have to let some things go, even if it really, really hurts and you don't understand why you couldn't make it all okay. Some things you just can't fix."

"I know," I say and squeeze her hand back gratefully, finally letting go to wipe my eyes. "I think I'm starting, at last, to learn that. God. Friendships can be even harder work than relationships!"

Lottie shifts around uncomfortably.

"I wasn't actually talking about Katie," she says carefully.

Her words hang in the air.

"I love Pete," I say quietly, and, just like delicate bubbles, everything she has just said bursts silently, vanishing without trace.

"Then I'm speaking out of turn, and I'm sorry." She stands up resignedly and starts to gather our cups before walking to the kitchen. She hesitates as she reaches the door.

"It's good to know that he's worth all of this; what you've put yourself through. After all, it doesn't matter what anyone else thinks. The only person you really can't lie to is yourself, and obviously you're not doing that, so . . . it's all okay, isn't it?"

I ignore her. "I think I'm going to pop out and get some milk."

"Look, Mia," Lottie interjects, "if I've crossed—"

"Do you want anything?" I cut across her desperately, begging her silently not to say anything else.

"No," she sighs. "You're all right."

I'm only slightly cheered when Patrick unexpectedly turns up at the office at about five o'clock, eating a bag of sweets like he's ten or something, wondering if I want to go out for a drink.

I've just finished the delighted "Hello!" and the "What are you doing here?" bit and he's done the "I finished work early and was up this way so I thought I'd pop in" bit. We have a slightly awkward "How's my sister?" and the "She's okay, thanks" bit, which is going to take some getting used to, and are just starting on the "So, how's work?" when Lottie, obviously tiring of chit-chat, says, "Hey, Patrick. What do you think about this?" She swings her legs out from under the desk and eyes Patrick steadily. "Pete says they . . ." she nods in my direction, "should formalize things."

I shoot her a surprised look as Patrick frowns and gives the matter his consideration.

"Oh, blimey. Big step. Hmm! I'm not sure now is a good time to buy, though." He chews thoughtfully on a blackjack and looks at me seriously. "The market's a bit volatile at the moment but it'll be an investment, I suppose. Just make sure you sign all the right stuff to protect what you put in and—"

"Not buy a house, they mean get married," Lottie interrupts bluntly. "Isn't it romantic?"

Except she says it again in the same sort of voice that someone might say, "Oh, a free holiday in Baghdad! How lovely!"

Patrick's chewing slows for a moment. His smile fades and he goes a bit still. Then it's as if someone plugs him back in again. The smile appears on his face from nowhere and he grins and says, "Well, bloody hell! Congratulations!" He comes over and gives me a hug. "Get all of us, happy and loved up!"

"He hasn't actually asked me yet," I point out, disentangling myself from Patrick, who smells quite lovely now I think of it: expensive sandalwood aftershave and aniseed. Lucky Clare. "But he as good as did. And I didn't say no. That's nice, isn't it?" I squint worriedly up at Patrick.

He glances at Lottie, who drops her gaze. "Hmmm," he muses under his breath. "Hmmm."

Then the megawatt smile is back. "Course it's nice!" he says. "If you're happy, I'm happy! You *are* happy, aren't you?" He looks at me searchingly.

I pause for a minute. Am I? Yes, I think so. I'm certainly relieved.

"I'm going to get married!" I say shyly.

Patrick nods slowly and says, "Yes, you are . . . Well, that's decided then. We *have* to go for a celebratory drink!"

"I can't," I say regretfully, getting up. "I've got to get home really. You're all right, though? My sister being nice to you?"

"She's fantastic," he says, popping a cola cube in his mouth and making toward the door. "I don't think I've ever been this happy. Anyway," he blows me a kiss, "you know where I am if you need me."

I nod gratefully and blow him one back. He winks at Lottie, gives me a salute, then he is gone. As ever, when Patrick leaves the room, it feels suddenly a little quieter and more boring.

Lottie sighs. "That's nice that Clare and he are together. Is it weird for you?"

"A little," I say honestly. "But Patrick's so lovely, I'm just glad they're both happy. Listen, I'm sorry about earlier. Thanks for today. I really appreciate it."

"No problem," she says, smiling a little sadly. "See you tomorrow. Have a nice night."

As I walk home from the station an hour later, I think about how we can start to spend more time together now, Pete and me. Maybe a shared hobby would help?

Once I'm in through the front door, I kick my shoes off, shouting, "I'm back!" I turn around.

There is a large cardboard box sitting in the middle of the floor with a big label addressed clearly to me.

My heart stops. Oh no . . . oh please no. Max said he'd sort it . . .

Totally aghast, I dash over to it and peer wildly at the delivery note. Pete signed for it at 2:30 p.m. I am too late. He's seen it. Oh Christ, I *thought* that stupid fucker sounded young. I probably got the office junior who didn't know his arse from his elbow. I should have called back and double-checked.

Pete appears at the top of the stairs to see me staring up at him, horrified.

"Do you know who that's from?" is all he says. "You expecting anything?"

I shake my head. "Did you send it?" I venture weakly.

He looks grim. "No, I didn't, but I think I know who did." We both know what he's suggesting.

"I think we'd better open it," he says uncertainly. "I'll get a knife."

THIRTY-ONE

As he slides the blade through the Sellotape, the cardboard flaps either side of the box open and two balloons rise silently out of the dark depths. One is a jaunty skeleton, and the other is just plain black with a white RIP across its proud, shiny front.

Pete blanches and whispers, "Fucking hell." I look at the balloons bobbing merrily and then I sneak a look at him. He is visibly shaken.

Then he springs to life and dives toward the box, tipping out the tissue paper, hunting for a card. But of course, I didn't order one, so there is nothing to find. He jumps to his feet saying, "She's pushed it too far this time. This is fucking mental. That's it. This stops *here*!"

He's really angry. I can see a small vein throbbing in his neck and his eyes have gone small, glittering like a snake's. He marches out of the room and I rush after him, shouting, "Wait! Pete! It might not be her! It might be a joke from someone else . . . What are you going to do?"

He's already got his phone in his hand, and is listening, waiting for it to connect. He ignores my flapping next to him, and I can hear his teeth grinding. I've never seen him like this. He's angry and yet scarily calm and focused.

"Never mind fucking hello," he says into the phone, his tone low and slightly wobbly with something more akin to total rage than anger. "Did you or did you not send the sickest balloons to my girlfriend today? One that said RIP on it?"

He listens for a minute, closes his eyes and says, "Don't lie to me, Liz. Don't make this worse, because I *will* find out. Did you or didn't you?"

I can't make out what she's saying, but I can hear a voice with a rising note of alarm on the other end of the phone. I stare at him and he stares back, listening to her and saying nothing.

Then he snorts a burst of laughter, but it's a bitter, aggressive "I don't believe you" laugh.

"Oh save it!" he says. "She knows all about you, so that won't work. In fact, she's standing right next to me if you want a word."

I shrink back, shaking my head violently. I don't want to talk to her! He looks at me and frowns at me in a sort of "don't be so silly, I had no intention of making you speak to her" way.

"Just tell me the truth. Did you send them?" he continues relentlessly. "Don't cry—it's pathetic," he almost spits down the phone. "Listen to yourself! You're so sad! Fucking get a grip!"

Even I'm a little shocked by this. Okay, so I don't like her. In fact I hate her, but didn't he say she was suicidal? I have never seen him like this—so harsh, so unkind.

"Just tell me!" he continues. "Did you send them?"

There's silence apart from a torrent of high-pitched squeaking down the phone.

Pete says nothing, he just lets her rant.

"Well, you know that's not going to happen. That can't happen. We talked about this," he says simply, no emotion in his voice at all now.

They talked about what?

"I'm bored now," he interjects rudely over whatever she is saying, and in a clipped voice that I've not heard before either, he says, "All I know is that someone sent some very unpleasant balloons, with all they imply, to my girlfriend, who I love." He reaches for my hand and squeezes it reassuringly. "And I'm not having it. Unfortunately, seeing as you've been wacky enough to send her all sorts of shit this week, which, whatever you say, could *only* have come from you, when some mad balloons turn up out of the blue, who do you think is going to spring to mind? Funnily enough, I'm not really convinced by you just saying, 'No I didn't, and you have to believe me.' I think I should call the police. This is getting out of hand."

This obviously has an effect; there's another high-pitched squeak. He stops and goes quiet again, and then shakes his head, listening to whatever she is saying.

Then he says, "Well, that's that then, isn't it? You said it, you don't understand it yourself. You're mad, Liz, mental." He taps the side of his head viciously. "You remember what I said to you. You don't come near us again, okay? It's over. It's OVER."

Then he hangs up and throws the phone across the floor.

"I'm sorry," he says simply. "I'm sorry you had to hear that. It's definitely her, though. When I said I'd call the police, she crumbled and said that an amount *had* appeared on her credit card, but she hadn't known what it was for, and that someone must have got hold of her card number and used it. Can you believe it? The lengths she's going to . . . my God! She's just insane—totally ga-ga." He shakes his head in disbelief.

But I'm not listening. Something in the way he said "It's over" did not sound right. He said that like someone would say "*We're* over." As in the end of a relationship.

"What's over, Pete?" I ask, ignoring what he just said.

He looks up and stares at me. "What d'you mean?"

"You said, 'Remember what I said . . . It's over.' What did you mean?"

He looks bemused. "This, her obsession with me. All this." He waves his hands at the box. "The cards, the fucked-up gifts."

"Not a thing with you and her, then? Not anything that would mean you'd lied to me and hidden something that I should know about? You wouldn't be making decisions about my life without me being in full knowledge of the facts? Would you?" I say quietly.

He looks at me straight, takes my hands and says slowly, "I love you and I've done nothing you need to worry about. It's *her* that's the nutter. I still think I should call the police. What if she really means to hurt you . . . or me?" He looks up at the bobbing skeleton worriedly.

With that unsettling thought, for him anyway, we sit there in silence, just looking at the balloons. I don't know what he is thinking, but all that is running through my head, on its now continuous and exhausting loop, is that even if he is lying to me, considering what I've done to Liz and how I've lied to him, am I any better? Or worse?

THIRTY-TWO

ater that night, we're trying to watch TV and not acknowledge the balloons in the corner of the room. I want to burst them and throw them away, but Pete thinks we should keep them in case they are needed as evidence. How did this slip so far out of my control and go so wrong?

The balloons are not the only thing setting us on edge. Since he hung up on Liz, his phone has rung almost continuously, until finally he switches it off, swearing under his breath, before staring blankly at the TV screen.

From the other sofa, I question how she has his number again, seeing as how he changed it. He, still clearly simmering with rage in the corner, says he was so angry when he called her earlier, he forgot to withhold his number. So that's how. "Not what you think!" he says, flashing me a hot, don't-go-accusing-me! look.

I apologize and say I wasn't accusing him of anything and that I'm going to get a drink, does he want one? He shakes his head silently and then says, "Sorry. I don't mean to take it out on you." I smile gratefully at him and walk out into the hall. My smile slips as soon as I'm out of sight and I pause to sigh, leaning my head on the wall for a moment. This is hellish. What have I done? Maybe if I just sit tight and say nothing, it'll just go away. There's nothing more to come, nothing more I've planned. It can be over now. Really it can. After all, he does think she's mad. I don't think he is interested at all now—even if he was before.

I think I'm getting a headache. I can feel a dull throb starting to pulse at my temples and spread over my brow. I might just take a paracetamol and go to bed. It'll all be better in the morning.

Since I've been in the sitting room it's got dark outside, and I can't see a thing in the hall without the light on. I'm fumbling around to find the switch when I happen to glance at the front door, the top half of which is frosted glass. There, framed in the eerie fluorescent orange glow from the street, is the distinct outline of a figure.

Someone is out there, just standing on the doorstep.

I freeze to the spot, completely unable to move or make a sound. I feel my chest constrict and my heart starts to thud. Then, as I watch in horror, the figure leans in slowly and silently presses its face up against the glass.

I can't see distinct features, just the impression of a nose, an eye and some long tendrils of hair. The head moves a little jerkily as I stand there in the dark, paralyzed with fear. I'm trying to scream but no noise will come out. I'm just making this hoarse, breathy rasp, too low to hear. "Pete!" I'm breathing frantically. "Pete!"

It's horrific, like all of my worst nightmares where I'm trying to run away from something that I know is going to hurt me. I'm trying to sprint, but inexplicably it feels like I'm wading through thick gel that is clinging to my legs.

The head twists back slowly and then the figure begins to sink down, crouching low, like an animal poised to spring. It just waits there for a moment, and then noiselessly, the letter box begins to hinge open and I see fingertips creep in round the edges. Still I find myself unable to make a sound. Then, as the fingers hold it open, I see eyes appear. Wide, mad, staring eyes; violent red rims. They roam quickly around, taking everything in—and then they alight on me. They stare at me for a moment and I stare back. Then, thank God, from somewhere I find some sound and just shriek, "Pete!"

As the sound of my voice cuts through the silence, the fingers shoot back and the letter box clatters shut. The figure draws away, and when Pete dashes into the hall to find me shaking and incoherent, pointing at the door, there is nothing for him to see.

Once he manages to get it out of me, he flings the door open and dashes out into the street, but there is nothing, and no one there. Just a deathly silence punctuated by the distant, mournful wail of a cat as a cold, damp rush of night air surges past me into the house.

Once he has come back in, hugged me, and assured me that it was probably just kids messing around, although he doesn't sound convinced himself, I calm down a little. He says he'll make me a cup of tea, but I send him back into the sitting room, assuring him that I'll be okay, I can do it. He kisses the top of my head—and after a worried look at me, he wanders back into the living room.

In the downstairs loo I take some deep breaths. After all, what *do* I have to be frightened of? *I've* done everything that he thinks is Liz. It probably was kids. Feeling a little better, I creep nervously into the kitchen. It's started to rain outside and I glance at the window as I pick up the kettle and wander over to the sink to fill it up.

Big fat raindrops slide down the glass. I can't see out into the dark garden, I can just see my reflection staring back at me. It's foul out there, so cold and miserable. Maybe a holiday would do me and Pete good. Help us put everything behind us? Somewhere hot. I need to feel some sun on my face. I turn to sit the full kettle on its base and grab a cup to wash up. As I rinse it off, I glance back up, out of the window again, and then let out a full scream as I jump and the cup slips out of my hands and shatters on the lino, because there, staring straight at me, on the other side of the glass, her hair plastered to her head and makeup starting to run down her face, is Liz.

The scream makes Gloria start barking in the living room and she comes dashing through, claws scrabbling on the floor. There are broken chips of china everywhere and I am suddenly aware of not wanting her to shred her paws. Liz just continues to stare at me, unmoved by Gloria barking and growling. Pete comes bursting into the room, saying, "What's happened? What's . . . fucking hell!"

He sees Liz and stops dead in his tracks, staring at her. She's not looking at me now—she's just gazing at him, and then she comes to life. She starts to bang on the window, bag in one hand, shouting. It's muffled, through-glass shouting. She presses up against the window and I can make out most of what she's saying:

". . . can't be like this, Peter! Please don't do this! Look! Come and . . . see what I've got!" She points at the bag. "It's hers! Her!" and she points at me and I look at it and realize it *is* my bag—the one I left in her wardrobe. I'd planned to call the police and use the bag being there as evidence that it was *her* that had done the break-in. OH SHIT—there *was* something I forgot about.

". . . got to believe me!" she's shouting, scraping nails desperately down the glass. "It's her!" She points at me. "Got to be her!"

Pete is moving to the door and unlocking it.

"Don't, Pete!" I shout, alarmed. "She might have a knife or something!" I think at this point I'm so caught up in everything I actually believe she might.

But Pete ignores me and flings the door open. She's through it in a second, flooding the kitchen, my kitchen, and imploring him, "Peter, I'm so sorry, I'm so sorry I'm doing this, but I don't know what else to do! You've got to believe me! I haven't done anything! I love you! You know I do!"

"Shut up!" he says harshly and grabs her tightly by the wrist. She yelps and he starts to drag her through the kitchen and out into the hall. She's sobbing now, pleading, "Please don't do this! . . . Ow! Peter—let go, you're hurting me!" I follow them, horrified. I never meant for this to happen. Did I?

He's dragging her so roughly and quickly, she stumbles over my shoes in the hall and falls to her knees. He holds her arm up like she's a child that has fallen over on purpose and gone limp, and says, "Get up, Liz, get up!"

It's hard to see what are tears and what is rain on her face. She is completely soaked through, with mascara streaks coursing down her cheeks. "Please don't, Peter," she bleats desolately. "What do I have to do to make you believe me?"

Pete flings open the front door and tries to force her through it.

"No!" she shrieks. "This isn't fair! You said you loved me! You said it! It's not me doing this, Peter—I promise you!"

"Liz, you need help!" he shouts at her. "Please—just get out. Leave us alone!"

"You promised me!" she continues, trying frantically to cling to the door frame. "I want you, Peter, I can't be without you!"

He wraps his arms around her tiny waist and lifts her up, pulling her away violently. Her fingers grab at the frame but slip off and she collapses on to him, flinging her arms round his neck and sobbing, "I love you, and I swear it isn't me!"

He sets her down and tries to pull her arms from him. "No! Please, no!" she shouts. Curtains are starting to twitch now next door and across the road.

He pushes her away from him and she stumbles slightly, swaying like she's drunk. Then she sinks to the ground and begins to cry as though her heart will break. "You said you loved me!" is all she says. "You said it would be *us*." She wraps her arms around herself as if she's literally trying to hold herself together.

I glance at Pete, just in time to see a look of utter pain pass over his face as he hears her words. He looks for a moment like he is about to speak, but then chooses not to. I'm rushed in my mind back to our bedroom, after we made love and I asked him if there was anything he wanted to tell me, and he hesitated.

"We were fine until all this started happening!" she bleats inconsolably, looking up at him. "I never asked you to leave her! I said I'd wait! Why would I do this? You'd still be with me if this wasn't happening. You know you would! Don't you love me at all?" she pleads.

"No, I don't love you!" He laughs incredulously and she cries out, as if he's hit her or something. His voice is a little unsteady for a second, as if he is choking something back. "How could I love someone who could do all this?" he says in disbelief. "You're mad!"

He takes a breath, tries to calm himself, lifts his head and eyeballs her.

"I don't love you. And I never did," he finishes simply. "Go home, Liz."

She slumps, defeated, and begins to cry racking, heaving sobs like a wounded animal.

He winces at the sound but nonetheless he turns to me. "Come on. We're going inside. Just leave her," he says.

But now I'm fixed to the spot, looking at her—this woman that I have hated. She's not the one I have obsessed about, the one in the cute hat who flicks her hair confidently and struts down the street. Not the one who looks out into the audience and flutters stuck-on eyelashes, not the one who smiles kittenishly out of the pages of the program, and certainly not the one I imagined wrapped around my boyfriend in bed.

She looks broken, she looks wrecked. Just like I have done this week.

Pete draws me gently back toward the house and she looks at me for the first time. "What has she got that I haven't?" she whimpers to Pete, gesturing at me. "I'll do anything, anything!" The humiliating desperation in her voice cuts through me like a knife. "I found her bag—she put it there. Oh God!" she sobs, sinking her head into her hands.

Then a car screeches up, a door slams and there is a clatter of heels. My heart stops as I see Debs come running up the drive. "Shit, Liz! I told you not to do this! I told you!" She dashes up to Liz and tries to pull her to her feet. "Are you happy now, you bastard?" she spits at Pete. "Look what you've done to her! Your boyfriend is a lying shit!" She spins round to face me.

"Whatever he's said to you, he's lying! You . . ." The words die on her lips as she recognizes me.

"Lotts?" she says, confused. "What are you doing here?"

She pauses, then it dawns on her. She is not as stupid as I thought.

"Oh my God! Liz, she's the girl that came to the flat. The one that was going to take the room!"

Liz is peering at me curiously, as if she's only just noticed I'm there.

"That's how your stuff got here. You were right! It wasn't you!" Debs says triumphantly.

There is a pause, and then Liz says slowly, "She came to our flat?"

"Yes she did," says Debs quickly. "She said she was Marc's mate. She's been in your room and everything!"

I say nothing, but my heart starts to pound. Oh no, oh no, oh no . . .

Then Liz gets it. "Oh my God. How could you?" She pushes her hair back and scrabbles to her feet, and I see a flash of hope spark in her. She turns to Pete. "She lied to you, Peter. *She* lied. Not me! See, this is her bag!" She holds it up eagerly. "She left it in the back of my wardrobe. She *planted* it there on purpose! How else would I have it? See, that proves it!"

Still I say nothing, I just stand there.

But Pete shakes his head. "Listen to yourself! You're both as mental as each other! Of course you've got her bag! You nicked it when you trashed our house! I know you know how much it's worth—what were you going to do? Flog it on eBay or something?" He looks at them both and shakes his head. "How many times do I have to say it? LEAVE US ALONE!" he shouts. "She's never been near your flat! Have you?" He doesn't look at me, just waits for me to back him up. Liz stares right at me. She is silently begging me to tell the truth while at the same time hating me every bit as much as I hated her.

Still Pete waits, and when I say nothing, he swings round and looks at me. "You haven't been there . . . have you?"

He doesn't sound as sure as a second ago.

I take a deep breath. Everyone waits for me to speak. I look at Debs, her arms wrapped protectively round her friend, obvious loathing on her face; then I turn to Liz. She knows the truth, knows what I've done, and meets my eye unfalteringly; this is her last chance for everything to be all right after all.

I stare stonily back at her. "No, I haven't," I say firmly "And I've never seen this woman before in my life." I nod toward Debs. "Come on, Pete. Let's go in." I take his arm. Liz reaches a hand out to him and insists desperately, "She's lying, she's lying! You know I love you, you know it!"

I tighten my grip and start to draw him back toward our house. Her fingers try to grasp his shirtsleeve, but I'm too quick for her, pulling him back sharply so she grabs only air. He's just watching her bleakly. I push him past me into the house, then, wedging myself between him and Liz, I pause and turn back to her and Debs.

"If I see either of you anywhere near my house or my fiancé . . ." I pause to let that sink in; Liz's eyes widen in shock and she slumps slightly. Debs has to grip a little harder to hold her up. "I'll call the police. Do I make myself clear?" I turn and start to go in through the door.

"Peter, please . . . I love you!" Liz shouts behind me. I see Pete's hand grip the door frame a little harder at the pain in her voice, and desperately I push him back into the hall, so I can get in and shut the door, drown her out.

"Go in the sitting room," I order him. "I'll finish this."

Looking drained, he just nods and disappears into the gloom of the house. I pull the door to and stride back out on to the drive.

Debs is trying to persuade Liz to get into her car. "Come on, baby, he's not worth it," she's saying in pleading and soothing tones. "You've got to move on, he's made his choice. I know it hurts, I know, but he's made it."

They are caught off guard to see me again, and freeze. Lowering my voice so Pete doesn't hear, I say in a strangulated tone, "If I do call the police, they will find what they're looking for in your flat. Proper proof that you did that burglary, understand? You think that bag is all I left there? Well, it's not. And you won't find it if you go looking. It's hidden, just waiting for if I need it."

I'm bluffing, of course; all I did was dump those two brooches right at the back of her wardrobe, but she doesn't know that. "You don't call him, you don't phone him. He is nothing to you any more."

Debs looks contemptuously at me. "She gets it," she says.

"No—*I* do," I say, fighting to keep myself steady.

Then I turn my back on them and start to walk up the drive.

"You bitch!" Liz shouts to my retreating back. "You've ruined my life and his. He should be with me. I really love him and he really loves me. You can't change that, no matter what you do. He'll never be yours. You'll never be right for each other."

I just carry on walking, my head held high, trying not to hear her.

Slamming the front door behind me, I find Pete just standing there, waiting. We listen until we hear the car pull away. Pete says nothing for a moment, then he speaks slowly and carefully. "I'm so sorry. She's mad. Completely mad."

I look at him sideways for a second, leaning against the wall. "Is it over, Pete?" I say tiredly, my eyes closing.

There is a pause, and then he says, "Yes. I hope so."

"I don't want 'hope so,'" I say. "That's not good enough for me. Is it over?" I open my eyes again and look directly at him, my stare unwavering.

"Yes. It is," he says finally, dropping his gaze first.

I nod silently, and close my eyes. Thank God for that. It's over. I won—I got him. I held on to our lives. It can all be okay again. It'll take some work, but it'll be okay. I can make this work, I know I can. I love him. He loves me. We can have it all.

Then Pete clears his throat nervously and says, "And great thinking about saying 'fiancé' . . ." and he laughs unconvincingly.

I open my eyes and look at him. "What?"

"Well, we haven't . . . I mean, I didn't . . . you know. Not exactly."

I'm not sure what to say to that, so I say what I feel. For once.

"Well, we love each other," I say simply. "We've been together a long time. Isn't that what people in love do? Get married, have children, grow old together. Be happy? Formalize it, you said. You do love me, don't you?"

But as I'm saying the words, all I can see in my mind is Liz, sitting brokenly on our drive, weeping desperately for him. I think of Patrick saying, "She's fantastic," and Clare saying simply, "I love him." I think of Amanda saying, "We're going to be a *family!*" And of Katie saying, "You're on your own." And finally

I think about Lottie looking straight at me: "It's good to know that he's worth all of this."

So I close my eyes really, really hard and force it all out of my head. All of it . . . the whole horrible jumbled-up swirling mess. When I open them again, Pete is still standing there and I realize he hasn't answered my question.

"I love you," I say softly, and I wait for him to say it back and set the seal.

"I know you do," he says. Then he walks past me into the living room, sits down heavily in his chair and turns the TV up, as if nothing has happened. Nothing at all.

LUCY DAWSON has been a journalist and magazine editor, and continues to work as a Pilates instructor, alongside writing. She is thirty-two and lives in Kent.

Lucy Dawson